Killer Lead

A DUPLICATE BRIDGE CLUB MYSTERY

BY
DOUG & SHERYL RILEY

Copyright © 2020 by Doug and Sheryl Riley

For information, email Cozy Cat Press, cozycatpress@gmail.com or visit our website at: www.cozycatpress.com

COZY CAT
PRESS

ISBN: 978-1-952579-09-7
Printed in the United States of America

10 9 8 7 6 5 4 3 2 1

Dedication:

For Augie, Wizer and Big-footed Long Boy who have grown up thinking that eating dinner while planning murders is completely normal.

Acknowledgements:

This book would not have been possible if not for the help and encouragement of family and friends. We would specifically like to thank our beta readers for their constructive criticism on an early draft as well as the folks at Cozy Cat Press for finding the book publishable. Our children's patience and faith in us during the writing process provided invaluable support during critical times. The timeless support of our parents in anything we have tried to accomplish in life provided the environment for success.

It is powerful to have the encouragement of knowledgeable colleagues when one embarks on a new venture, and Doug would like to thank the folks at Birmingham-Southern College, specifically Kent Andersen, Tynes Cowan & Susan Hagen. Thank you also to Sam and Debbie Pezzillo not only for backing anything we do, but also for their monthly bridge playing. Our bridge playing hobby would not have been possible without the initial tutelage of Jon Edwards, and the hours of practice with Jon and Liz Prather.

Lastly, thank you to the members of the Birmingham Duplicate Bridge Club for encouraging us, making us better bridge players, and providing inspiration.

Table of Contents

Chapter 1

The clap of the Seven Clubs bid card hitting the table felt louder than the train going through the Ol' Chasm Bridge above Cacanaw Creek north of town, although I knew it wasn't. I glanced from my cards to my right-hand opponent's smirking face. "Your bid, sweetheart," said Clovis with a smile, his bushy mustache twitching.

We'd just been skeetered.

Clovis "Skeeter" Jones was known for making wild bids, but also known for succeeding at a few of them. He had been playing bridge for years, but only recently had moved to town and picked up duplicate at the Alpine Duplicate Bridge Club. His face was rugged, what some would deem handsome, and his body was muscular from years of working outside in the field raising tobacco, or "bacci," as Clovis would say. The women in the club whispered and giggled about him, making noises like high school girls with a crush. Clovis had made the rounds, being one of the few eligible bachelors in town of that certain age. In fact, his only real competition for the ladies was Edward Schultz, an elderly attorney we had already played that day. With his full head of white hair and his habit of dressing nicely even on his days off, Edward was the epitome of the Southern gentleman. The two men were complete opposites in manners if not in looks, yet both seemed to be considered quality catches, although for the life of me, I couldn't understand why. Fortunately, Clovis had not yet set his sights on Mamaw. Unfortunately, he seemed to have set his sights on me, despite the over twenty-year age difference.

I ignored the man and studied my hand. More precisely, I studied that annoying singleton four of clubs in my hand. It was a quick loser, especially if Clovis held the ace of clubs, and from his bid, he almost had to. Mamaw and I had only tentatively reached the small slam in hearts and we were missing one key card. If it was the ace of clubs and Mamaw had a club, we couldn't take all thirteen tricks. At this point there was no way to find out. Seven Hearts appeared out of reach.

I couldn't risk it, and placed the Double card on the table. Disappointment dawned on Mamaw's face, but there was nothing we could do. This should have been our board, but Clovis had stolen it, fixin' us again. One maxim of good bridge is to take the biggest positive score your opponents will allow, and in this case that meant setting Clovis on his wild Seven Clubs bid. Unfortunately the positive score from setting Clovis wouldn't match the bonuses we should have gotten from bidding and making Six Hearts. It was a classic Clovis move, one that he was known for. It happened so frequently that I had privately co-opted Clovis's preferred name, Skeeter, to describe the phenomenon. We had been skeetered all right, skeetered good.

My bid was followed by a quick Pass on my left. I wasn't surprised. Clovis had bludgeoned Wilhelm Bea into being his partner today. Wilhelm was a good player, but not inspired and certainly not as bold as Clovis. He owned the Pole & Arms, a small downtown shop selling an eclectic combination of gardening equipment, fishing tackle, and guns. The store had always seemed a little strange to me until Papaw had explained that all three could put food on the table, and in Alpine, where cash was scarce, such an establishment had its own clientele. Wilhelm usually partnered with his wife of thirty years, Ida, but today Ida was playing with her mentor, a more experienced player who could help improve her play. Wilhelm seemed a bit shell shocked—Clovis had a way of doing that to his partners.

Mamaw passed as well. She rarely second-guessed me at the bridge table, although she seemed to question every other decision in my life. Papaw and Mamaw took me in at the tender age of eight after the automobile accident that killed my parents. It was a bad time in my life, and if it wasn't for their love and support, I don't know if I would have made it. Later they taught me to play bridge; my boyfriend, Hank Waderich, and I against Mamaw and Papaw around the kitchen table on Sunday nights after supper. Papaw was gone now, but those Sunday evenings remained among my fondest memories of that time—well, those, and a few more private memories involving Hank.

Of course, Clovis passed. He had gotten what he wanted.

I was on lead and didn't want to give Clovis an extra trick, so I played that offending singleton club. The dummy was better than Clovis deserved, and when I saw Mamaw was void in clubs, I almost threw my cards in disgust. We could have made Seven Hearts. Sometimes I hated this game. I heard Clovis snicker and wanted to pelt him.

The play progressed and we collected four set tricks. Not enough.

"That's down four, doubled but not vulnerable. Correct?" gloated Clovis. "So that's what, 800 points fur ya?" I nodded and the man entered the result into the Bridgemate. "Well, that should be a top for us, pardner. Looks like they can take all thirteen tricks in Hearts." He looked so smug I wanted to reach over and rip that annoying mustache off his tanned face.

"You made a good bid, Skeeter," replied Wilhelm as he placed his cards in the plastic container in the center of the table. "I believe that was the end of the round. If you will excuse me, ladies." He stood and I nodded, but Wilhelm was already gone.

"It was a pleasure, gals," added Clovis as he stood, favoring his bum leg. He flashed a practiced smile, and I felt my irritation grow when I saw Mamaw smile demurely in response. The man was a menace. Why couldn't he find another hobby, like bingo? "Maybe sometime you'll agree to partner me, Gracie."

"I have a partner, Clovis," I said using his given name. I knew he preferred Skeeter and it was petty, but it was the closest I was going to get to revenge today. As for partnering, I wanted nothing to do with the man, either at the bridge table or away from it.

"Never hurts to try another. Ya might find ya like it." He waggled his eyebrows suggestively, and the glint in his brown eyes told me he wasn't just talking about the bridge table.

"When pigs fly, Clovis." For heaven's sake, he was old enough to be my father. The thought made bile rise in my throat.

Clovis blinked in surprise at my rudeness. He was used to being fawned over, not shut down. His eyes turned cold, but he directed that smile to Mamaw and I swear I heard a sigh escape her. "Nora, it was a pleasure." He limped away, and I glared at his retreating back.

I needed some air and a cigarette. I had quit smoking once before, but when my life fell apart with The-Event-That-Changed-My-Life, I had picked it up again. I wished I had never started, but then again, I had plenty of regrets in my thirty-three years on God's good Earth. I knew I needed to put the cigarettes away for good, but not today. Not after getting skeetered. We had finished the round a few minutes early. I had time for a quick smoke break. I stood up and turned towards the door.

"Grace Amelia Theis, you sit back down. How dare you be so rude to that nice young man?" scolded Mamaw.

I slumped back into my chair. Mamaw was like a bulldog with a bone when it came to manners. I might as well hear her out now rather than later. However, that didn't mean I had to like it. "Young? Skeeter is what, fifty-five, fifty-six?" Her bright blue eyes flashed, her white eyebrows pulled into a frown. I remembered that look from my teenage years. I hadn't been as rebellious as some of the kids in town, not anything like my childhood best friend Emily, but I hadn't made it overly easy on Mamaw and Papaw either.

"That doesn't matter. You were still rude. Gracie, you can't afford to be that way in a town the size of Alpine. Word will get around. How will you ever get a man and give me a grandchild?"

"I am your grandchild, Mamaw, remember?" I almost rolled my eyes, but luckily stopped myself in time. It would only make matters worse.

"You know what I mean. I want to have little ones around the house again before I join your Papaw."

"Not now, Mamaw," I muttered as I stood. She let me go this time, but she was probably just rallying her forces for the next you-need-a-man discussion. I really needed that smoke now.

I hurried to the central table, where everyone kept their purses and other items during the match. The table was filled with belongings: bags, umbrellas, raincoats, and even a pair of red galoshes like I once wore to grade school. I had to dig to find my petite handbag, a leather Louis Vuitton I picked up second hand on the back streets of Paris before The-Event-That-Changed-My-Life. I finally located it tucked between the red galoshes and partly under a box of tomatoes that someone had brought to give away. My pack of cigarettes was in the very bottom of the bag and had been smashed by the tomatoes. I know the forecast said rain, but really? The amount of gear collected on the table could shelter a small village from a monsoon.

I went around the remaining tables in my path and through the double doors that led out of the building. In seconds I was outside listening to the construction noise across the street at the old Carlyle Hotel. Scaffolding covered the red brick building, and they had sandblasted the top two floors with three more to go. *The Alpine Tribune* said the new owners planned on bringing in some big name artist to restore the murals that had faded over the years. The town was undergoing something of a resurgence. For years, Alpine had sat unchanging, nestled in a hidden valley on the edge of the Appalachian Mountains in northeast Alabama. It had been a wealthy community once, back in the 1830s, when German settlers came planning to farm but ended up making furniture from the abundant hardwoods instead. Those wealthy days had disappeared with the hardwoods, and in the 30s, Alpine had entered a period of decline that had lasted for decades. Now Alpine was coming alive like the fabled Brigadoon in the Scottish foothills. The new game in town was tourism, and a lynchpin of that plan was the renovation of the Carlyle.

Personally, I would miss the sleepy little town I had grown up in.

The wind was blowing for real now, and the grey cloud mass approaching from the west looked ominous. With my luck it would be pouring rain by the time the game was finished. I wished I had had the forethought to bring a raincoat. I needed to take a lesson from all the older bridge players and bring rain gear whenever there was a single cloud in the sky. However, remembering my purse was about all I could handle after four hours of bridge. I turned to shelter my cigarette so I could light it, and a strong gust of wind made me stumble. Before I could recover, I felt a hand on my elbow steadying me.

"You okay, miss?" asked a deep voice I had not heard in fifteen years.

I looked up into eyes greyer than the clouds coming in from the west. They were a bit wiser now, with hints of wrinkles around them. The face was the same though—and the smile. I knew Hank lived in the area, but I had not seen him in the six weeks since I had moved back home. I was not sure I was ready to see him now.

"Hank? Is that you?" I feigned. It wasn't as if I didn't already know, but sometimes you have to play games, even if it's just against yourself.

"Gracie?" he laughed. "I can't believe my eyes. I never expected to see you here." The words had barely left his lips before his gaze wandered from me to the door of the bridge club. His eyes used to never leave my face, or at least not my body. I was still the same size as in high school, if a bit more filled out in a few areas and with shorter hair. I had cut my red tresses after Paris in a need to change everything, but otherwise I looked much like I did back when we dated.

"What are you doing here?" I asked, cringing at the tone in my voice. Sure, I was annoyed, but Hank didn't need to know that. Even after all this time, the man could still raise my ire.

"Nothing." But his answer was too quick, too clipped. Hank was up to something, I knew him too well. His gaze returned to mine, and his smile broadened. My heart skipped a beat, despite how desperately I tried to clamp down on it. How the hell could he still look so good? "It really is nice to see you, Gracie. Are you visiting Mamaw Nora? I haven't seen her in months, since around Easter, I think."

"Not visiting. I've moved back home for a spell." I giggled. Giggled? I hadn't done that in ten years. What was wrong with me? I took a deep breath trying to pull myself together, and continued, in a calmer voice, "I'm renting a small house over on Elm, across the street from where Jimmy Griece used to live. You know, the one with the green shutters." I willed myself not to stare into those grey eyes.

"You've moved back to town? I can't believe it. The last I had heard you were living in Paris, married to some Frenchman?" He looked over again at the bridge club door.

Just like the Hank I knew in high school, barging in like a bull in a china shop. "Pierre was a pilot. He died six months ago in a plane crash." I felt the tears gathering in my eyes, but I refused to cry again.

"Oh Gracie, I am so sorry. I didn't know," replied Hank, and then he gathered me into his arms.

I allowed it, inhaling the scent of him and taking what comfort I could. After a few shaky breaths, I pulled away. It was too dangerous to stay there. I looked at the Carlyle to get Hank off my mind and lit a cigarette. Workers were scrabbling along the scaffolding like ants to prepare for the upcoming storm.

I took a puff or two to calm my nerves before glancing back to Hank. I was surprised by the look of disappointment I witnessed on his face.

"When did you start smoking?" He frowned and coughed as the wind swirled the smoke his way.

"It was something that I picked up in Paris," I explained, dryly. How dare he judge me that way? He had no right to act all high and mighty with me after what had happened between us.

"Right," he drew the word into three syllables with a fake southern accent and smiled apologetically. I guess he could still read me pretty well too. "I'd better get going. That storm looks like it's going to be nasty. You be careful going home." He looked into my eyes and I thought I saw regret, but he blinked, and the moment was over. Maybe I had just imagined it.

I watched as Hank walked away, his shaggy brown hair blowing in the wind. He had gotten a little thicker in the middle and lost some of the spring in his step. But I could still see a remnant of the high school football linebacker I remembered. He got in a beat-up black F150 but did not start the engine. For some reason he just sat there, staring at the club. Hank was definitely up to something.

I put out my cigarette. I didn't feel like smoking anymore, and the next round would be starting soon anyhow. I entered the club and was surprised to see everyone milling around. Quite a few people were going in and out the back door, and the box of tomatoes had vanished. Most members parked in the lot behind the building, but I preferred the spots along the street in front. Apparently, Gladys Chisholm, the club manager and director for the game, had called for a short break to allow folks to prepare before the rain started. The central table had even more raincoats and umbrellas than before. It looked more like a mountain of supplies for hurricane victims than it did an actual table at this point. I stuffed the pack of cigarettes into my back pocket; it was not worth digging for my purse now.

The last round of bridge was uneventful. Our opponents were a pair of octogenarian spinsters, the Strange sisters, who had partnered together their entire lives. One would think that after playing together for sixty years the two would have gotten pretty good at the game, but apparently not. They bickered the entire time with neither quite knowing what the other was doing. I figured the sisters had remained partners because no one else in the club was willing to deal with either of them.

After the game, I stuck around for the scores while Mamaw and many others hurried home to beat the worst of the storm. The rain had begun to fall by then, so I knew I was getting wet regardless. Clovis crowed in delight at coming in first, just ahead of Ida and her mentor, Edward. Mamaw and I were fourth in our direction, just out of the points. I sighed and Gladys wished me better luck next time as she finished counting the money from the game. Most of the card fee went to support the club, but Gladys also received a small portion, as did the national organization that sanctioned the game.

Disappointed, I retrieved my purse from the central table and wished again that I had bought a raincoat, or even an umbrella. I opened the front door to the club and was hit by a gust of wet rain. I would get soaked getting to my car.

"Gracie, don't you have an umbrella?" called Clovis from across the room, interrupting his conversation with Greg Jergensen. "Let me escort you to your car. We can share mine."

"I'll be fine, Clovis."

"I insist. No use in getting wet when you don't have to," he said, stroking his mustache.

I sighed. Mamaw would want me to accept the man's help. It would be rude not to, and I did have a life to build in this town. I nodded my agreement and Clovis hurried over to hold the door open for me. The rain was coming down hard at this point, and Clovis's definition of sharing meant using the umbrella while I walked beside him only partially covered. By the time we got to the car, I was soaked. My blue silk blouse clung to me like I had entered a wet T-shirt contest on the Redneck Riviera, more formally known as Alabama's Gulf Coast. True to form, Clovis could not keep his eyes off my chest. I wanted to scream at him to get a good look now as he would never get another, but my better senses prevailed.

I slammed my car door shut and lit a cigarette, thanking him only with a thin smile. Clovis stood there for a minute before hurrying back into the club. That man could move when he wanted to, racing to the door like a track star. I finished the cigarette and prayed that my 1972 Mustang would start. I had bought the car on impulse in Atlanta after returning to the States and had regretted it ever since. Oh, I loved the look and it was fun to drive, but the beast would sometimes leave me stranded, and it had been in the shop already. The last thing I wanted to do was asking Clovis for a ride home.

Luck was with me, or God had finally listened to one of my pleas, because the engine roared when I turned the key. The radio was playing classic rock songs this afternoon, and the song that came on reminded me of when Hank and I used to park out by the lake. I turned on the wipers, and through the periodic clearing of the windshield, glanced to where Hank's F150 had been parked. The truck was long gone. What had he been up to?

It didn't matter. I wouldn't be seeing Hank again anytime soon if I could help it.

I put the car in gear and headed through downtown Alpine, pleased to see a sign on an empty storefront next to the Pole & Arms indicating that a new Chinese restaurant would be opening in a few weeks. The renovations had begun shortly before I moved home, and apparently were going well. The street was flooded at the corner of Main and Maple, but I was able to slowly cruise through the intersection without killing the engine. I had just passed through the worst of it when my cell rang. The ring tone identified the caller as Mamaw, and I suddenly worried she had had trouble getting home.

"Mamaw, are you all right?" I asked after fumbling to answer.

"Not at all, Gracie. I forgot Grandma Mable's cut-glass platter."

"What?" I thought I had misheard her.

"Grandma Mable's platter. I brought a plate of homemade peanut butter cookies to share at the club and used Grandma Mable's platter. I can't believe I left it. Where has my memory gone? Can you pick it up?"

"Mamaw, I'm almost home." Surely she wasn't that concerned about a plate. The woman sounded as worried as if she were missing a dog out in the storm.

"It's the only thing I have left of hers—well, beside the sideboard—and I guess the dining room table was hers as well—but neither are truly as special as that platter."

I sighed, dreaming of melting into my turn-of-the-century clawfoot tub. The tub was so tall I could literally soak up to my eyebrows. And afterwards I would curl up on the couch with a glass of Merlot and the Agatha Christie mystery I had picked up at a used bookstore in Gadsden. I had devoured all of the Hercule

Poirot and Miss Marple mysteries in my teens, but somehow had missed the four Tommy and Tuppence books Christie had written. It felt like I had discovered a new Monet when I came upon them. "Can't it wait until tomorrow?" I pleaded.

"Oh. Well, that's okay, Gracie. You head on home," Mamaw continued. Her voice quavered, and I knew I was being played. "I had hoped to catch you before you left the club, but I guess I was too late. I'll just head back out in the storm and get it myself. I won't be able to sleep a wink until Grandma Mable's platter is safe. To think one of those thieving Mexicans over at the Carlyle could simply walk into the club and take it!"

Inwardly I groaned. I knew that if I didn't retrieve the platter Mamaw would do exactly what she had threatened and get back out in the storm. She had been fretting for weeks about the construction workers, despite the fact that none had ever entered the club, let alone stolen anything. Mamaw was convinced they were criminals simply because many of them looked Latino, and nothing I said to the contrary mattered. The inherent racism bothered me, but Mamaw wasn't about to change at her age. There was no way I could enjoy either bath or book now, not while worrying about Mamaw. Both luxuries would just have to wait a bit. I took a deep breath and said, "I'll get the platter. No need for you to get wet when I'm already soaked."

"You're soaked? You should have worn a raincoat. Go on home and get dried off before you catch your death of cold. I'll go get it myself," said Mamaw.

"No, Mamaw, I'll get the platter. No big deal," I growled. Here I was doing as she asked and yet she had to almost make me beg to do it. The woman was a guilt-trip master.

"Well, perhaps that would be best. Just be careful and get dry soon. Summer colds are the worst."

We said our goodbyes, and I debated heading home to change first but decided that was pointless. With the way the wind was blowing and the rain was pouring, even with a raincoat anything dry I put on would be soaked the minute I stepped outside again. Instead I looked for a good place to turn the Mustang around and ended up pulling into Margaret's Diner. I saw Margaret looking out the window, and I gave her a quick wave as I circled the parking lot. She waved back, looking disappointed that I wasn't coming in for a late lunch as I often did after a morning bridge game. The flooding at the corner of Main and Maple had lessened, but shortly after going through the intersection, I passed by a blue sedan that threw up enough water to make me curse. The Mustang sputtered as if the water had entered a fuel line, but thankfully did not die. I pulled up in front of the club, and there was not a car in sight. I waited until the rain slackened and then made a dash for it. The front door was locked, but I knew there was a key beneath the doormat.

The club was dark when I entered. I had no idea where the main light switches were located, so I pulled out my cell phone to light my way, carefully heading straight through the main playing area and around the dozen or so tables to the back hallway. The back hall led to the rear exit and the parking lot beyond, with mirrored bathrooms on the right and the kitchen and small office off the left side. When I reached the kitchen, I tucked the cell back in my rear pocket and flipped on the kitchen light.

The light revealed a man lying in a pool of blood on the kitchen floor. I was so shocked my screech could have woken the dead.

Chapter 2

Whoever was lying there did not react to my scream, and that only made my heart beat faster. I rushed over and grabbed his shoulder, causing the man to roll over onto his back. There was blood on his shirt and his pale face had unstaring eyes. I grabbed my cell out of my pocket to call 911, but the phone slipped from my trembling fingers and landed in a pool of congealing blood underneath his body. I leapt away before the blood touched me, and the room darkened as I experienced a sudden case of vertigo. I was not fond of blood. I closed my eyes and leaned against the wall until the dizziness faded. When I felt ready, I opened my eyes and recognized the still face staring up at me. It was Edward Schultz. I needed to call for help, but I sure wasn't going to touch my cell now. I couldn't even reach it safely—not while surrounded by all that red. I canvassed the kitchen looking for something I could use to fish my phone out. "Focus," I muttered as I began to tremble. I looked again and saw an old-fashioned phone on the wall. I could use the cord from the landline to drag my cell from the crimson pool.

The cord was just long enough that I was able to lasso my cell and pull it free, although it took me three tries. I still wasn't going to pick it up; the trail of blood was loathsome. With the cell phone on the floor, I gingerly hit the on-button with my forefinger while I held the phone in place with my thumb, making sure to not touch anything red. Nothing happened—the phone was dead. I felt a rumbling of nausea in my stomach and willed myself to stop thinking about how the crimson liquid might have seeped in and shorted it out. How was I going to call for help now?

I felt pretty foolish when the receiver I was holding began to beep indicating it had been left off its stand too long. A hysterical giggle escaped me and I knew then I was close to losing it. I hadn't felt this freaked out since the night in Paris when I had heard about Pierre. I took a deep breath to calm myself as I dialed 911.

"Alpine Police, what is the nature of your emergency?" asked a female voice that seemed vaguely familiar.

"I need help. I'm at the Alpine Duplicate Bridge Club off of Main near Oak Street. I found Edward Schultz lying on the floor in a pool of blood. He's badly hurt. I think he might be dead." I got it all out, proud at how calmly I stated the facts, and then it hit me I was in a room with a dead body. I wobbled a little and hoped the dizziness would pass.

"I'm sending the police and paramedics now. Is there anyone else there with you?" The voice was matter-of-fact and composed.

"What? Someone else? No. Wait, I don't know. I haven't seen anyone, but I haven't looked." I glanced around, half expecting to see someone in the doorway, laughing.

"Just stay there and do nothing. I'm sending help now. I'll stay on the line with you until they arrive." The voice continued to portray a sense of calm, but I heard the underlying concern.

I felt the goose bumps as fear blossomed within me. Had someone attacked Edward? Was a murderer lurking in the club, hiding in the bathroom? Would he come for me now that I'd seen the body? I plastered myself against the wall and scanned the dark hallway outside the kitchen, hoping that I wasn't going to spot a guy dressed in black with a hockey mask coming towards me like in a B-horror movie. I saw nothing and no one, but I looked for a weapon regardless. The best I could find was Grandma Mable's cookie platter that someone had thoughtfully washed and left in the drying rack next to the sink. I grabbed it, the weight of the cut glass feeling good in my hand. I was pretty sure Mamaw would forgive me if I broke it over the head of a killer.

"Are you still with me?" asked the woman on the other end of the line, and I realized she'd asked me a question while my brain was occupied with my choice of weapon. I gave myself a mental slap. Even psychotic killers weren't stupid or crazy enough to kill someone while that person was on the phone with the police—or at least I hoped not.

"Yes, I'm still here," I said with a tremble in my voice. I felt suddenly foolish. Any self-respecting killer would laugh if I tried to smack him with a cookie platter. I needed to pull myself together, to focus on something I could control. I was sure this was an accident anyhow. Edward was going to be fine; he was probably just unconscious. I set the platter down and decided to reclaim my cell. I could wipe the blood off and see if it was busted or if the battery had just popped loose. I snagged a wad of paper towels, grabbed the phone from the floor and started to clean it, holding the landline to my ear with my shoulder. I kept on glancing to the darkness beyond the kitchen door just in case there was a psycho killer milling about, but no one appeared. When I saw that I had smeared blood onto my hands, I almost let out a scream. I tossed the phone onto the kitchen counter and shoved my hands into the sink, using my wrists to get the water running. The water was cold, but I couldn't wait to get the red off.

"What's that noise? Please don't do anything. Chief Doeppers and the paramedics should be arriving any moment."

"Who?" I asked. I didn't care if Inspector Japp was coming; I was going to wash my hands.

"Jon Doeppers, the Chief of Police."

I felt like I'd been slapped. Jon Doeppers was the Chief of Police? The man who had ruined my senior year of high school was now the Chief of Police. He had been a God-lovin' tea-totalin' judgmental jerk back then, drunk on his own power as a newly-hired officer of the law, as he used to drawl. The man had had a vendetta against me and anyone else he deemed a miscreant. In many ways it was because of Doeppers that I fled the state upon graduating high school, going to college on the east coast, where I met Pierre. Hell, Doeppers was the root cause of all my problems in the last fifteen years.

I heard the front door open and a man called out, identifying himself. I called back in response, then thanked the dispatcher on the other end of the line before hanging up. I turned the water off and used another wad of paper towels to dry my hands. Only then did I notice my cell in the bottom of the sink. I must not have tossed it far enough onto the counter. Crud, if the circuits hadn't been fried before, they sure were now. At least the blood was gone. I grabbed it and shoved it into my back pocket, only then remembering the cigarettes I'd stashed there earlier. The club was nonsmoking, but surely this would justify breaking that rule. I grabbed a cigarette, but my hands were shaking too much to light it.

I would not have recognized the man who appeared in the entryway to the kitchen if I hadn't known whom to expect. The Jon Doeppers I remembered was tall and athletic, with thin blonde hair, an unforgiving gaze, possessing a confidence that was palpable to the point of arrogance. The man who appeared was still tall, but the athletic grace I remembered had fled, leaving a noticeable paunch around the middle. What hair he had he kept clipped short as if to hide how little remained upon his head. The biggest difference was in his brown eyes. Doeppers looked world-weary, still confident but no longer eager, as if he'd seen too much in all of these years.

He glanced about the room, looked at Edward, and without saying a word stepped aside to let the paramedics through. Two paramedics dashed to the man, but in a few seconds the taller of the two admitted there was nothing they could do. They had a quick whispered conference with Doeppers, gesturing at the body, and then one pointed at his chest. Doeppers grimaced and used his radio to summon additional officers to secure the building. Only after the paramedics left did his gaze shift to me.

"Were you the one who called? Did you find the body?" he asked, taking a small notebook out of his rear pocket to take notes. He frowned at the cigarette in my hands, and then his gaze shifted to my wet blouse. Apparently I was giving a free peep show today. I shoved the cigarette in a front pocket and then crossed my arms in front of my chest, with a pointed look at him that let him know I'd caught him. He didn't look ashamed, just looked at me expectantly; after a moment of silence, he barked, "Well?"

"Well, what?" I replied somewhat annoyed. Who was this man to disapprove of my smoking while he was ogling me?

"Were you the one who placed the call?" He stared at me as if wondering if I was mentally disabled. He had moved on to business.

"What? Oh yes," I admitted. "He's dead, isn't he? Was it an accident?" God, I prayed it was an accident. The thought of someone I had played cards against less than an hour ago being murdered unnerved me.

"Humpf, and your name, Miss?" he asked, looking down at his notebook and jotting something.

"Gracie Theis," I replied. That got his attention. He stared at me for the longest time, and I could tell that he was connecting the face before him to the high school student from years past. I liked to think that I had aged well; I had certainly aged better than he had. I just hoped the jerk wasn't going to bring up what happened back then. I stared back at him, my resentfulness plain on my face.

Doeppers lowered his eyes first, jotting something into his notebook, and then approached the body. He didn't bother to kneel, but frowned at the blood smears my cell phone had made.

"That's from my cell," I offered. I didn't want him to think the marks were somehow relevant to his investigation. "I dropped it when I found the body and—"

"Later, Miss Theis. I'll want to hear the whole story from the beginning." He knelt then, careful to avoid the pool of blood, and used the pen he'd been writing with to gently pull the shirt away from the bloody area on Edward's chest. He grunted as if he saw what he expected to see. He looked at me and said, "Do you own a gun, Miss Theis?"

"No," I said, and then it clicked. "You mean he was shot?" My voice went up a couple of octaves. This was no accident: it was murder.

He groaned and stood. I heard a pair of voices call from the front door followed by a crash and a curse. Doeppers flinched at the noise, then sighed. The lights came on in the main part of the club and a pair of officers arrived at the kitchen door, one rubbing his knee. "Secure this room," ordered Doeppers. "And call the State Police to see if they'll send a forensics team. I'm sure they'll be too busy to grace us with their presence," he intoned sarcastically. "Once they refuse, we need to send in our team to do the best they can. And call the coroner. I need an estimate for a time of death, ASAP." He turned to me and said, "Miss Theis, let me escort you to the other room. I believe you have a statement to make."

I started my story at the beginning. How after playing bridge I'd started to drive home, only to have Mamaw call and ask that I return to pick up Grandma Mable's cookie plate. I could tell from his expression that he found it hard to believe she was that attached to a platter, or that I'd go out in the storm just to keep her happy. Clearly the man didn't know Mamaw and therefore had no idea of the guilt she could lay down when motivated. Considering his attitude fifteen years ago, he was probably raised by wolves. That would explain a lot.

I switched my mind back to the topic at hand, and had barely begun again before Doeppers interrupted, probing for superfluous details. He seemed to want to keep me off-balance, which didn't surprise me with our history. He didn't really need to try so hard though, I was pretty unsettled already just from finding the body. Add into that seeing Hank and Doeppers again for the first time in fifteen years, and my brain and stomach were both in knots. Did it really matter if I had the radio on in the car, and how could it possibly be relevant what songs I heard while driving home? And if Doeppers wasn't interrupting me with ridiculous questions, we got interrupted by one of his men. He had five different officers present; two of whom had cameras and were taking snapshots of everything in sight. Every time one of the men discovered something, he would come and whisper in Doepper's ear. The room was worse than the Gadsden Mall at Christmas time.

When I finally got to the part about unlocking the club door with the key under the mat, Doeppers shook his head in disbelief and let out an audible sigh. At this point a thirty-something blonde woman in a lab coat arrived, and Doeppers watched as one of his officers led her to the body. He turned back to me and told me to stay put, even motioning for one of his men to keep an eye on me. I groaned and settled back in my chair, really just wanting to go home and forget this ever happened. Doeppers headed for the kitchen, and once he was out of sight, I stood to go take a smoke, but my guard wouldn't let me. I considered objecting; they couldn't keep me here against my will, or at least I thought they couldn't, but decided I was better off cooperating. Doeppers returned after about a half hour when the woman in the lab coat left with the gurney holding a large black bag. I turned my eyes away; I didn't want to picture Edward inside it.

Chief Doeppers sat back down and glared across the table. It looked like his mood had worsened, if that were even possible. He let me finish my narrative without any further interruptions, which surprised me. The annoying man kept jotting things down in his little notebook and somehow managed to deepen his frown as I talked. After I finished, he just sat there and stared at me. I felt a sense of déjà vu; he had looked at me just the same back when I was in high school.

"So let me get this straight," he drawled. "You found someone lying in a pool of blood on the kitchen floor, and instead of calling 911 immediately, you rushed to the body."

"I thought I could help him," I explained.

"And then you moved the body…"

"That was an accident, I touched his shoulder and he rolled over."

"…dropped a personal possession in my crime scene…"

"I was trying to call 911!"

"…and then conveniently retrieved that item and washed up before the police arrived."

"I…" Drat. I was in deep… again. I should have known when I heard the name. Doeppers was looking for an easy answer, and what could be easier than pinning the murder on the poor sot who found the body? This was starting to look like fifteen years ago: framed for something I didn't do. And here I thought I could come back home and make a life for myself, or at least take a breather until I decided what I should do next. I should have known better. There was clearly no place for me in this town as long as he was in charge. Damn him. Damn this town. Damn Edward for getting killed, and damn Grandma Mable's platter.

"Nice little story, Ms. Theis. It explains very nicely any trace of evidence we might find on the body. Having an excuse to wash up afterwards is awfully convenient; any blood we might find in the sink, presto, explained. And, of course, washing removes any gun residue from your hands. Bravo." His brown eyes bored into mine, looking for any sign of weakness or guilt.

I straightened up in my chair and stared right back. I was not that girl anymore, and I wasn't going to roll over and take it this time. "Look, Doeppers, I don't know what you have planned here, but let's get this straight. I didn't kill that man." *I didn't do anything fifteen years ago either,* I thought to myself, but I knew better than to bring that up now.

"What I have planned? It looks to me like you were the one with the plan. Commit murder and then try and hide the evidence by 'dropping' a cell phone in the blood, pulling it out with the cord from another phone, instead of just using it to call the police, and then washing both the cell and your hands? What kind of story is that? Just tell me what happened. The truth this time," he said, staring at me intently.

"What I told you is the truth! I wasn't thinking clearly, okay? I had just found a body and I panicked. I didn't do anything wrong."

He glared at me. "We'll see about that. Your story had better check out perfectly, and even then, I may not be convinced."

"I am not a naïve high school student anymore, Doeppers. You can't pin this on me. You have a real killer on the loose, and you'd better do your job instead of looking for a convenient patsy."

"Ms. Theis, let me assure you that I have no intention of 'pinning' this—"

"You've done it before," I snapped. From the silence that followed, I immediately regretted my interruption. I could tell from the shocked look on his face that I had misstepped, and badly. This man was the Chief of Police, and I was a nobody who had just moved back to town. As much as I hated him, it had been stupid to bring this up now. "Look, that was a long time ago, let's just forget it."

Doeppers fixed me with a stare and snarled, "You accuse me of being a dirty cop and then tell me to just forget it? Not going to happen, Miss Thies. You were trouble fifteen years ago and I can see you haven't changed. I'll check out your flimsy story and if there's one thing, one tiny detail out of place, I will bust your ass and charge you with murder so fast your head will spin."

Now I was just mad, and my Irish temper got the best of me. "You planted the drugs, Doeppers. You know damn well I did not have any marijuana in my car. You set me up just to make a name for yourself. You and your petty war on drugs at the high school. You needed a bust and you arranged for one at my expense. I spent 120 hours in community service because of your shenanigans. I was shunned my senior year at school. This time I'm not going to take the fall just so you can tie a nice blue bow on a murder case and get a commendation!"

"Ms. Theis. Let me be blunt. I did no such thing then, and I have no intention of doing so now," he growled. I was so angry I could spit. The nerve of that jerk to think that I would believe his lies. "Shall we go over your statement one more time? I want to make sure I have everything, exactly like you claim." He jotted something else in his notebook, but with such force that I could almost hear the paper rip.

"Look, I had blood on my hands, okay? I don't like blood and I needed to wash it off. What was I supposed to do, just stand there and wait?"

"Yes! That was exactly what you were supposed to do!" he screeched like a barn owl spotting a mouse. "That was what the dispatcher told you to do. Do nothing and wait for the police."

"Well, I didn't. What are you going to do? Arrest me?" I stood and glared at him. I'd had enough of Chief high and mighty Doeppers.

"Don't tempt me." He met my stare and I saw something deep in his eyes, something unexpected.

They didn't look like the eyes of a liar to me. I wilted back into my chair. I needed time to think. God, I needed a smoke.

Doeppers must have sensed my confusion because instead of questioning me further, he put on a pair of latex gloves and asked to see my phone. He fiddled with it for a few minutes trying to get the phone to turn on with no success, and then placed it into a plastic bag as evidence. I was annoyed but couldn't very well object as I had dropped it in the victim's blood. He then asked whether an officer could search my purse and car. I knew I couldn't refuse without rousing additional suspicion, but I sure wasn't going to let Doeppers do it. I wanted that smoke, and so I agreed to the searches as long as I could stand witness. Doeppers delegated the task to a young black female officer who introduced herself as Officer Yancey. After she checked my purse, I followed her out the door and unlocked the Mustang. The rain had stopped, although the clouds remained, and the temperature had plummeted, making it unusually pleasant for an Alabama summer afternoon. I lit my cigarette and watched as the officer checked under the seats and in the trunk. I felt a bit of embarrassment; I really should clean the beast more often. She did not take long and found nothing, of course. She closed the doors and trunk and escorted me back into the club.

Doeppers had claimed a bridge table at the far side of the room and was reviewing his notes. Officer Yancey took me back to where I'd been sitting previously and left me there. Occasionally Doeppers would use his cell, but I was too far away to hear anything. After hanging up, he would scribble, scribble, scribble in that little notebook of his. I wanted to go over and smack the pencil out of his self-righteous hand. I glanced around the room, but there was little to see. On the wall near the front doors were posted advertisements for various bridge events; sectionals and regionals mostly. I noted that Birmingham was having a regional this year in August and wondered if Mamaw would want to go. She was still a few gold points shy of Life Master. Of course, that was assuming I wasn't in prison by that time. Could a man look so sincere and still be lying? I wasn't good at spotting liars, I knew that all too well.

On the wall opposite from me and nearest to Doeppers, Gladys had posted the results from the most recent games. The murder couldn't have anything to do with the bridge results, could it? Edward had been a good player, generous with his time and willing to play with and mentor players much less experienced than him. It just didn't make any sense. I could see someone murdering Clovis for his hijinks at the bridge table, but not Edward. Yet it was Edward's body that had been on the kitchen floor. What could have been a matter of life or death for Edward Schultz?

The far corner of the back wall held the pass-through from the kitchen, although from my angle I couldn't see into the space, and the near corner sported a bookcase holding a scattering of outdated bridge books. Technically, the club required members to check out the books like a regular library, but in reality, holdings tended to ebb and flow like the tide. Between the two corners, centered in the wall, was the hallway that led to the bathrooms, office, proper entrance to the kitchen, and the back door. Occasionally I would see a flash from one of the officers taking a picture in the kitchen area, the light leaking equally from the pass-through and hallway.

After perhaps fifteen minutes, Doeppers returned and asked to go over my statement once more. We remained civil to each other, much to my relief; neither of us mentioned the unpleasantness from before. He truly seemed to be interested in the truth, and I had a fleeting hope that this time it would be different. I was able to add a few more details, and Doeppers added these tidbits to his notebook like he was gathering precious gems.

Towards the end of my tale, Doeppers' phone rang. He indicated that he needed to take the call and left me once again, much to my dismay. I was past ready to go home, that clawfoot tub was pulling me like a lodestone. He wasn't on the phone ten seconds before he dashed out of the room like—well, like a policeman, actually. I sighed and my stomach gurgled. I suddenly realized I hadn't eaten since this morning and was ravenous. I wondered if any of Mamaw's peanut butter cookies were left in the kitchen. Would the officers let me check, or were the cookies now evidence too?

I asked for some coffee and something to eat from the officer left to mind me, and before I knew it, I had placed an order for a Rueben and a piece of pecan pie from Margaret's Diner. Margaret's pecan pie was the best this side of the Mississippi. I rarely indulged, as I knew it would go straight to my waistline. Yet after what I'd gone through today, I felt I deserved it.

Doeppers returned before the officer with the food, and he approached my table saying he had a few more questions. He showed me a handgun within a plastic evidence bag and asked if I'd ever seen it before. I shook my head no, and he jotted that fact down in his notebook; yet another precious gem, I supposed. I wondered if it was the murder weapon and where they'd found it. Doeppers glanced through his notebook again, and I dreaded the thought of going through my statement for a third time.

"Just a couple more questions, and then I believe I'll be finished with you for the moment," he said, to my shock. He was actually going to let me go home. "According to your statement, the victim spent the last three hours before his death playing bridge, and was still at the club when you left with a Mister…"

"Jones. Clovis Jones. He goes by Skeeter," I offered. Was I really going to be able to leave? Maybe Doeppers had mellowed with age, or maybe he was getting ready to pull the rug out from under me.

"Yes, left with a Mister Jones, who walked you to your car. It was raining, correct?"

"Like cats and dogs." I shivered slightly in my still damp shirt.

"My question is this: during those three hours, were any of the bridge players behaving strangely? Were any of the players acting suspicious or doing anything out of character?" he asked, piercing me with his gaze.

I felt my pulse quicken and prayed it didn't show on my face. I should have seen the connection earlier— Hank. Did he have something to do with Edward's murder? The Hank I once knew would not, but what about the Hank I ran into this afternoon? Fifteen years was a long time, and people change. I thought that Hank had left by the time the leering Clovis had escorted me to my car in the rain, but he could have been hiding. "No, I don't remember any of the bridge players acting strange," I replied as calmly as I could. It wasn't a lie, not really; Hank had not been playing bridge. "Well, strange in the sense of different. Some of them are pretty strange generally," I snickered, but Doeppers didn't respond to my humor.

"Are you sure?" he asked, fixing me with a quizzical stare.

"Yes," I replied, hoping I wasn't blushing too badly.

"Thank you, Ms. Theis. That will be all for now," he said with a fake smile, shutting his little notebook. "We have some checking to do to confirm your version of events, which may lead to more questions. Thus, I ask that you do not leave town without speaking with me first. I want you to understand that at this moment you are still a person of interest in this case. Also, speak of this to no one. *No one.*"

I said I understood, although I didn't know if I should be relieved or if I needed to call a lawyer. I still didn't trust him, but apparently Doeppers would look elsewhere. Either that or he needed the time to build a case against me. There was nothing I could do regardless; a lawyer wouldn't help now that I'd already given a statement, not that I knew of anyone besides Edward Schultz, and he certainly couldn't help me. If Doeppers charged me with murder, I'd have time then to get a lawyer and mount a defense. I just wished I knew whether Hank was mixed up in all of this. I needed to talk to him, while I still had the freedom to do so. I needed to know. If he could give me a good reason for hanging out in front of the club, then I wouldn't ever need to mention his name to Doeppers. If not, then I would fess up. Edward deserved justice, even if that meant Hank also became a person of interest.

I gathered my belongings and exited via the front door. The sun had made an appearance and the temperature had risen significantly as a result, turning the day hot and muggy. The work across the street had started again, but I could tell that little would be done in this heat. I had to wait for the officer to return with my late lunch and debated going back into the air conditioning, but decided to have another smoke instead. I needed to think. How should I approach Hank? Did I really know him anymore? If he was involved, was it even safe for me to talk to him? By the time I finished the second cigarette, I still had no answers, but the officer with the food had returned and I was ready to go home.

As I drove off, I realized I had forgotten Grandma Mable's cut glass plate.

Chapter 3

I woke to a screaming phone. I glanced to the clock, surprised to see that it was already well past dinnertime. After getting home from my ordeal at the club and eating my Rueben and pie, I had drawn a hot bath in the clawfoot. I had hoped for some inspiration on how to approach Hank, but instead of answers, all I got was more wrinkles than a Sharpei puppy. After the bath I had considered calling Mamaw, but I hadn't wanted to go into the whole story until I had the time to think it through carefully. I knew it would worry Mamaw to no end, and I was half convinced she'd blame the whole thing on "the Mexicans" renovating the Carlyle. So instead I'd curled up on the couch in my nightgown with a glass of Merlot to think. I must have been more tired than I realized and had fallen asleep.

I got to the phone on the third ring, an old fashioned wall-mounted device like the one I'd spent hours talking on as a teenager. The number was unlisted and only a few people knew it, so it had to be important. "Hello," I queried.

"Gracie! Thank God I reached you. I tried your cell first, but it went to voicemail. The police are here. They want to take me in for questioning."

"Mamaw?" I tried to shake the cobwebs out of my brain. What were the police doing at Mamaw's?

"I can't talk long. I told them I needed to visit the powder room so I could call you. But I've got to go now. That nice young policeman, Bert Lancaster, is waiting. You'd like him. He isn't wearing a wedding ring."

"Questioning? What?" I asked, still trying to wake up. The wine had gone to my head, or maybe I was still in shock from seeing a dead body in a pool of blood. Maybe it was a late reaction from confronting Chief Doeppers. In any case, I wasn't at the top of my game and what Mamaw was saying made no sense.

Mamaw rolled right on over my fumbling. "I really should go. I just called to make sure you found Mable's platter. I've been worried sick over it. I know it's foolish to worry, but that platter is special."

"Mamaw. Stop. What exactly do the police want?" The woman was like a dog treeing a coon sometimes, so focused on one thing that she was unaware of anything else. Unfortunately, in this case, the anything else might be Doeppers trying to ruin my life again by pinning a murder on me.

"Well, I don't know, dear. Bert did ask about my revolver, but when we went to look for it, the gun wasn't in the glove compartment of the car, and I swear that was where I'd left it. I don't know where my mind has gone; first Mable's platter, now the revolver."

"You own a gun?" I was appalled. What was my seventy-seven-year-old grandmother doing with a firearm?

"Of course, dear. You know a woman can't be too careful nowadays, especially without a man in the house."

It clicked, and I suddenly knew what the police wanted. I needed to warn her before it was too late. "Mamaw, listen—"

"I really must go. I think you'd like Bert; he's such a nice young man with a good job, and your age, too! Oh, he's calling for me—I'm almost finished, Bert!—bye now, dear."

"Mamaw!" I cried. The dial tone sang in my ear. She had hung up on me.

I tried returning the call, but Mamaw wasn't answering her cell. I needed to talk to her before the police asked too many questions. Who knew what she would say to Doeppers? That man was a menace and would take Mamaw's comments out of context to hang her if he could.

I changed from my nightgown into an old pair of jeans and a knit tank top in sixty seconds flat. The top and jeans were a little loose, but I needed the comfort of old clothes at the moment. I pulled back my hair into a messy ponytail; I still wasn't quite used to it being this short and glanced into the mirror on the way to the door. Luckily, I'd been blessed with good skin and only a smattering of freckles across my nose. I rarely wore makeup other than lip-gloss. I thought about doing a little more for appearance's sake, but decided I looked good enough. After all, I was there to save Mamaw, not to impress a date.

I drove the Mustang as fast as I dared to the police station. I arrived just as a dark-haired officer opened the back door to a police cruiser and Mamaw stepped out. I slammed the Mustang into park and jumped out calling for her. Mamaw looked around startled as I ran to join them. The officer who had opened the door tried to guide Mamaw to the station, but thankfully she shook her arm away to wait for me.

"I warn you to say nothing," preempted the officer at Mamaw's side when I arrived. I glanced towards the man while I tried to catch my breath from the dash I'd just made. He was an inch or two taller than me, with a prominent nose and a military haircut. I realized that this must be the Bert Lancaster Mamaw had been so enthused about. His partner, who was standing on the other side of the cruiser, was the female officer who'd searched the Mustang earlier in the day. Lancaster had also been at the club, I realized—one of the officers taking pictures.

It didn't matter what he said. Nothing was going to stop me now, not with Mamaw's freedom on the line. I caught enough breath to begin, "Edward Schultz has been shot!"

"One more word and you will be…"

"They think he…"

"…arrested for interfering…"

"…was murdered…"

"…with an investigation," continued Lancaster.

"…with your gun," I gasped, still trying to catch my breath. Mamaw gulped, pulling her hands to her mouth in shock. I could almost hear the crickets chirping in the silence left by my announcement. I saw the realization blossom in Mamaw's eyes. She had read enough mysteries to know that she was now a suspect.

"Yancey, detain her," demanded Lancaster.

Before I knew what happened, I was slammed face down onto the patrol car. I protested as my arms were pulled cruelly behind my back and my wrists cuffed. I could hear Mamaw crying behind me, pleading with Lancaster to let me go. Then I was yanked up and pushed towards the station by Yancey, ahead of Lancaster, who now had to handle an indignant senior citizen. I was barely able to kick the door to the station open with a foot before Yancey opened it with my face.

I stumbled into a lobby area. Chairs lined the two walls on either side and a high counter on the far end guarded the double doors leading deeper into the building. At first, I couldn't place the woman in blue sitting behind the raised front desk, but when she looked towards us, it clicked. It was Emily Huntsman, a classmate from Alpine High and a childhood friend. I realized she was the one on the other end of the line when I'd called after finding the body. The voice had sounded familiar, but I would never have guessed that it was Emily. She'd been much more of the rabble-rouser than I and had a tongue that used to make the boys blush. Back then she was like a Tasmanian devil on speed. Mamaw and I had to come to her rescue more than a few times in those days. I never expected to see her in a uniform.

Yancey pushed me towards Emily and the desk. I could hear Lancaster struggling with Mamaw as they entered behind us. Mamaw was screaming about police brutality and how she was going to sue the city for all it was worth. Lancaster cursed under his breath, and Yancey sighed but kept me firm in her grip. Emily was downright laughing now, trying to hide her smile behind her hands. Mamaw created such a racket that a couple of officers appeared at the doors behind the front desk to watch. I was able to turn my head enough to catch a quick glimpse behind me, seeing Mamaw flailing her arms in an effort to get Lancaster to release her. The poor man looked overwhelmed, completely flabbergasted while trying to keep Mamaw in hand. I couldn't help but laugh and yell in encouragement, earning a nudge in the back from Yancey and a snort from Emily.

Doeppers appeared from nowhere and somehow cowed Mamaw with a look. He then turned his gaze to me; I swear I could feel daggers in my flesh. He ordered Yancey to take me to a holding cell, saying he'd deal with me later. That just set Mamaw off again, claiming that I'd been wrongfully detained. I yelled my agreement as Yancey pushed me through the doors behind Emily's desk.

Yancey led me past offices and interview rooms toward the back of the station. We went through a barred door, entering a small chamber with three cells along one wall and little alcoves along the opposite wall. I gagged from the foul smell, tracing the stench to the snoring man in the first cell. Thankfully Yancey took me to the third one, farthest from the drunk, and released my hands prior to shoving me in. There were four bunks, stacked two high along the back wall, and a curtained area that I assumed hid a commode. I tried breathing through my mouth; the smell was overwhelming.

I settled upon one of the bottom bunks, worried about Mamaw. I prayed she had the sense to watch her tongue, or better yet, to ask for a lawyer. I wondered who she'd call; Edward Schultz had been the only lawyer I knew in town, but Mamaw knew everyone, of course, and would know who to call in her moment of need. I feared that Doeppers was going to try and pin the murder on one of us, but at least I'd been able to warn Mamaw about how serious the situation was. I wondered what Doeppers would do now that I'd interfered with his case, and whether I'd be spending the night here. If it weren't for the smell, I wouldn't have minded so much. The cot was comfortable enough and I had the cell to myself, unless I found myself sharing it with Mamaw. Come to think of it, I had no interest in staying if that meant sharing with Mamaw. This would be a prime opportunity for her to nag me about a husband, children, and anything else she felt like discussing while I couldn't escape. Maybe I could claim sharing a cell with Mamaw was cruel and unusual punishment.

I stewed for perhaps fifteen minutes until I heard someone walking my way. I looked up and a grin escaped me as I saw Emily bearing two coffee cups and a smile that brought back memories. She wordlessly offered one of the cups to me and pulled up a chair just outside the cell.

"Well, I'll be a hog's tit, it *is* you. Gracie Thies back in town," said Emily. There were a few laugh lines around her eyes, and her figure was fuller, but otherwise she was the same Emily I remembered. Dirty blonde hair to her shoulders with a full mouth and glint in her light blue eyes like she was planning mischief. God, I missed those days.

"In the flesh," I replied.

"I swear I almost pissed my pants when I saw y'all come through that door. And with Miss Nora screeching like a dog in heat, I think y'all may have damn near given the Chief a heart attack."

"Is Mamaw all right?" I was much more concerned about her situation than mine. After all, I knew to what lengths Doeppers would go to get a conviction.

Emily nodded reassuringly. "She's with the Chief, answering a few questions. Don't get your panties in a wad."

"Emily, it's Mamaw."

She nodded and fixed me with a firm stare. "Exactly! And when have you ever known Miss Nora to be in need of help anyhow? I seem to remember she was the one always bailing out your sorry butt. She'll handle the Chief. He won't know what hit him."

"Uh, Emily, I think that was you who got bailed out."

"Damn straight. Miss Nora did me right." She grinned, clearly remembering a few of those episodes.

"And she needs you now," I pleaded. "You could repay that debt."

"Hogwash. Miss Nora will be fine. Better than you in fact. She'll answer a few questions and be home in time for *Matlock*, or whatever the hell she watches nowadays."

"Then why was she brought in for questioning? You tell me that," I pleaded. I needed Emily to reassure me that Doeppers wasn't going to pull a fast one on Mamaw. Her reassurance would allow me to sleep tonight, wherever that happened to be.

"Because it was her gun that was found today, you nitwit."

"Exactly," I said with satisfaction. "Which was why she needed to be told. Doeppers will try and pin this murder on her!"

"I think you need to be worrying about your own self, and let Miss Nora take care of her business," Emily warned.

"Crap," I muttered. It seemed Doeppers had me pegged for his patsy. This time I would go to jail. No community service for a murder rap.

"Listen, Yancey spits fire and pees vinegar. She's the first black woman hired by the Alpine Police Department and constantly thinks she has to prove herself. She has a chip on her shoulder as big as this jail cell, and she has this mad idea that you committed the murder. Luckily, the Chief disagrees."

"What?" I asked stunned. Doeppers thought I was innocent? It was Yancey who wanted to arrest me?

"Yancey thinks you staged it, and she's been fit to be tied ever since the Chief let you go. She would have hauled your ass in here faster than you can spit. Doeppers though—he doesn't think anyone who committed murder would have been as stupid as you were at the crime scene." She laughed. "Fishing a cell phone from a pool of congealing blood using the cord from a wall-mounted phone…"

"Listen, Emily," I interrupted, ignoring the jibe. "You know I didn't do it. You know how I am around blood. You know me. I just happened to be unlucky enough to find the body. I wish I'd never gone back to the club this afternoon." I grinned ruefully. "And I forgot the damned platter when I left again. If it's gone or broken, I'll never hear the end of it from Mamaw."

"Oh, I know you didn't do anything. Doeppers had me do the callin' to check out your alibi. Margaret over at the diner remembers you turnin' around in her lot, and the radio station confirmed the songs you mentioned in y'alls interview. We have the times. We got a pretty tight timeline goin' and it looks like you couldn't have done it."

I felt the blood rush to my face at how foolish I'd been. Doeppers knew his stuff, pulling enough details out of me to confirm my whereabouts during the time in question, and here I thought he was just being annoying. "But then Yancey…"

"Oh. She thinks you shot Schultz, drove off to establish an alibi and dump the gun, and then returned to 'discover' the body and see how the investigation progressed."

"What?" I asked, pondering whether what Yancey thought was even possible. There were still people in the club. I told Doeppers about everyone I could remember. "Clovis Jones—Skeeter—escorted me to the car," I reminded her. "How was I supposed to have shot Edward without him or any of the others noticing? And why would I want to shoot Edward in the first place?"

"Beats the hell out of me. It makes no sense for you or Miss Nora to knock off Schultz. We haven't tracked down this Clovis Jones yet for a statement, but we have officers out looking. He's a person of interest as well."

"Well, that's a relief. Maybe Doeppers will start looking outside my family for suspects." Could Clovis have done it? He was one of the last people in the club.

Emily shook her head. "You didn't help things along, you know."

"What do you mean?" I asked.

"Yancey thinks maybe you and Clovis have a thing and you worked together to kill Edward. Or maybe you drove off and returned to kill Schultz once everyone left. Your little act out front doesn't help matters. Rushing around like a chicken with its head cut off, saying it was Miss Nora's gun that was used in the murder."

"Well, it was, wasn't it? Or at least it could have been her gun." God, I hoped it wasn't, for Mamaw's sake. And a thing with Clovis, really? Did anyone actually see that man for who he really was? Besides, he was old!

"We don't know yet, but you seem to think so. Why would you assume that?" asked Emily, peering intently.

"It just fit," I explained. "I didn't even know Mamaw owned a revolver until she told me on the phone maybe an hour ago. When she said it had gone missing and the police were asking about it, it clicked. I assumed it was her gun that Doeppers had shown me this afternoon at the club. I figured it had to be the murder weapon."

"I see. And when did you talk to Miss Nora?" She pulled out a slim notebook and flipped it open.

"She called me from the bathroom on her cell, when the police arrived to bring her in for questioning—Emily, why are you writing this down?"

"Why do you think?" She laughed, but I could see her blush, and her eyes didn't meet mine.

"This is a police interview!" I should have known not to trust her. Emily had been my best friend in school, but that was clearly ancient history now. Today she was simply the employee of the man who ruined my life. "Emily, how could you? I thought you were my friend."

"I am your friend. Don't be an idiot, Gracie. Just tell me what happened." She looked at me, pencil poised.

"I can't believe this. Don't you have to warn me or something? Read me my rights?" I was aggravated beyond belief. Was there no one in this town I could trust?

"You aren't under arrest, not technically, so no, I don't have to read you your rights," she said smugly. I remembered that look from grade school, when Emily knew she was right and I was wrong.

"Then why the hell am I in this cell?" I demanded, returning her superior stare with one of my own.

Emily laughed and closed her notebook. For some reason that made me feel better. "Because of your stunt out front. What were you thinking?"

"I was thinking I needed to warn Mamaw to keep her mouth shut."

"But why? What could she possibly say?"

That took me aback. I thought about it and realized I'd been a fool. It wasn't as if Mamaw was going to lie. They had found her gun, of course the police would want to ask about it. "Crap."

"You sure stepped into a nice stinky cow pie."

I had to laugh. "Do you remember when someone broke into Hank's car and filled the back seat with cow pies?"

Emily blushed and looked away, and it struck me.

"It was you, wasn't it?"

"I plead the fifth."

"Emily! He was convinced it was his cousin John from down Gadsden way. He figured John did it when Hank refused to go along with some scheme of his."

"Come on, Gracie, you know how Hank was then, strutting his stuff all around school because he was going to Tech to play ball. I figured he needed to be taken down a peg or two."

"His car stunk for a month! We had to drive mine around everywhere. I gave him my extra set of keys while he was still trying to get the smell out." The mystery of who had filled the back seat of his car with cow pies had driven Hank crazy. He claimed he'd cleaned it, but it still stunk worse than a chicken coop, and I refused to go anywhere near his ride until after the smell was completely gone. In the meantime, we used the old Buick Mamaw and Papaw had given me for my seventeenth birthday, although Hank still insisted on driving most of the time.

"I remember. But that was then, and this is now." She flipped back open her notebook, and I knew she needed to know the truth. "Why did you do it, Gracie? Why did you have to meddle with this investigation?"

"I don't trust Doeppers," I confessed.

"Why ever not?" asked Emily.

"How can you ask that? After what happened in high school?"

"You still wound tight about that after all this time?" she asked, surprised.

"I spent every Saturday of the spring of my senior year picking up trash at the side of the road. I lost all my friends, except for you. Hank's father forbade him from seeing me. And why? Because that man planted dope and framed me."

"Gracie, are you really that naïve? You think a cop could be crooked in a town this size without word getting out? Hell, you fart in Margaret's Diner on a Friday and someone asks about it Sunday mornin' at church."

"I didn't put the marijuana there—"

"And neither did Jon Doeppers," finished Emily boldly. "I should know. I was married to the man for three years."

"What?" I asked aghast. "You were married to Doeppers?"

"Yep, seemed like a good idea at the time, being knocked up and all. Jon Junior is seven now and the biggest brat y'all will ever see, but I love him."

"I can't believe you have a kid."

"A kid? Gracie, I got two. Little Eliza Anne is two and a half, and a sweetheart. Here, let me find a picture." Emily fumbled in her wallet and pulled out a creased snapshot that she handed to me through the bars. I looked at it and felt my chest tighten. There Emily was, holding a little blonde girl dressed in pink and white lace with a little boy standing beside her in a blue suit. Behind them all was a tall man with dark hair. He had one hand resting on Emily's shoulder and the other on Jon's. They looked so happy I wanted to cry. "That's Henry in the background. He is an over-the-road trucker. We've been married for a little over three years now. Eliza Anne is his."

"You've got a beautiful family," I said, handing the picture back as I tried to blink away the sudden moisture in my eyes.

"And you? Last I heard you moved to Paris with some Frenchman. Any kids?"

"No children," I replied in a clipped tone. That was not a subject I wanted to discuss, now or ever. "Pierre died six months ago in a plane crash," I continued as calmly as I could.

"Oh, honey, I am so sorry," she said softly.

I wasn't going to cry. Not here, not now. The Event-That-Changed-My-Life would not keep its hold forever. I took a shuddering breath—and somehow the pain of the loss and betrayal was less. For the first time I realized that I would heal. It would take time, but I would get through this and build a new life. If not in Alpine, then somewhere.

"So, let me make sure I got this straight." Emily glanced down at her notes before continuing, "Miss Nora called you on her cell when Lancaster and Yancey went to pick her up. She told you about the gun then. You did not know anything about a gun before that time?"

"That's right. I've only been in town for a few weeks. Mamaw must have purchased the gun before then. I had no idea she owned a firearm." I watched as Emily scribbled down a few details.

"And then you put two and two together getting five, and decided to head down here to tell Miss Nora before we could interview her."

"Yes. I was afraid that if she didn't know she might say something stupid and get arrested for a crime she didn't commit," I explained. It sounded so foolish now that I said it aloud. What had I been thinking?

"Alrighty, then. Listen, I have to get this to the Chief. I've been gone too long the way it is. I'll try and convince him that you meant no harm; it shouldn't be too hard to confirm the facts of your story with Miss Nora."

"Thank you, Emily," I replied.

"I'm off on Saturday, and Henry will be home to watch the kids. What say we get together for lunch at Margaret's? Around eleven?"

"I'd like that. Very much," I replied. "I want to hear how you ended up as a police officer. I sure never would have predicted that!" I grinned at her and truly felt relieved. I knew that Emily would fight for me, be on my side, just like back in school. "But no little notebook," I warned.

Emily laughed as she stood, flipping the notebook open and showing a page of doodles. "The Chief says it can be disquieting to take notes. Half the time I think he's just making a grocery list. Now how I earned a uniform, that's quite a story." She scooted the chair back into the cubby in the wall where she had found it, and then turned back to me. "Y'all hold tight, hear. It shouldn't be too much longer."

I had waited perhaps a half hour when the drunk in the first cell woke with a groan. I averted my eyes when he stumbled towards the commode in his cell and pulled down his trousers, but I couldn't help but hear the sound of his relief and his satisfied sigh. Unfortunately it reminded me that I had not used the bathroom since before my nap, and with that realization came the urgent need to do so. I pulled back the curtain that separated the bath area from the rest of my cell. I discovered an ancient, chipped commode that had clearly seen better days. I couldn't quite tell if it was clean and stained, or dirty and stained. The thought of perching there was not appealing.

I returned to the bunk and started rocking back and forth, trying to think of anything but the need to pee. I couldn't believe how my day had gone. Seeing Hank Waderich again after all these years, discovering a dead body, running into Jon Doeppers and then Emily Huntsman. It felt like a bizarre *Twilight Zone* version of a high school reunion. When I had moved back to Alpine, my plan had been to spend some quality time with Mamaw while I got back on my feet before deciding what was next in my life. I knew Mamaw didn't have that many years left, and I'd gotten enough from Pierre's life insurance policy to take some time for her now. I hadn't realized how much of my past I'd be forced to confront by doing so. At eighteen I had run from Alpine never intending to look back. Now here I was, fifteen years later, back to where I'd started. It wasn't a pleasant feeling.

When the time came, it was Officer Yancey who showed up to get me. From what Emily had said, I knew Yancey suspected me of the murder, and I suppose I should have taken that threat seriously. I should have been dignified, stoic even. I don't know what came over me, maybe a bit of Emily had rubbed off, but I just couldn't behave. Instead, I greeted Yancey like an old friend. When she unlocked the cell and said I was free to go, I thanked her sincerely and started chatting about the sudden thunderstorm this afternoon. I asked to use the restroom, of course, and asked Yancey to wait, saying I was afraid I wouldn't be able to find my way out of the station otherwise. Once I'd finished, I asked her what salon she used and where she got her nails done. Yancey remained silent throughout, but I saw a slight tightening around her eyes; my efforts at annoying her were paying dividends.

Yancey left me in the lobby, almost fleeing back into the depths of the station. I asked the officer manning the front desk about Mamaw, and he replied that Lancaster had taken her back home already. I felt the tight muscles in my back and shoulders loosen. Grinning, I said goodnight and left by the front door, only slightly disappointed I hadn't seen Emily again. When I reached the Mustang, I was surprised to see something pinned under the wipers on the windshield. I yanked it free and cursed. Yancey had gotten the last laugh.

It was a parking ticket with her John Hancock.

Chapter 4

I slept in the next morning; I deserved it after the day I'd just had. Around 10 a.m. I rolled out of bed and took a shower in the clawfoot. It had one of those detachable showerheads that was reminiscent of a prior time, but in truth was new. I hadn't quite figured out the trick of using it, even after three weeks of renting the house, and once I'd finished water covered the bathroom floor. I grabbed a clean towel from the stack on the shelf over the commode, dried myself, and then dropped it on the floor to mop up the tile with a foot. It helped a little, but I almost slipped anyhow. The tile was slick when wet. I decided I'd let the rest air-dry.

I found an old pair of jeans and a T-shirt from a concert I didn't remember attending. I made a cup of Fresh Mornin', a coffee blend I'd picked up in Gadsden in bulk on my last shopping trip. When I first saw the coffee machine capable of making one cup of coffee from an individually wrapped little plastic cup, I bought it on impulse, thinking it would be perfect for my lifestyle. Of all the things about Paris, the one I missed the most was the variety of caffeinated drinks: espressos, cappuccinos, lattes, and more. However, I should have realized that in Alpine I wouldn't be able to find the plastic refill cups.

With coffee in hand, I sat at the kitchen table and reached for the receiver of the wall-mounted phone. I dialed Mamaw's cell but it went to voicemail; she'd probably forgotten to charge it. I tried her home number next and got a busy signal. I needed to talk to her about what happened yesterday. I wanted to know what she told the police. If I couldn't get her on the phone, I'd just have to drive over and see her in person.

I finished the coffee, locked up, and left by the back door off the kitchen. It was a typical Alabama summer day, hot and so muggy from the rain overnight that I swore I could almost steam some greens if I set a covered bowl out in the sun. The Mustang was in the carport where I'd left it. I crossed my fingers, turned the key, and breathed easier as it fired right up.

I detoured downtown on my way to Mamaw's house. The parking lot at Margaret's Diner had only a few cars, about normal for midmorning on a Friday. The club still had the yellow crime tape blocking the door and there was a police cruiser parked out front. I wondered when, or if, we'd be playing bridge there again. I turned on Pine and worked my way over to East, where Mamaw lived. I pulled up in front of her place, a two-story Victorian that was built in 1874, painted baby blue with yellow trim. The ginger-breading around the windows needed a little bit of work, and it looked like the chimney could use a tuckpointing. Papaw had always done the house repairs, and since his passing, Mamaw had tried to keep it up to his standards, but she didn't have the eye for it. In truth, neither did I.

When I'd scurried home like a dog with its tail between its legs after the Event-That-Changed-My-Life, Mamaw had offered me the second floor of the house. She had converted a small sitting room off the dining room into a downstairs bedroom so she could avoid the stairs, which left the whole upstairs free for me. Part of me yearned to move back in, but the stronger half rebelled. Maybe it was pride, or maybe I just knew that I needed my own space. In any case, after a few weeks of living with Mamaw, when I had discovered that the cottage on Elm was available, I had leapt at it. That meant Mamaw was alone in the Victorian. It worried me some, and I wished Mamaw could find a roommate that wasn't me, but she refused to share with anyone who wasn't family, saying "her home wasn't some boarding house for miscreants."

I went to the back door, as did everyone, and let myself in. Mamaw was sitting at the kitchen table talking on the phone. I was surprised to find her still in her nightgown. Normally she'd have been dressed for the day hours ago. I grabbed a coffee cup and poured my second cup for the day from Mamaw's pot. It was off-brand generic, plain and simple but good. I then joined Mamaw at the table.

"I talked to Evelyn Franklin earlier," said Mamaw to the phone. She flashed me a grin and then continued, "She is just devastated. Uh huh… Edward was her beau back in the day. You didn't know?" Mamaw motioned to the coffee machine with her cup and a frown. I took the hint and got her a refill. She rolled her eyes at me when I returned. Whoever was on the other end of the line was talking her ear off. "Ida, I really must go… uh huh… I'm sure they'll let us back into the club soon. Uh huh… you should talk to Gladys, she's the club manager after all… Oh it couldn't have been anyone at the club… I agree… it must have been those hooligans at that beastly old hotel…. well, that was why I bought the gun in the first place… exactly… Ida, I really must go. Gracie just walked in… of course I'll ask what she saw… I'll talk to you again soon. Bye-bye now… I'm devastated as well… I sure will… bye now."

Mamaw replaced the receiver on the wall and turned to me with a sigh. "That was Ida Bea. Oh my goodness, I didn't think I would ever get off the phone with her. That phone has been ringing off the hook all morning."

"No wonder I couldn't get through earlier." I took a sip of coffee and saw Mamaw's demeanor change. She crossed her arms and fixed me with a stare.

"Gracie Amelia Theis, I'm cross with you!"

"What?" I asked. This was not how this conversation was supposed to go.

"I'm cross with you. How dare you discover a body, at the bridge club no less, and not call me immediately?"

"Mamaw…" Really? She was upset that I hadn't called her? The woman had almost been arrested. Her gun had been stolen and probably used to kill someone, and she was upset with me?

"And what were you thinking last night? Here I had almost convinced that nice young policeman Bert Lancaster to look you up, and what do you do? Dash in and get arrested."

"I was not arrested—"

"Well, certainly not. I told Chief Doeppers that if he didn't release you, I'd picket the station. I have connections in this town. See how far…"

I tuned her out. God, I needed a cigarette. I let my mind wander to that little café off of Mode de Blanc in Paris where I used to spend a lazy morning while drinking a cup of espresso. I could almost smell the freshly baked croissants that permeated the small nook. The cafe had room inside for only three small tables, with maybe half a dozen tables on the sidewalk out front. It had been a favorite getaway when Pierre was flying. I sighed, letting the image fade. It was from another time, before the Event-That-Changed-My-Life. I took another sip of coffee, thinking how Alpine needed a haven like that, or maybe I just needed one.

"...and so he agreed," finished Mamaw triumphantly.

I had no idea what she'd just said, but from her look I knew she expected some kind of response from me. I don't know how Mamaw did it, but whenever I tried to have a conversation with her, it always went off kilter. Here I had come over to her house to learn what she'd told the police, and instead found myself defending my actions. It was time to draw a line in the sand. I had my own questions that needed answers. "Mamaw, when did you get a gun?" I asked.

"You still haven't answered my question, Gracie."

"Which question is that?" I had lost my patience. The phone rang just as I was about ready to let her have a piece of my mind. On the second ring I realized it had saved me from saying something I knew I would have regretted. Mamaw looked torn. I could almost see the wheels turning inside her head. Should she continue to put me through the ringer or gossip on the phone?

The phone won out. She reached for it, saying she wanted to talk to me again later. I stood and rinsed the coffee cup in the sink. I wouldn't get any answers out of her now, not with the gossip mill turning and Mamaw's own agenda for our conversation. The answers I sought would have to come later. She was still on the phone when I finished. I waved my goodbye and left by the back door. I reached for a cigarette once I was on the back stoop, but somehow found the will power to shove it back into the pack. I walked around front and started up the Mustang.

I drove back by the club, seeing the same police cruiser parked out front. I slowed and pulled the Mustang into a shady spot under an old oak tree so I could think. The club looked innocent enough, no dark shadows or menacing clouds on the horizon. Yet someone had committed a murder there yesterday and I had stepped into the middle of it. Who would want to kill Edward Schultz and why?

Part of me knew the sane thing to do was to let the police handle it, but to do that I had to trust Doeppers, something I was not yet prepared to do. Despite what Emily had said, I still felt that Doeppers was to blame for what happened when I went to Alpine High. I pulled out my pack of cigarettes and cursed at how crushed they'd become over the last twenty-four hours. I pulled out the best of the lot and lit it, tossing the rest of the pack onto the passenger seat. I ignored the pang of guilt I felt at succumbing to the pull of my addiction. I thought back to that pivotal day over fifteen years ago, the beginning of when my life went to the dogs.

Hank and I were in the same History class in seventh period, where we usually spent more time passing coded notes back and forth under the nose of Mr. Klink than paying attention to the lesson. We'd been going out since the start of the football season, and we couldn't keep our hands off each other. I'd just gotten a note from Hank saying he wanted to talk about something after school but needed to stop by the locker room first. I flashed him a smile, and we enjoyed a quick kiss after the bell rang, ignoring Mr. Klink's protest. I told Hank that I'd meet him at my car later and stopped by my locker to gather my things, where I ran into Emily.

"So, you still hauling Hank the Hunk's ass around?" she asked while opening her locker, which was two doors down from mine.

"Emily," I laughed. "If Mamaw heard you she'd wash that filthy mouth out with a bar of soap!" While we'd been best friends in grade school, we'd grown apart some in high school. I was the prim and proper type, while she was more on the wild side.

"Good thing she isn't here then, ain't it?" she replied smugly. Emily had dated him before Hank and I became an item and was always harassing me about taking her "leftovers." "Griece and I are heading to the lake tonight," offered Emily. "Care to join us?"

"You be careful with him. He's the type who wants a bit more from a girl than is appropriate," I warned.

"Hell, he's like a dog in heat. That's partially why I like him, and why you and Hank should join us. I might need a bit of support if his engine gets roaring too high. And you know I'm high octane fuel," crowed Emily with a flick of her hair.

Laughing, I replied, "I'll ask Hank if he wants to go. We're meeting by the car later. I think he's finally going to ask me to prom." I felt the silly smile on my face but couldn't stop myself.

"You mean that dog hasn't asked you yet? I figured he manned up weeks ago."

"It hasn't arisen," I replied primly.

"Too easy," replied Emily.

"What?" I asked.

"I said 'Too easy'. Talking about you, Hank and something rising."

"Emily!" I gasped appalled. I could feel the heat on my face.

"That blush says it all." She laughed. "Call me about tonight. Griece is coming to pick me up about 7 p.m." I watched as Emily sauntered away, flicking her hair.

I gathered my things and headed towards the parking lot. Every few feet there was someone to talk to. The school was abuzz with gossip: prom, weekend parties, classes, all the normal high school stuff. I made arrangements to meet Jill Stupiansky and Catherine Dooley on Sunday afternoon to talk about prom decorations. I talked to Sam Pezzillo about Hank's Pontiac and the smell. He suggested tomato juice, of all things. I told him that would just make Hank's car smell like an Italian chicken coop. I even commiserated with Ellen Kelper on the math test we'd taken that day.

I left the school in a good mood, hoping that Hank hadn't been waiting by the car too long. I turned the corner and was surprised to see a police cruiser in the student parking lot. I was even more surprised to see a hound dog sniffing around my Buick. A small crowd had gathered but parted like the Red Sea as I walked up.

"What's going on here?" I asked.

A tall policeman I didn't recognize turned toward me. He had thin sandy blonde hair cut in a military style, and the blue uniform stretched across a muscular physique that would make Emily swoon like a Goth girl meeting Johnny Depp. He flipped open a small note pad that he pulled from his back pocket as he asked, "Is this your car, Miss? And your name is?"

"Yes, this is my car. My name is Gracie Theis. What's happening here?"

The man jotted something in his notebook and closed it before answering. "My name is Officer Doeppers and I'm with the Alpine Po-lice." I'd lived in rural Alabama my entire life, but this man's southern accent was thicker than the humidity on the Alabama coast in July. "We received a tip down at the station about illicit drugs in student cars, and our hound has gotten a hit on this here ve-hic-le," continued Doeppers, savoring every word. "That's probable cause to demand a search of said ve-hic-le."

"You want to search my car?" My heart felt like I'd run the mile at a track meet even as I stood with feet frozen on the asphalt. It didn't seem possible for a dog to smell anything in my car. There were no drugs. I was Gracie Amelia Theis, class treasurer, cheerleader, planning on going to college at Georgia Tech in the fall with Hank, where he'd gotten a football scholarship. My future was set; no way would I jeopardize all that with drugs.

"That is cor-rect," drawled Officer Doeppers. "If you would be so good as to unlock this here ve-hic-le."

I glanced around at the murmuring crowd, looking for advice on what to do. All I saw were shocked, scared faces, and no sign of Hank. Part of me screamed to refuse this outrageous demand, but the man said he had probable cause, and I was afraid refusing would make me look guilty of something. I opened my purse and found my set of keys. I shoved them towards the officer like I was holding an old smelly sock. The sooner he finished, the sooner I could go home and forget all about this.

Officer Doeppers smiled and took the keys from my outstretched hand. He turned and said something to his partner, who was holding the dog, and before I knew what had happened, the dog was in the police cruiser and my car was sitting with all four doors, the hood, and the trunk open. At this point the crowd had increased and there were a few teachers scattered among the students. Mr. Klink was standing by my side, murmuring something about staying strong. Hank still hadn't arrived, and I was beginning to wonder if something had happened to him.

Doeppers was crawling around in the backseat, while the other officer with the dog stayed outside the vehicle keeping the crowd away. My fear had abated, but my embarrassment had only grown as the afternoon sun crossed the sky. This incident would be the talk of the school for days. Thankfully it was the weekend, so I wouldn't have to deal with the gossip until Monday morning.

I was about to demand he stop when Doeppers hollered from the backseat and held something up in his hands as if he held a live water moccasin. It was hard to see through the thick glass of the back window, but it appeared to be a plastic sandwich bag filled with herbs. My heart leaped in my throat as Doeppers crawled out of the car, said something to his partner, and turned to address me.

"Is this yours, Miss Theis?" he asked.

"I've never seen that before in my life," I replied, taking a step backwards. I felt the world closing in and feared I would faint.

"Now listen here," began Mr. Klink. "Gracie Theis is an excellent student and in no way could be held responsible for whatever it was you claim to have found in her car."

"And you are?" Doeppers asked, pulling out and flipping open his little notebook.

"George Klink, the History teacher, and I tell you Miss Theis is innocent!" I had never heard such a passioned tone in Mr. Klink's voice and felt relieved that someone was defending me.

Doeppers jotted something in his notebook, and then turned his icy stare back to me. "So, Miss Theis, you deny that this belongs to you?"

"I already said that I have never seen it before. Of course it's not mine," I replied in a shaky voice.

"But this is your ve-hic-le, which was locked before the search. This bag did come from your locked car."

Taking my cue from Mr. Klink, I found my courage and replied, "Or so you claim." I heard snickers and glanced around me. I'd almost forgotten about the crowd; this show would be meal for the gossip mill for weeks, not days.

"I think we should continue this discussion down at the station," stated Doeppers menacingly. "Come with me."

"I don't want to go," I whispered, taking another step backwards.

Doeppers followed, stepping towards me as he said, "I'm afraid you have no choice, Miss Theis. You've been found in possession of marijuana, and as an officer of the la-aw, I do declare that you shall accompany me back to the station to answer my queries. Now you can either do so under your own free will, or I'll cuff you and drag you there myself." He grabbed my arm and I could see the shocked look on my friends' faces as he escorted me to his patrol car. I remembered looking out the window of the police car as we began to pull away, seeing Hank's solemn face staring back at me from the crowd.

Sighing, I returned to the present. My cigarette was finished and the inside of the Mustang was turning hot despite the shade. Hank and I didn't make it to the lake that night, nor did I meet with Jill and Catherine that Sunday to talk about prom. Hank did ask me to prom that next week, but it wasn't the same between us. When I got sentenced to 120 hours of community service a month later, Hank's father, Harry, banned him from seeing me and I ended up not going to prom at all. My so-called friends at school treated me like I had head lice; only Emily stood by me. I went to a small private college that fall in upstate New York where no one knew me, instead of Georgia Tech as I'd planned. Those last months at Alpine High were some of the worst of my life.

And it was all Doeppers' fault, or so it seemed at the time. Now Emily was claiming that Doeppers hadn't planted that marijuana to make a name for himself, like I'd thought. There were only two sets of keys to that old

Buick: I had one and Hank had the other. As Doeppers said, the car had been locked. Hank had denied having anything to do with the drugs Doeppers had found, but he did have that football scholarship, the first in his family to make it out of Alpine to go to college. Could he have lied to me all those years ago? Had I been betrayed then, for the first time, and not even known?

I fired up the Mustang and did a U-turn to go back the way I'd come. Hank had been outside the club yesterday and he was acting suspicious. I couldn't see him as a murderer, but then again, I didn't think he would have hung me out to dry on a possession charge either. He had some questions to answer about yesterday and about that day fifteen years ago. I was sick of being the patsy to any man's shenanigans. He needed to answer some of my questions. It was time to exercise those "little grey cells," as Hercule Poirot would say, and solve this mystery to clear both my name and Mamaw's.

It didn't dawn on me until much later that I was potentially on my way to confront a killer.

Chapter 5

I hadn't been out northeast of town on Roundbarn Road since I'd moved back. It looked like little had changed in the fifteen years since I'd fled. The barn the road was named after was still there; a wooden structure 73 feet in diameter that Hank and I spent one musty afternoon exploring. Small tobacco plots broke the lightly wooded areas on either side of the road. I passed a cornfield on the left, and then turned onto the county road that Hank's family farm was on. It hadn't occurred to me until now to wonder if Hank lived elsewhere. I stepped on the gas and felt the Mustang roar beneath me. I would just knock on the front door and see.

Turning into the Waderich driveway gave me a sense of déjà vu. Ancient pecan trees lined the gravel lane. Hank had told me once that his grandfather had planted the trees back in the 1940s with high hopes of another cash crop, but that dream had failed like so many others. Even fifteen years ago, what little the trees had produced was of poor quality and had been dumped in the hog feed.

I pulled into the farmyard and gazed at the white farmhouse surrounded by a picket fence. A twin pair of windows on the second floor overlooked the yard. The covered porch had a swing on the far end and a door in the center. I remembered the long spring evenings sitting with Hank on that swing talking some and kissing more. That was before the arrest, of course. After the scene with Officer Doeppers, I hadn't been welcome at the Waderich home. After the conviction, I hadn't been welcome anywhere.

I checked in the rearview mirror and put on fresh lip gloss, reasoning I'd do it for anyone, although deep down I knew I wouldn't. I got out of the Mustang and marched through the gate and up the walk to the front door. The door was propped open, leaving just a screen as the only barrier between inside and out. The place had no air, not even window units. I could hear a TV playing, which gave me hope of finding someone at home. I knocked.

I glanced around the yard while I waited for someone to come to the door. The flowerbeds needed to be weeded; actually, it looked like the beds hadn't been touched in years. I remembered how they'd looked before—a rainbow of flowers from white to purple. Now only a few plants peeked through the grasses that had taken over the bed. In fact, the whole place was in need of some care. The bushes on either side of the front gate were overgrown and beginning to encroach upon the walk. One of the redbud trees along the north side was dead, and none of the others looked healthy. Even the house needed some attention. Now that I was close, I could see the peeling paint.

I knocked on the door again but heard no one. I tried the screen door. It was unlocked, so I let myself in. The front room hadn't changed; the patterned sofa was still sitting proudly in front of the fireplace. Guarding the sofa on either side were two antique end tables, both in an Alpine design from the glory days. The matching high board gracing the far wall held a scattering of artfully displayed Depression glass. I stepped over to admire the pieces and noticed the dust. The room hadn't been cleaned in months. I knew that Mildred would never have allowed her house to degrade so far and wondered what could have happened.

I marched through the house back towards the sound of the TV. I passed through the kitchen, flabbergasted by the array of dirty dishes, scraps of food, and wrappers left on the counters. The back room was somehow worse; I couldn't see the floor on account of the mess, a scattering of shoes, blankets, papers, and empty bottles. The TV on the far wall was turned up so loud that it hurt my ears, and in the middle of it all sat someone unmoving on a recliner facing towards the television. For a second I was fearful I'd discovered my second dead body in two days, and then I heard the snore.

I picked my way to the sleeping figure and gazed down upon my once-upon-a-time nemesis. Harry Waderich had not aged well. His once strong frame had shrunken into a shadow of itself. Wrinkles etched his brow like the carvings in the more intricate pieces of Alpine heritage. He was wearing a plaid shirt whose pattern couldn't hide the stains of sweat and wear, and even with the heat, his legs were covered by an afghan that once had graced the back of the sofa in the living room. On the table beside the chair sat an untouched Salisbury steak in a cardboard container. Beside the microwave meal was an empty rum bottle and the remote for the TV. From the smell it looked like Harry had drunk his lunch.

I shook the man, intending to ask about Hank, but he just muttered in his stupor and squirmed in the chair. The afghan slipped when he rolled to the side and I saw a grimace flash across his face. Something looked wrong, and when I reached to adjust the afghan, I knew what it was. A quick peek confirmed my suspicions: Harry had no legs beneath either knee.

Once I was sure Harry was comfortable, or at least as comfortable as he could be passed out drunk, I used the remote to turn off the TV and tiptoed my way back to the kitchen. The man could be out for hours, there was no telling how much alcohol had been in the bottle when he started. Yet someone had to be caring for him, if you could call leaving him with a bottle of rum and a TV dinner in front of the television all day caring. There was no way Harry could have heated the meal in the microwave, let alone gotten it to his chair. And that Salisbury steak was still warm, perhaps not appetizing, but warm. And where was his wheelchair? Shouldn't he have one if he had no legs?

I needed time to think this through, and at least here I could do some good and avoid Mamaw's harping for a bit. I began by hunting for the coffee machine, finding it tucked away in the cabinet beneath the sink. I got a pot brewing, knowing that Harry would need a cup when he woke up. I then began on the dishes. Of course the dishwasher was full, so I started by unloading and loading another set. That took care of maybe a third of the dirty dishes lying about. I piled the rest in the sink and then found a box of trash bags in the pantry. I filled two 50-gallon bags and began to find the red countertop beneath the mess. I piled the trash on the back steps and continued to clean.

When my stomach growled, I realized I'd skipped lunch. I glanced into the refrigerator and immediately went for another trash bag. I'd lost my appetite. After piling a third bag on the back step and adding to the dishes in the sink, I heard a sound from the back room. I rushed to check on Harry and almost gagged on the smell—the damn man had puked in his sleep.

I went to the laundry and luckily found a stack of clean towels and a bucket. I couldn't find any hand soap in the kitchen, so I used dish soap with hot water. There was no way to do this gently—and frankly I wasn't that interested in being gentle with Harry—so I just started scrubbing the filthy man. He didn't remain asleep long, and woke with curses, flailing with his arms. He glared at me, claiming he could do it by himself. I left him to it and returned to the kitchen.

I unloaded and loaded the dishwasher again. I might be able to finish with one more load, if I was lucky. The counters were clean and I recalled seeing a pack of Pillsbury cookie dough in the refrigerator. Maybe the cookie smell would mask the stench.

As the smell of cookies filled the air, the man called for me. I entered, seeing the pile of filthy towels beside the bucket on the floor. Harry had sat up in the recliner, but didn't look that much better. His eyes wavered as he looked at me; the man was still drunk as a skunk. "So, are you one of the damn Baptists?" he slurred.

"Nope," I replied.

"Well, get the hell out of my house, whoever you are. I don't need y'all's damn charity," he said, flailing his arms like he was shooing away a fly.

"It looks to me like you could use some help," I replied. The old goat was as ornery and stubborn as I remembered.

"Looks can be deceiving. The boy and I are doing fine on our own. We don't need nobody." His bloodshot eyes glared briefly at me, and then lost focus again.

"The boy?" I asked.

"My son, Hank. He's around here somewhere and we be doin' fine. Don't need no damn church folk sniffing about."

So Hank did live here after all, and he was the one responsible for his father. I would have words with him about that. "I've been here for a while and I haven't seen him. Why don't I just stay around for a bit?" I offered. "Just in case you need anything."

Something inside of Harry broke, or perhaps it had broken long ago. He wilted before me and looked away as he mumbled, "Do whatever you want, not like I can stop ya."

I took it as permission and grabbed the towels and bucket from the floor. I threw the towels in the wash and added a few other items from the laundry room floor before starting the machine. I then returned to the kitchen and pulled the cookies from the oven, setting them on the counter to cool. It was time to tackle the back room.

I grabbed a trash bag and started with the liquor bottles. In addition to the empty rum bottle on the table, I found three empty vodka bottles on the floor and another rum bottle stuck between the cushions of the couch. I couldn't count the number of beer cans. I then added the empty food wrappers, newspapers, and a few unidentifiable items that made me wish for gloves. Harry had turned on the television, but spent more time looking at me than at the screen.

I kicked the two pairs of shoes, obviously Hank's, to the side of the room and tossed the blankets on the couch, leaving the floor relatively free of clutter. I then turned to Harry and realized that the smell of the place was not entirely Harry's fault. I should have realized it sooner. There was no way Hank could leave Harry immobile this long without taking into consideration his bodily needs. Hank had rigged a bedpan for Harry if he needed it.

"I suppose you're expecting me to thank ya. Well, I won't do it. I didn't ask for y'all's help." Harry growled from his recliner.

"Where's your chair?" I asked. If I was going to clean this room, I needed to get Harry and his smelly self out of the way.

"What?"

"Your wheelchair, where is it?" I demanded.

"I don't need no damn chair. I'm perfectly content to stay where I am. I have everything I need right here."

I ignored the man and went to the kitchen. I grabbed a clean plate from the cabinet and piled a dozen chocolate chip cookies on top. I poured a cup of coffee and returned to the back room with coffee and cookies in hand. I could see Harry salivating, but placed the plate out of reach on the coffee table in front of the couch. I grabbed a cookie from on top and made a big show of eating it in front of him.

"Hand me one of those, will ya?" Harry asked.

"I thought you had everything you needed?" I wasn't above a little torture after what he'd done to me all those years ago.

"I'm a bit hungry," admitted Harry.

"Well, your lunch is sitting right beside you. Salisbury steak, right?" I could see the man stiffen, and he grabbed the remote and turned the volume of the television to the point I swore my ears would bleed. I felt a stab of guilt, but I couldn't let Harry bully me like he was obviously accustomed to doing to others. I stood and walked over to the TV; the plug was easy to find.

"Why the hell'd ya do that?"

"I'll make a deal with you, Harry. You tell me where your chair is and I'll give you one of these cookies. I'll even throw in this cup of coffee."

"Ah, hell. The chair's in the bedroom, second door on the left past the kitchen."

I handed the plate of cookies to Harry, who immediately stuffed one into his mouth. I placed the cup of coffee beside him and then followed his directions to the bedroom.

Fifteen years ago the room served as a dining room, with a large table centered in the middle and a china cabinet in the left corner, which balanced the fireplace on the right, with a window between them. A slew of family photographs on the walls and an overhead chandelier had completed the space. The fireplace remained, but that was all. The table had been replaced with a double bed centered on the left wall, and where the china cabinet used to be now stood a dresser with drawers hanging open and clothes sticking out like a cracked overripe tomato leaking juice. The bed was drowned by laundry, and the wheelchair was jammed in the near corner under siege by old jeans, socks, and underwear that were as ripe as—well, an overripe tomato leaking juice. The chandelier had been replaced as well, by a ceiling fan that was losing the battle to cool the space.

I retreated to the laundry area, where I remembered seeing a basket, and this time searched the cabinets for the elusive rubber gloves. Armed for battle, I returned to the room and gathered the laundry, freeing the wheel chair and discovering the oval hand-knotted rug that used to lie under the table. I guess it too had survived the bedroom conversion. I placed the basket in the laundry area, tossed the comforter on the bed and wheeled my prize to Harry now that the path was clear.

Seeing the chair, Harry reared like a coon confronting a hound dog. "Why'd ya bring that out here fur?" he demanded.

"I thought you could use some fresh air," I replied.

"Open your eyes, girl. The damn window's letting in enough air to suit me."

"Look, Harry," I said, losing my patience. "The recliner you are sitting in reeks. You reek. If you get in the chair, I'll wheel you out to the front porch and then I'll see what I can do with your recliner. Afterwards maybe we can see what we can do about you."

"Damn rude Baptist. I don't need this crap. Who do you think you are walking in here and being so high and mighty?"

Good question. What the hell was I doing cleaning up after Hank and Harry? This wasn't my problem, why should I care? But I knew the answer. "Because it's a job that needs doing, and my Mamaw raised me to do what needs to be done. Besides, Mildred would be ashamed to see you like this."

At the mention of his wife's name, Harry blanched whiter than a Yankee on spring break on the Redneck Riviera. "You knew my wife?" he asked tentatively.

"A long time ago," I said.

He frowned. "Maybe some air would be nice," he replied. "That damn chair can be a nuisance."

Now that Harry was amenable, it didn't take long to get him into the chair and wheeled to the front porch. I parked the chair near the swing and turned to go back into the house. Maybe if I mixed the laundry bleach with some water, I could get the chair disinfected and remove the smell emanating from the back room.

"Wait," called Harry as I opened the door. "Sit a spell, will ya?"

"Let me get the cookies." I smiled. I got the plate of cookies, only half full now, and poured both Harry and myself another cup of coffee. I came back to the front porch, sat on the swing, and returned Harry's stare.

"I don't know ya, do I?" asked Harry. "How did ya know Mildred?"

"We've met before," I replied. "It must be fifteen years since I last saw Mildred." I was not ready to mention my connection to Hank, not with how it had ended. Better to leave it vague for now. I took a sip of my coffee while I waited Harry out. The man used to like talking.

"She passed five years ago this August. Worst day of my life, coming home from the fields to find her lying in the begonias just over yonder," he said, waving to a patch of tall grass on the far side of the yard. Now that he mentioned it, I did remember a flowerbed there. "Doctors said it was a heart attack," he murmured.

"I'm sorry to hear that," I replied. And I was. Mildred had always been kind to me, at least before I was banned from the property. Her passing did explain the state of the house and yard though.

"Place just wasn't the same after that, like a peapod without the peas, just an empty shell remained," continued Harry. He took a stuttering breath, then said, "She went to First Methodist, sang in the choir for years and taught Vacation Bible School in the summer. Preacher used to come around after she passed. Haven't seen him now for a couple of years. He put ya up to this?"

"Nope," I replied with a smile.

"Damn then, girl, whatcha doing here? Haven't had company in I don't know how long."

I knew if Harry remembered who I was, he would clam up and I wouldn't learn anything. I had too many questions, about what Hank had been up to recently and about the Hank of years ago. I needed a reason for the visit, one that didn't spook Harry. Time to fib a little, and maybe get Harry to talk about Hank during his high school years as well. "Actually, I came looking for your son, Hank. I spoke with Samuel Olgaman a few days ago and he told me this story involving Hank from his high school days," I lied. "I'm writing a book on Alpine High's football teams and wanted to make sure I got the details of the story right. It's part of the town's push to become a regional tourist center, you know, add a little local flair with a history book on the town's football teams." It was a ridiculous lie, but I hoped Harry would buy it.

"Seems like a damn fool thing to me," he said, taking the bait hook, line and sinker. "Who'd buy such a thing anyhow? Just like those idiots on the town council, thinking of Alpine as a tourist center. Damn crooks all of them. This one of Edward Schultz's ideas?" he asked. "He's the worst of the lot. A damn rotten apple, that one."

"Nope," I said. "This project has nothing to do with Mr. Schultz." Apparently Harry had not yet heard of the murder. Not really surprising, considering how isolated he was. Time to pry a little. "But I thought Mr. Schultz was a well-respected citizen of Alpine. Is there something I don't know?"

He looked at me sideways, studying me like a cat before pouncing. Eventually I knew he'd tell me what I wanted to know. "After Mildred died, I had a rough spell. Drank too much, caused a stir once or twice. Somehow I ended up in an auto accident off of State Road 43, down on the curve where those two ol' silos used to sit on either side of the 'bacci shed. The damn accident cost me both my legs, but the other driver walked away. And ya know what happened then? The damn idiot who hit me claimed I was on the wrong side of the road. Said I was drunk. Schultz represented him in a civil case and took us for all we had. Said I had a 'history,' the damn fool. The man who hit me claimed he couldn't work no more; him there standing on his two good legs while I'm sitting there in this damn chair. We had 'ta take a loan on the farm to pay 'em. Barely could make ends meet the way it was and now we gotta pay on a lien 'cause he said he can't work no more.

Hank had to move back home afterwards to help out. Lost him a good job on an assembly line down in Gadsden, he did."

I felt the world close in. I'd read enough Agatha Christie novels to know that to solve a mystery you look for motive, method and opportunity. From what Harry just said, Hank had the motive to wish Edward harm, and he was present at the bridge club, two of the three. Did he know about Mamaw's gun? Could he have succumbed to murder?

"What day is it anyhows?" asked Harry. "They alls run together something fierce anymore."

"Friday."

"Well, Hank musta gone down to the car lot off of the ole Gadsden road. Ya know the place; ol' Henry Watson runs it. Hank goes down on Fridays to detail cars before the weekend rush. Should be back anytime. Lookie there, that's his F150 now." Harry pointed down to the road.

"What?" I turned and saw the same truck that Hank had driven yesterday. I could place him at the bridge club around the time of the murder, and I now knew about the court case. Could Hank actually be a murderer? Would he see me as a bit of unfinished business? Was I destined for a shallow grave?

Chapter 6

My first thought was to run like a chicken from a coon. Harry couldn't stop me and I could reach the Mustang before Hank arrived, if just barely. The trouble was the single lane driveway, and those pecan trees lining it. I couldn't make it to the road before Hank cut me off. If I ran and he was a murderer, I knew he wouldn't hesitate to block my way. I could place him at the crime scene with a motive, after all.

"Well, I'm sure me boy will regale ya with stories of his glory days. He got a football scholarship ya know, down at Georgia Tech," said Harry.

I mumbled something to Harry and tuned him out as he continued to ramble about Hank and his glory days on the gridiron. I hadn't told Harry my name, fearing that he would recognize it and kick me out for old perceived sins. I certainly wouldn't get him to talk about Hank's high school days if he knew I was prying into what happened back then. And I needed to keep Harry in the conversation. Hank wouldn't try anything with his father around. At least I hoped he wouldn't.

"Got hurt in his senior year of college and couldn't play no more. Damn shame that," continued Harry. "Did get him a degree though, majored in Anth-er-polgy of all things. Don't know what that is exactly, but he can't seem to get a job doing it. Hank was the first Waderich in history to get a college degree, and he wasted it on Anth-er-polgy."

I ignored Harry's mumbling about Anthropology—I needed to think. If Hank would go along with the football story, maybe I could fool Harry. And talking about high school might keep Hank from getting wary that I was suspicious of his actions yesterday afternoon. I took a drama class in college; I could do this.

I needed a smoke.

I grabbed at my pockets for a cigarette, only then remembering that I'd left the pack in the car. I plastered a smile on my face and departed the front porch like a soldier marching to the battlefront—or maybe more like a sheep to the shear-pen. I needed to take charge before Hank said something to blow my cover with Harry. Hank had parked his truck next to my Mustang and he was busy admiring the car.

"Hank Waderich," I called drawing his attention. Before he could say anything, I continued, "My name is Emily Klink. I'm writing a story on Alpine High's football teams. I understand from Sam Olgaman that the team had developed a code to talk in secret." I had emphasized all the right words. Now if only Hank would play along.

"Gra—"

"Klink, Emily Klink," I repeated interrupting him. I gave him a wink and quick head nod towards Harry sitting on the front porch. I saw the light dawn in his eyes and I almost sighed in relief.

"Emily, you say, pleased to meet you," replied Hank, putting his hand out. I took his hand and he gave a firm shake. "Sam Olgaman. Now that's a name I haven't heard in a while. We did have a history of using codes to keep secrets."

"That's what Sam told me," I confirmed, thankful that Hank seemed to understand.

"Last name is Klink? I had a history teacher with that name in high school. A relation of yours?" he asked mischievously.

"An uncle," I said with a glare.

"Interesting. He was always full of surprises, old Mr. Klink." Hank laughed as he walked towards the porch. "Hi, Pop. Glad to see you up and about."

"The damn girl wouldn't leave me in peace," grumbled Harry. I gave Harry a glare and he returned a sheepish grin. Somehow both the Waderich men could draw the looks out of me.

"How'd you get in the chair, Pop?" asked Hank, glancing between his father and me.

"I helped him a little," I interrupted before Harry could answer. "The front porch seemed cooler than the house at this hour, and Harry agreed."

Hank seemed to accept it, and then turned to me. "Sam Olgaman. I thought he moved down Birmingham way. What's he been up to?" asked Hank with a twinkle in his eye.

"This and that," I replied coldly. *Idiot.* "We mostly talked about old times; football, in fact."

"Can ya believe it, son? The damn city council wants a tourist book on Alpine football," contributed Harry. "She be writin' it," he said with a nod towards me. "Damn foolishness if ya ask me."

"It does sound pretty far-fetched, Pops," agreed Hank with a grin as he glanced to me.

"Well, I get paid regardless," I said with yet another glare. "Why don't we all sit around the kitchen table. Hank can tell me about his high school football days and you can keep him honest, Harry."

"Well, I don't know how easily I can do that." Harry laughed, maneuvering his chair towards the screen door.

"Pop, I'm not too certain the house is in any shape for company," said Hank, putting a hand on the screen door to keep it closed. At least he had the decency to look embarrassed.

"Hell, son. She's been all over the place. Even made some cookies—not that there's any left!"

"There's some dough left in the fridge," I said warmly. "We can always make more."

"Open the door already," demanded Harry.

Hank did as commanded, but put a hand out to delay me as Harry worked his way down the hall. "Gracie," whispered Hank, "what in the world are you up to?"

I shushed him, motioning to Harry and mouthing, "He might hear." I then pushed my way past Hank's arm and followed Harry back to the kitchen. I felt like I'd just bid to Seven No Trump, my heart was beating so fast. I hoped I could keep the charade up, and that Hank would play along. It only took a moment to get some more cookies into the oven, but I felt better when I sat down at the table with Hank and Harry. Harry had a roguish smile on his face like he'd snuck a piece of pie before dinner. Hank, on the other hand, looked just like he did back in high school when Mamaw caught him with his hand up my blouse while we were kissing on the front porch. He kept looking around the kitchen, a much cleaner kitchen than when he'd seen it last. Sure, the counters could use a good scrubbing and the chrome edging needed polishing, but at least you could see the countertop was red. I felt a smile creep onto my face and ruthlessly banished it. This was not some game. I took a deep breath. "Let's talk football. You played linebacker for Alpine High?"

"Yep," chimed in Harry. "He shore did. Best damn linebacker this state has ever seen, if you ask me. Got twelve sacks in a game once, and got the all-time season sack record in the state for triple-A in his junior year. Then he went an' broke that damn record as a senior."

"Pop, that was all a long time ago," demurred Hank, looking around. "What's happened to this place?"

"Well, she's here to talk about ol' times, you nitwit. She's trying to write a football book, for God's sakes," replied Harry. "And she cleaned a bit. The place needed it."

"What if I don't want to talk football?" asked Hank, meeting my eyes with a questioning look. I could still spend hours looking into those grey eyes. I gave myself a mental shake; I couldn't afford to get distracted now.

"Oh hell, son. Give the poor girl a story or two. She's been waiting for ya, and made herself useful in the meantime," said Harry. I gave Harry a smile even while part of me smirked at the irony of Harry Gutlope Waderich coming to my rescue.

Hank turned to look at his father and I saw his expression soften. He then turned back to me saying, "Well, Emily, I don't know what you're after here, but if Pop wants me to tell you a story or two about high school football, I guess I can oblige." He paused then, and from the smile on his face, I knew to expect a curveball. "You know, you should just write about your own high school football team. Somehow I think those stories would be identical to what I could tell you."

I forced a laugh. "Oh, I doubt that, Hank. I'm sure what I remember about high school and what you remember would be significantly different," I rejoined. I felt my stomach drop like I was riding a rollercoaster when I saw a puzzled look blossom on Hank's face. I almost smiled, as I stood and took the cookies out of the oven. It was a bit early, but I remembered Hank liked them gooey. I grabbed the plate from the sink, dried it with a cloth, and arranged the cookies before returning to the table. "They're still hot," I warned.

"Don't you need a notebook?" asked Hank as he grabbed a cookie and shifted it from hand to hand as it cooled. "You know, for taking notes on the stories, just like a detective would use."

"I have a good memory," I said. I needed a smoke. "And besides, I can always come back and ask again."

"Don't think ya will always be welcome here, girl," barked Harry. "I don't need no one sniffin' round my place."

"What if I bring a homemade apple pie?" I winked and smiled at the old curmudgeon.

"Well then, that might be a different story," growled Harry. "I'll see how good that pie is first."

"Let's get on with this," interrupted Hank.

I wished I'd paid more attention in journalism class in high school. I didn't know how to conduct an interview, not to get to what I really wanted to know. At least Hank was still playing along, even if he seemed to doubt my motivations. I had to ask something. "So," I said, "what was your most memorable moment in high school?"

Hank laughed and leaned back into his chair. I remembered that look, and knew I was in trouble. "Well, there was this sweet little thing of a girl, about your height and coloring, and we spent this fall afternoon exploring that round hay barn on..."

"I meant on the field," I interrupted, giving Hank an icy stare. I hoped I wasn't blushing. I heard Harry chuckle and turned that stare to him as well. They looked like a pair of dogs that had treed a coon. Unfortunately that made me the coon.

"Ah, on the field," said Hank. "Well, after the last game of the season, we met on the 50-yard line at midnight—"

"On the field while playing football," I clarified. I could feel the heat on my face, and it wasn't from baking cookies. If Hank planned on bringing up every tryst we had in those days, it was going to be a long interview.

"Hank, tell her about the night the scout was here," interrupted Harry. I flashed Harry a smile, thankful for the help.

"Not much to tell. I played ball and the scout liked what he saw."

"You shut down Walter Riley that night, and he was All-State. Went to play for the Tigers, he did," countered Harry. "Ya earned yourself a scholarship that night."

"Your father told me you earned a scholarship to play for Georgia Tech. What was it like going from small town ball at Alpine High to play Division One college ball?" I asked.

Hank stared at me for the longest time before speaking. "You want to know what it was like to go from Alpine to Atlanta? To leave behind everything and everyone I knew here to go there? To lose you?" Hank stood, and I knew he was no longer interested in continuing the charade. "It felt like I had lost part of my soul," he said.

"Boy, what're ya talking about?" asked Harry.

"Pop, I think I know a bit more about what Emily here is after than you do," countered Hank. The look Hank gave me made a chill go up my spine, even on this boiling Alabama summer day. I knew the game was up. "Enough of this crap. Pop, it's Gracie—Gracie Theis—sitting there. You know, my girl from high school that got busted for pot, and who you banned me from ever seeing again."

"What?" asked Harry, stunned.

"Harry," I explained, turning to the man in the chair. "I didn't mean to mislead you—"

"I ran into her yesterday in town, and I guess she decided to look me up," explained Hank. "There is no book. She's just trying to dredge up crap from high school."

"Now, wait a minute…" I said.

"This that girl that coulda cost you your scholarship?" interrupted Harry. The shocked look turned to anger in a flash like a sudden storm. "You get outta my house, girl. Go on."

"What? I didn't almost cost Hank anything," I replied.

"Pop, that was a long time ago," soothed Hank. He almost looked remorseful, for what good that did me now.

"I said get out," snarled Harry. He pushed the kitchen table towards me, striking me in the gut while simultaneously pushing his wheelchair backwards, hitting the wall. Harry recovered before I did, and prepared to ram me as I stood doubled over, dazed and trying to catch my breath.

"Gracie, watch out," yelled Hank as Harry launched himself across the room. "Enough," yelled Hank, grabbing the back of Harry's chair and stopping him mere inches from my shins. I looked at them in shock. I knew Harry hadn't wanted me seeing Hank in high school, but how could he still hold this hatred after fifteen years? If Hank hadn't intervened, Harry could really have hurt me. Tears pricked at my eyes as all the old emotions of loss and loneliness threatened to bubble up to the surface, no matter how hard I tried to keep them down.

"Get out of my house now! No damn drugs in my house, ya hear?" replied Harry.

"I don't have any drugs, and I never did!" I heard the screech in my voice and almost winced. I sounded like Mamaw when a neighborhood dog got in the trash.

"Drugs? Pop, you're blitzed most of the time," complained Hank. I appreciated him trying to stand up for me, even if it was too late.

"Liar!" screamed Harry at me. "Damn police found drugs in your car. Illegal drugs." His gaze shifted to Hank and he spat, "And I'll drink if I want to. I'm entitled and there's nothin' wrong with it. Alcohol is legal the last time I checked, unlike marijuana."

"The drugs in the car weren't mine," I said, forcing myself to remain calm. I had come here thinking the danger might lie with Hank, but it was Harry who looked ready to kill.

"Likely story. What woulda happened if Hank here was driving and got pulled over? Bye bye, scholarship. Bye bye, college," retorted Harry.

I stared at him with a long hard look. "Look, Harry, it wasn't mine. I didn't do drugs then, and I don't do them now."

"Gracie, I think it's time for you to leave," interrupted Hank. I saw him flinch when I looked his way and wondered what he saw in my face. This was a fight that had been brewing for over fifteen years. I grabbed the front of Harry's chair at the armrests, partly to protect myself and partly to look the man in the eyes. I leaned in mere inches from his scraggly beard, and as calmly as I could, said, "I was innocent. It wasn't my weed that the police found."

"Then whose was it?" whispered Harry. As I straightened up and took a step back, I saw him inadvertently glance towards Hank.

My knees became weak as understanding hit me. I realized that Harry never truly believed I was guilty; deep down he'd always had doubts. That was why he wouldn't let me explain, banning me from the farm and from Hank. He was afraid I might convince him I was innocent. He knew that Hank was the only other one who had keys to the car. So if I hadn't been responsible for the marijuana in the car, it must have been his son. Even now, Harry was turning violent instead of facing the possibility of that harsh truth.

I turned and faced Hank, knowing that it all depended on him now. I saw his eyes shift from me to Harry and back again. Hank looked as overwhelmed as a Southerner driving in a blizzard. I knew that this moment was as painful for him as it was for Harry and for me. All three of us had held delusions of that time, and the truth was still hidden. Harry had forced himself to believe I was guilty. I had thought it was Doeppers who'd planted the evidence. What did Hank believe? Was he responsible? Did he know the truth?

"I never asked," began Hank in a whisper, reluctantly. "But I think it was John's dope."

"What?" I asked. "John Waderich? How did his pot get into my car?"

"That boy was always an idiot," added Harry. "I could see him messed up with something like that. I always knew it wasn't you, son." He looked relieved.

"Why didn't you say anything back then?" I was confused and getting angry. Why wouldn't Hank have cleared my name? Surely I'd been more important to him than his cousin.

"I didn't figure it out until afterwards. And by then you'd gotten off with community service, so I figured it didn't matter," explained Hank. He avoided my gaze as he spoke.

"So you let me take the fall for him," I seethed. "And how did he do it anyhow? I always kept the car locked. Only the two of us had keys." Hank was nothing but a coward who'd known I was innocent and yet let my life be ruined. What had I ever seen in him?

"Gracie," pleaded Hank. I wanted to punch him. "Don't be mad. It all happened such a long time ago. It's ancient history now. No one cares about it anymore."

"I care. You let me believe that Doeppers planted the evidence on me to make a bust. You let it ruin my senior year at high school. I had to change my college plans. That one lie changed everything." *And led to the Event-That-Changed-My-Life,* I admitted to myself. Obviously I had always made poor choices in regard to men. Unfortunately, my choices had not improved with age. "Well, Hank Waderich, I think it's time that you explain what happened," I said, crossing my arms in front of me. I still wanted to smack him.

"Some of this is guesswork. Like I said, I never did ask. And Gracie, truly, I didn't figure it out until much later, after you'd already started community service."

"That's no excuse, son," added Harry. I could see the shadow of a smile on the old man's face. He was so relieved it wasn't his son's fault that he'd completely changed from the angry lunatic who'd tried to ram me with his wheelchair just a few moments ago.

"Pop, stay out of this," warned Hank. He looked down at his father, and then back to me. "I think perhaps this is something that Gracie and I should discuss privately. Dad, why don't you go to the back room and watch the tube?" From the look on Hank's face, I figured there was more to this story than just him being late reckoning the drugs were John's. Hank knew more than he was letting on and was sending Harry away so as not to disappoint him. But the Hank I knew back then didn't do drugs, I was as sure of that as the fact that Hank had gray eyes.

"That's not fair. This is still my house, and I'll stay here if I damn well please," complained Harry.

"Then perhaps it's time that Hank and I leave," I said. Now I wanted to punch Harry too, the conniving old goat. I wasn't going to let Hank off the hook that easy, and if he didn't want to talk about it in front of Harry, that was fine by me. I wasn't happy with either of the Waderich men at this point. They deserved each other. Stamping down my irritation, I motioned to Hank. "Shall we go for a walk?"

Hank nodded, and while Harry argued loudly, it wasn't as if he could follow in his wheelchair. Hank wheeled Harry into the back room while I went toward the front of the house and out onto the front porch. Hank joined me soon enough, and we walked side by side down the porch steps, past the cars down the lane beside the pecan trees. I was still spitting mad but was able to wait silently until Hank was ready to begin.

He stopped walking and turned to face me, fixing me with those gray eyes. He bent down towards me and smiled, but I could see the regret in his face. "I wanted to thank you for all of the work you did..."

"Forget it," I snapped. "No more delays. I've waited fifteen years to find out what happened and why. Time to spill your guts, Hank."

"Okay, okay," mulled Hank. "So, you remember when someone stole the keys to my Pontiac, and filled the thing with cow dung?" He looked my way and I nodded. I now knew that had been Emily, but I wasn't about to tell Hank. Maybe later, depending on his story. "Well, the weekend before that, Griece and I met my cousin at a party in a barn off of the Ole Gadsden highway, about twenty miles from here. John wanted me to introduce him to some girl, but I refused, and he got pretty upset about it. That's when I lost my keys, or they were stolen. Griece drove, so I didn't even notice that the keys to my Pontiac were missing until later."

"That was the weekend of my cousin's wedding," I said, thinking back.

"Yeah, you were in Birmingham. I figured my keys would turn up, so I just used the second set I had back at the house. I reckoned they fell out of my pocket at the party, and I'd probably get them back from whomever found them the next weekend. Well, that Monday someone filled my car with cow pies. I always figured it was John paying me back for not helping him out at that party. And besides, I saw him a couple of times in town that week. I figured he had the chance to punk me that way."

"Continue," I urged him, still not hearing anything that made me want to forgive the idiot.

"Anyhow, that was when we started driving your car around, you know, because of the smell."

"I remember," I said. That was probably the worst thing I'd ever smelled in my entire life, other than perhaps the Alpine jail.

"On Thursday we went to the drive-in off Highway 43, and you remember John was there. I confronted him about the cow dung and he denied knowing anything about it. He laughed about it and blew me off." Hank still looked angry. He'd been truly peeved about the prank.

"Maybe because he didn't know anything about it," I supplied, trying to mollify him. I was the one who should be angry, not Hank.

"Well, while you were in the bathroom, I dragged John into the back of the car where we could have a little more privacy to 'discuss' what he knew or didn't know about my Pontiac. I think that was when he stashed the marijuana in the car. At least he got a fat lip out of it."

"You hit him?" I asked, appalled.

"He laughed when I accused him of putting the cow manure in my car. I loved that car."

"So you hit him for laughing at a prank." Now I remembered how ridiculous teenage boys could be. I was glad I didn't have to deal with that drama anymore.

"Putting cow manure in a car is no prank. That's vandalism."

I was confused. This sounded like the beginning to a story that ended with "…and that's why I reported him to the police." However, my criminal record proved that was not the case. "So, why would you protect him when the police found weed in my car? Why not tell what you knew? He was a jerk and I was your girlfriend." I was getting angry again, my Irish side starting to show. I took a few calming breaths and looked away from those eyes.

"Gracie, I didn't know then, I swear. I only figured it out later."

"When, Hank? When did you 'figure it out'?" I asked.

"Okay, so about three months after the cops found that bag of dope in your car, John got busted for dealing down in Gadsden. Apparently he'd been selling weed all over the place, including here in Alpine. That's when I put two and two together. He was in town that night selling dope and I think he stashed some in your car. I'm not sure if that was by accident when I hit him or if it was on purpose. You'd already started your community service. I never asked him about it."

"Why didn't you tell anyone?" I asked, still confused. If he had, maybe we could have stayed together.

"Because if I ratted on John, he would have ratted on me. I couldn't afford that, not with heading to Atlanta at the end of the summer. Besides, you and I had gone our separate ways by then."

"Rat on you for what?" I asked, ignoring for the moment that the only reason we'd split in the first place was because of the drug bust.

Hank looked uncomfortable then, and I knew there was something more to the story. Something I might not like. "Gracie, Mom and Pop never had nothing. Here I was a football star with a car and I was dating the best looking girl in school. How do you think I paid for all that?"

"You were dealing drugs?" I concluded appalled. I couldn't believe it. I had dated this man, had planned to go to college with him and perhaps build a future. We were as close as possible, and I'd never seen any signs of drug dealing. How had he hidden that from me?

"No, of course not," replied Hank, shaking his head, much to my relief. "But I did work for John in a way, although at the time I didn't realize he viewed me as an employee. He used to slip me cash, and in return I'd introduce him around. You know, vouch for him with my friends. That's why we'd met at that party; he was paying me that night to show him around, and when I refused to introduce him to Sarah Klink, he thought I'd reneged on our deal. I didn't realize until later that he was using those connections to sell weed."

"And so if you fingered John for the pot in my car, he would have named you as an accomplice." I couldn't believe it. Jon Doeppers hadn't planted that marijuana; it was Hank's fault all along. Well, not Hank's fault directly, but certainly he deserved some of the blame.

"Exactly, Gracie. By the time I figured it out, you and I had split and I saw no reason to stir things back up, and besides, John could say I helped him. Honestly,

I still didn't know for sure. I never asked John about that night at the drive-in. I did discover that John had been the one behind the sudden rise in marijuana use in the school that year, and that I had unwittingly helped him do it." He shook his head ruefully. "I can't believe how clueless I was."

"You sold me out to protect your scholarship, Hank. I hope it was worth it." It really had been my first betrayal, the one that all the others followed. I'd been a fool even then. The tears came to my eyes and my voice trembled. I turned to walk away, but Hank put a hand on my arm.

"Wait, Gracie, don't be that way. I have regretted it ever since. I was selfish and stupid, and I'm sorry." I pulled my arm away but did not storm off like I had intended. After a minute, we began walking again.

"Well, you can fix it now," I said. "I'm trying to build a life in this town, and cleaning that stain from my past will make a difference in certain circles." I doubted I would stay in Alpine that long, but I wanted to be able to hold my head high while here. Mamaw deserved it, even if it made no long-term difference to me.

"I can't do that, Gracie. God, I wish I could, but I can't," replied Hank.

"Why the devil not?" I asked. "It was fifteen years ago. You already got your scholarship and your degree. Why does it matter to you anymore?"

He paused, finding the words. "Life's been tough. Hell, downright hard. After Mom passed, Pop got depressed and started drinking more. While driving drunk one night, he had an accident. If it wasn't for the fact that he lost his legs, I think he'd be in jail now," explained Hank. We'd reached the end of the lane by now and turned to head back to the house. "The man Pop hit, he sued us."

"Harry mentioned that," I said confused. The sudden change in topic made no sense. I still didn't understand why Hank didn't want to clear my name. It wasn't like I wanted him to take an ad out in the paper; just a few words to the right people.

Hank took a big breath and then continued, "The case didn't go well. We had to get a loan from the bank to pay the award with the farm as collateral. That monthly payment is killing us; the money is just not there."

"Didn't the insurance cover it?" I asked. That's what the blasted stuff was for after all.

"Pop forgot to pay his premiums and the policy had lapsed a few months before, so the insurance company refused to pay. We're close to losing the farm."

"Oh, Hank, I'm so sorry," I said, and I truly was. I didn't want to see Hank or even Harry suffer; I just wanted my reputation back. "But what does this have to do with John and the marijuana bust in high school?" We had reached the parked cars now and stopped by the Mustang.

"Nice car, Gracie. What is it, a '72, '73?" Hank asked.

"Hank," I said. "You owe me this." He was clearly trying to stall, but I'd come this far. There was a connection here somewhere; I just couldn't see it. The picture was too fuzzy.

He looked into my eyes for the longest time, and I could almost see him making up his mind to tell or not. Hank took a deep breath and said, "We need the money, Gracie. We need cash to make the payments or the bank will take the farm. I couldn't let that happen to Pop, not after he'd lost his legs. This place is all he has left."

"Hank, what did you do?" I asked in a shaky voice. The picture was becoming clear, but I didn't want to see it.

Hank opened my car door and gestured for me to get in. It was clear he wasn't going to continue until after I got into the car, so I followed his lead. Once I sat down, he leaned into the Mustang and said, "Pop can't get around the place no more and it's always been quiet. We're far from town and nobody comes out here to visit. A few folks used to try, but Pop is a mean drunk, and ran them all off." He took a deep breath, lowered his eyes, and continued, "I grow marijuana for John and get a cut of the sales. It pays the bills, barely. I'm only telling you this, Gracie, so you will know to stay away. We Waderich men are no good for you. All we can do is cause you grief. For your own good just leave us alone. Just stay away." He slammed the door then and marched up to the house. I didn't even get a chance to reply.

Chapter 7

I debated chasing Hank back into the house, but my better senses prevailed. Now was not the time for more talk. I turned the key—thankfully the car started. Having car trouble at the Waderich farm would've just been icing on the cake after the day I'd had. I drove slowly down the pecan-lined drive and thought about my next move. I couldn't tell Doeppers about seeing Hank at the club now. Not only would the man be irked that I hadn't told him earlier, but then Hank would become a suspect for murder and the police would search the farm. With what Hank had just told me, he'd go to jail for growing marijuana even if he were innocent of murder. They'd lose the farm, and Harry would probably go into a home for the elderly and disabled. I had watched a documentary about a few of those places and, without money, Harry wouldn't be much better off than Hank. I wouldn't only be punishing Hank, but Harry as well. As upset as I was that Hank had known I was innocent and said nothing, I couldn't do that to him or his father.

Yet what if Hank had committed the murder? What if Hank was trying to get rid of the need to grow drugs by murdering those to whom he owed money? I shook my head as I realized that the theory made no sense. Hank and Harry had lost a civil case, so there would be legal documents. They'd already paid the award anyhow with the bank loan. The money would just transfer to the heirs, whoever they were, and Hank would still owe the money to the bank. Maybe it was subtler than that; Edward was a smart man, with exceptional logic that helped make him a good bridge player. Maybe he'd discovered that Hank couldn't afford the payments he was making and got suspicious. Maybe Edward had deduced that Hank was growing drugs and was blackmailing him. That would explain why Hank was at the club and why he'd want to see Edward Schultz dead. Maybe Hank was the killer. Didn't I have an obligation to tell the police what I'd seen? Wasn't it the right thing to do, the honorable thing to do?

I turned onto Roundbarn Road on my way back to Alpine while my mind raced. I was in a pickle. If Hank was guilty of murder, he needed to be caught before anyone else got hurt. Heck, considering what he'd just told me, I might be pretty high on his list. Yet if Hank was innocent, or at least only guilty of growing marijuana, then he needed to stay out of the spotlight. If I said anything to anybody, then Hank could be brought up on drug charges like I was so long ago. Somehow, I didn't think Hank would only get community service either.

The barn for which the road was named was approaching on my left. I turned onto the gravel drive, which opened into the field with the historic structure, and threw the Mustang into park. I grabbed a cigarette, lit it, and sat there staring at the round hay barn. I remembered when Hank and I had explored it so many years ago. It had been a lazy fall afternoon; back when we'd just begun dating and were getting to know each other better. Hank had suggested the outing and I remembered accusing him of taking all his girls there. I remembered that he blushed then, trying to deny it, and that only made me giggle like the schoolgirl I was at the time. We only spent about a half hour exploring the structure until we found a pile of hay streaked with golden bars from the sun shining through the slats in the wall. The next two hours were spent on that hay pile, talking and kissing and touching. I think I fell in love with Hank that afternoon; at least I was smitten with him afterwards. He asked me to be his steady girl that day, and I remembered how happy that made me feel, and how I'd said yes with a kiss that took his breath away. I remembered him taking me home afterwards, telling Mamaw and Papaw, and how happy they had been for us. I remembered getting ready for bed that night and realizing that my face hurt from all the smiling that I had done that day. It was, perhaps, the happiest day of my senior year.

"Damn him!" I screamed, and then felt embarrassed at yelling at a barn.

I couldn't do it. I couldn't turn Hank into the police. Yes, he could have committed murder. Yes, he was guilty of growing pot. But several states had recently legalized marijuana use; Alabama just hadn't gotten the memo yet. What Hank was doing wasn't that much different than tobacco farmers, I rationalized. Both grew crops that did more harm than good. It was somewhat arbitrary that one was considered legal while the other was illegal. Was what Hank doing really that bad?

"Crap," I muttered under my breath. Yes, it was. Hank was breaking the law and now he'd involved me into his mess again. If it weren't for Hank and his cousin John, there would've been no marijuana in my car that day. I wouldn't have had my car searched, and I wouldn't have a criminal record. I wouldn't have gone to New York for college and I wouldn't have met and fallen for Pierre. I wouldn't have moved to Paris, and I wouldn't have gone through the Event-That-Changed-My-Life.

I ground the cigarette out in the ashtray and threw the Mustang into reverse. Once on the road, I continued on my way back to town. I didn't like it, but I could only come up with one solution. I needed to solve this murder case, or at least investigate enough to determine whether Hank was involved. If he'd committed the murder, then I'd tell Doeppers all I knew and let Hank rot in jail. If not, then I'd somehow convince Hank to stop growing weed. There had to be another solution to his money problems. By telling me, he'd made me into an accomplice of sorts. And who was he to determine who I could see or not see? If I wanted to speak to him again, by God, that was my decision. Hank couldn't just announce that he was "bad for me" as if I was a toddler. How dare he try and make those decisions for me? And to announce all high and mighty that I needed to "stay away." Idiot! Did he actually expect me to obey him? I didn't take commands well. He should have known that.

I'd made it to the edge of town and decided that I'd done enough woolgathering. I needed to make a plan. I was no detective, but I'd read enough mysteries to have some idea on how to move forward. Unfortunately, I couldn't depend upon stumbling across clues like the amateur sleuths so often did in those books. I needed to make opportunities to learn more, about the victim and about the possible suspects. And I needed to learn more about Hank and the type of man he'd become, even if he wanted me far from him.

I pulled into the Piggly-Wiggly and parked the Mustang a couple spaces from the front door. I didn't normally do my grocery shopping on a Friday, but I needed to pick up a few things if I was going to make that homemade apple pie for Harry. I figured that if I brought him the pie while Hank was working, perhaps I could get the old goat to tell a few things about what Hank had been up to recently. I also wanted to pick up the *Alpine Tribune* and see if the paper had anything about the murder yet. Most news in town traveled more quickly by rumor, but occasionally I learned something from the paper before hearing it from Mamaw.

I grabbed a cart, thankful I could find one with four wheels that worked properly, and made my way to the produce section. The apples they had didn't look very appetizing, but I figured they'd do well enough for a pie. I bagged a half dozen, picked up a bag of green beans that were on sale, and made my way to the back of the store. I was surprised to find Gladys Chisholm chatting with the butcher. I'd said I needed to make my own opportunities, and this seemed like a prime one. I rolled my cart over, making sure that Gladys saw me.

"Gracie, I'm so glad you're here," said Gladys. "I was just telling Frank about how Edward Schultz was murdered at the club. God rest his soul."

"Amen," said Frank as he leaned on the butcher's counter.

"Nora told me earlier that you discovered the body. Was it very grisly?" asked Gladys, with a light in her eyes.

"There was a lot of blood," I replied. I didn't like thinking about it.

"You don't think he suffered, do you?" asked the butcher.

"Oh my," shuddered Gladys. "I didn't think of that." She looked whiter than a new pair of Fruit-of-the-Looms on Christmas morning.

"My guess is that he died pretty quickly," I replied, "without much pain." Not that I really knew anything about gunshot wounds and how fast they could kill a person. It just seemed like the right thing to say. I was grateful to see Gladys accept my words and decided to turn the conversation in a more useful, and less upsetting, direction. "But I can't imagine why anyone would want to hurt Edward."

Gladys and Frank exchanged knowing glances before turning back to me. The two seemed to be in cahoots; maybe there was more to Edward Schultz than I'd thought. I could tell Gladys was itching to talk. She always seemed to be in the thick of things, and so I waited patiently with an expectant look on my face.

"Well, I don't like to speak ill of the dead," Gladys began as I nodded understandingly.

"And I'm not a rumor-monger," added Frank. I managed to hold in my snort. This town was full of the biggest gossips this side of the Mississippi.

"But we were just talking..." continued Gladys.

"You know, comparing notes..."

"And we think there are several people who won't be too upset about Edward's passing," they said together as if rehearsed.

"Really?" I said. Jackpot! Maybe I'd learn something after all. "Like who?" The two exchanged glances for a second time, and I was momentarily afraid that they wouldn't confide in me.

"Well, Edward was a lawyer, and he'd sued several folks around here," began Gladys tentatively. I really shouldn't have worried. Gladys couldn't help but share anything she knew.

"He even sued the Pig once," added Frank. "Some joker walked in from the rain, slipped and fell on the wet floor. We had the warning cones up and everything. The insurance company decided to settle, and they were the ones paying the bills. But our premiums went up afterwards. Made things a lot tighter around here."

"I had no idea," I said. I couldn't believe my ears. Frank had just admitted to having a motive of sorts. How many other suspects were there?

"He threatened to sue the city over the renovation of the old hotel," said Gladys. "I heard him talking about it at the club."

"What was his problem with the Carlyle?" I asked.

"Edward was the owner, is what I heard," explained Gladys. "At least one of the owners."

"I read in the paper that the renovation had been delayed," added Frank. "Something about inspection issues. They wanted to open before the fall leaves turned to try and get some tourists, before Oktoberfest for sure, but it didn't look like they were going to make it even before Edward died. Now with his death, who knows how long it will take?"

"That's right," said Gladys. "I overheard Edward complaining about the building inspector, and the delay in getting permits. He threatened to sue the town for the higher construction costs and lost earnings. At least that was what he said to Tommy Hilgeman at the bridge table. Tommy works for the city, you know. Edward laughed as he said it, but Tommy wasn't smiling."

"A lot of the construction workers come in here at lunch time to buy sandwiches and chips from the deli. Well, anyhow, I overheard a couple of them talking the other day about how one of the owners was yelling at the site manager, blaming him for the delays and threatening to sue," interrupted Frank.

"My guess is that was Edward," stated Gladys. "He always visited the construction site before playing bridge. I would often see his car in the lot when I arrived to set up, you know, about a half-hour before each game. He'd park at the club and walk over to the Carlyle to see how the project was progressing."

"With Edward, someone was always getting sued," complained Frank.

"I had no idea. He was always so nice at the bridge club. A ruthless player, but pleasant enough," I said. "Was his car there when you arrived yesterday?" I asked.

"It sure was. Chief Doeppers asked me that same thing and I told him it was there," confirmed Gladys.

"So he may have gotten into another argument with the site manager then," I said. "The site manager would certainly be a suspect." My suspect list was growing by leaps and bounds.

"You don't think he killed Edward, do you?" asked Frank, looking excited. "I heard from my cousin's boy that the police found the gun in a construction dumpster." Gladys was looking at me with a new fascination in her eyes. She'd just gotten herself some new gossip.

"I have no idea," I said quickly. "I was just speculating." I almost kicked myself. I needed to be more careful what I said and to whom. The detectives in my mystery books never had problems spreading more gossip than they received. This was harder than it looked.

"I just hate that this has happened. For all his faults, Edward was such a generous bridge player," said Gladys. "Always willing to help beginning players. You know he was willing to partner with just about anyone. He was even mentoring Ida Bea, and she's a mess at the table. And the ladies swooned after him, almost as much as dear Skeeter. I swear, between Skeeter and Edward, those two added an extra table of ladies to every game."

"I never understood what you women saw in that man," said Frank. "He was just an old codger with a serpent tongue from what I could tell." I assumed he was talking about Edward, but I had the same feelings myself about Clovis.

"Frank, you almost sound jealous." Gladys laughed. "What would Margaret say to that?"

"I think my wife would agree with me," retorted Frank. "She knows what a real man is like," he snorted.

Gladys and I joined in on the laughter for a minute, although I didn't find the comment particularly funny. Clovis was a menace, and while I hadn't found Edward particularly attractive, I knew some female players who did. Now with Edward gone, Clovis would be even more of a miscreant at the club. "Hey, maybe Clovis murdered Edward to reduce the competition for the ladies," I joked.

Unfortunately, I found myself laughing alone. Gladys looked at me like I had a pimple on the tip of my nose, and Frank began wiping down the counters. My attempt at humor had fallen flatter than a Coke purchased at the county fair. I needed to recover or the conversation would die and I would learn nothing more. "Serpent tongue?" I asked. "What did you mean by that, Frank?"

"Well, in that court case against the Pig, I was one of the witnesses. I don't know how he did it, but during my deposition he got me all turned around. He chewed me up and spit me out. And I didn't do anything wrong," added Frank. "I'm sorry that someone felt the need to kill the man, but I'm not sorry he's gone."

"God rest his soul," murmured Gladys again.

"Amen to that," added Frank. "Gracie, you need any meat this fine Friday?"

I ordered a couple of pounds of beef, and Frank went to the back to wrap it up. I was hoping Gladys would have more to say about Edward, but as I feared, she was finished with that topic. I guessed she'd decided I didn't have any further gossip to provide, so I was of little use to her. I did learn that Doeppers told her they'd be finished with the club that evening, and that Gladys had arranged for some professional cleaners to come for a thorough once-over to remove any trace of the crime. She also told me about a special Edward Schultz Memorial Game she was organizing for Sunday afternoon. She was trying to get the word out and had told Mamaw already by phone but wanted to tell me in person. I thanked her for the information and promised to come and play on Sunday if I could. By that time Frank had returned with my beef, and we said our goodbyes.

I picked up a few other items I needed, paid for my merchandise, and as I left the store, I noticed that a police cruiser had parked behind my Mustang, blocking my exit. I glanced around, and then walked over to see why.

"Officer Yancey," I said, as I recognized the woman behind the wheel of the cruiser. She took her time getting out of the car, and even polished the edge of the door with the sleeve of her uniform before addressing me.

"I looked up your record, Miss Theis," she drawled, her eyes seeking mine with a vengeance. "Even at Alpine High you were a bad seed. You had a drug charge while still in school. And then you up and disappeared, only turning up back in Alpine about a month ago. I wonder where you spent all that time. Fifteen years is a long time to not come home." She paused, and I could almost hear her counting for the dramatic shift. "Why don't you just save us the trouble and tell me why you killed Edward Schultz."

I sighed. This was just what I needed. "I had nothing to do with Edward Schultz's death," I said. "I was just unfortunate enough to discover his body. Why don't you go and find the real killer?"

"Oh, I have. I'm looking at the real killer right now," she replied.

I ignored her and maneuvered the cart to start putting my groceries into the backseat of the Mustang since I couldn't get to the trunk. I knew I should defend myself; I just didn't have the energy to do so. It wasn't as if I was going to convince Yancey of anything anyhow.

"I was talking to you," said Yancey to my back.

"Well, I'm done talking to you." Without looking, I placed the last of the bags in the back of the car. I felt a hand on my shoulder and stumbled against the Mustang as I was forcefully turned. Yancey was inches away from me and radiated anger like a tomcat cornered by dogs.

"You'd be wise to show some respect," she seethed. Her breath was hot on my face, and I really wanted to just shove her away. This had been a disaster of a day, and I really didn't want to deal with a police officer who had a gun in her holster and a score to settle. I didn't even know what the score was, let alone how to settle it.

"Look." I stood fully erect, holding my ground and causing Yancey to backpedal a step. "I made my statement to Chief Doeppers. I'm happy to answer whatever questions he has, but I'm not going to be harassed by you for something I didn't do." I turned back to my car and opened the door.

"I should run you down to the station," muttered the woman. "Showing me lip like that."

"Go ahead. Arrest me." I'd lost what little control I had. I was done with her and her attitude. I turned back to her, my eyes flashing. How dare she accuse me of murder and then harass me? "I know my rights. Arrest me, and let's see what Doeppers has to say when I charge the department with false arrest. You've got nothing on me because I did not kill Edward." I met her eyes with my own and was pleased when she looked away first.

Yancey retreated to her cruiser and opened the door to the driver's seat. She looked my way and said, "I'm keeping my eye on you." She got into the car and drove away.

I shuddered and wanted to curse. Only then did I notice that there were several people looking my way, plenty of witnesses to the confrontation. I was sure that word would get around, and I'd have to explain myself to Mamaw. I smiled and waved, like I'd put on a show, rolling the cart back to the storefront. A few folks waved back.

I returned to the Mustang, got in, and pulled the last usable cigarette from the pack. I'd need to get more cigs soon. I lit it and then turned the key in the ignition. The tears came unbidden when all I heard was clicking.

Chapter 8

Seventy-five dollars and two hours later I'd made it back to the cottage. The AAA guy had claimed I needed a new battery. I was thinking I needed a new car. I unloaded the groceries and poured myself a glass of Merlot. Grabbing my wineglass and the small notebook that I'd purchased at the Piggly-Wiggly, I headed to the couch to relax and think. I opened the notebook and on three separate pages wrote the headings: Motive, Opportunity, and Means. Time to do some figuring on the murder case.

On the Motive page I wrote the names: Frank, Hank, Tommy Hilgeman, the unnamed site manager, and after a minute, Clovis. I admitted that Clovis murdering Edward to have less competition for the ladies at the bridge club seemed ridiculous, but I wasn't willing to rule out anyone at this point. I couldn't think of anyone else to add, although from the conversation with Gladys and Frank, I figured the names on this list would grow rapidly, so I turned to the next page.

I knew that my list would be shorter on the Opportunity page, and began to think about who'd have had access to Edward around the time of the murder. Hank, obviously, but also Clovis as he'd returned to the club after escorting me to my car. I added Gladys' name—she was still at the club finishing the scores and posting them online when I left. I had no motive listed for Gladys, and she hadn't mentioned one at the Piggly-Wiggly, but then again if I'd committed murder, I wouldn't be advertising my motive in a casual conversation either. She and Frank had said that Edward had sued a lot of people in this town. Maybe Gladys was one of those. I made a note to myself to somehow check the court records to see who Edward had filed lawsuits against in the last few years. I figured if that were the motive, it would be a recent case. I couldn't imagine someone waiting twenty years after a lawsuit to kill the attorney involved, but then again I couldn't imagine murdering anyone either.

I closed my eyes and tried to picture the scene at the club. Most players had hurried home, trying to beat the worst of the rain. I'd stayed to see the scores, and Edward had been there as well. It looked like he'd been going through the mail looking for bills. Edward had been the club treasurer for several years and stayed after a game once or twice each month to pay bills and balance the books. I could remember Gladys, of course, and Clovis, crowing about coming in first place. For the life of me I couldn't remember anyone else, just the four of us. I decided to add "site manager" to the list. There were men working on the Carlyle that day; I remembered seeing and hearing them sandblasting the outside, so presumably the site manager was working as well, and thus had access to the club and to Edward. I'd need to figure out who was managing the work on the old hotel, so I had an actual name instead of a title. I wasn't sure how to do that either. Being a detective was definitely harder than Miss Marple made it seem.

I gave up on Opportunity, and turned to the Means page. Edward had been shot, presumably by Mamaw's gun. I still needed to confirm that fact and hoped that my lunch date with Emily tomorrow would give me that opportunity. I hated to use my friendship with her that way, especially as we'd just begun to revive it, but knew that I needed to take advantage of every resource I had. I just hoped that Emily would be willing to confide in me. Now, if I assumed that Mamaw's gun was the murder weapon, who knew she had it and knew where she'd kept it? The only name I could add was Mamaw's, but I couldn't make myself write it. I left that page blank, closed the notebook, and tossed it onto the coffee table.

My stomach was growling, so I fixed myself some cheesy eggs and grits, good southern comfort food, and enjoyed my meal watching a zombie invasion flick on the television. I wasn't much of a sci-fi fan, but occasionally enjoyed immersing myself in something that had nothing to do with reality. When the show finished, I headed to the kitchen, rinsed the dishes, and began slicing apples for the pie that I planned on making. I figured that after my lunch date with Emily, I'd head back to the Waderich farm for a nice long conversation with Harry. Only after slicing the apples did I realize I had no pie pan. When I returned home from Paris, I'd shipped only the most sentimental of items, and had sold the bulk of my kitchen hardware. I hadn't yet replaced everything I needed for the kitchen, including a pie pan.

I knew the apples would go brown and be worthless unless I baked them tonight; they weren't that good in the first place. At this hour in Alpine there was no place where I could buy a pie pan, so I grabbed my wall phone and dialed Mamaw's number. Amazingly, I got through, and after I explained my problem, Mamaw said I could bake my pie at her house. I changed quickly out of the lounge clothes into something more presentable, gathered up the necessary ingredients in a small crate, and headed to the Mustang, trapping the crate between my left arm and hip while carrying the bowl of sliced apples in my right hand. I got everything stowed safely in the backseat, turned the key, and was thankful that the beast started without trouble.

"I have some coffee brewing," Mamaw called to me as I got out of the car. She was waiting for me at the door. Mamaw was still wearing the same nightdress she'd been wearing that morning, which made me wonder if she'd changed that day. "And what in the world made you want to bake a pie at this time of night?"

I smiled and handed her the bowl of sliced apples, so I could use both hands for the crate of other ingredients as I made my way into the kitchen. I saw that Mamaw had already cleared the counter and had even begun mixing up a crust. I shook my head ruefully, as I realized that I wouldn't need half of the ingredients I'd bought. I set the crate aside and took over making the crust, explaining to Mamaw about my trip out to the Waderich farm earlier that day and the state in which I found Harry. I told her of my plan to visit him and wanting a pie to bring along.

"Well, I'm glad you've reconnected with Emily. She was always such a dear friend of yours. I think her last name is Stevenson now," Mamaw said, taking a seat at the kitchen table with a cup of coffee, as she watched me work.

"You always called her a hell-raiser," I replied. "I distinctly remember you warning me away from Emily a few times in high school, saying that she'd be nothing but trouble." I scattered some flour on the countertop, plopped half the dough in the center, and used the wooden rolling pin to flatten it.

"And she was trouble back then. Lord, I remember some of the things she did, and I'm sure I didn't know nearly all of them. She was trouble, but she had a kid, got married, and has matured a lot since those days. Having a kid changes a person." She paused and looked meaningfully at me, but I avoided her eyes and kept rolling. If I didn't quit pushing so hard on the rolling pin, I was going to end up with Filo dough instead of a pie crust. I took a deep breath and released my death grip on the rolling pin as she continued, "I know how lonely you've been since moving back. It's good to have friends, even if they were hell-raisers. Heck, some called me that back in my day." She grinned.

"Some still call you that now." I laughed.

"True," chuckled Mamaw. "I do have my ways."

I transferred the overly flattened dough to the pie pan, spraying it first with butter-in-a-can, and then used a table knife to slice the excess off the edges. I then grabbed the bowl of sliced apples and began adding the necessary ingredients to turn the mixture into pie filling. "You haven't said anything about the Waderichs," I said.

"Oh, Gracie. You can't go back home again," murmured Mamaw.

"What do you mean by that?" I asked.

"You and Hank. That's an entirely different animal from you and Emily. You and Hank have both grown and changed in too many ways. You can't go back to the way things used to be between you two," she explained.

I stopped mixing and turned to Mamaw in disbelief. "You can't think that Hank and I... Mamaw!" That was the last thing I needed, for Mamaw to think I still had a thing for Hank and that we were getting back together. If the gossip mill got hold of that, it wouldn't matter if I stayed away from him. As soon as Yancey connected me to Hank, she'd be all over him like mud on hog. Besides, I had no intentions of ever dating him again. I wasn't that much of a fool to think that he wouldn't put his own interests over mine again if the opportunity arose. He'd already done that to me.

"Then what were you doing out there?" she asked. "There's only one reason a girl goes to her high school sweetheart's house when she moves back into town, and it's never a good one."

I did have a good reason, but I couldn't mention my suspicions concerning Hank and the murder; I couldn't ask Mamaw to remain silent after learning that Hank was present and acting suspicious around the time someone shot Edward. I already felt torn in not mentioning the encounter to Doeppers, although I did still feel somewhat mollified since he hadn't exactly asked. Mamaw didn't need that burden too. I could see that from Mamaw's perspective, it did look like I was trying to reconnect with Hank. Hell, it probably looked that way to Hank as well. And here I was baking a pie as an excuse to visit the farm. It sort of looked like a courtship ritual to me now that I thought about it. I let out a small groan that I hoped Mamaw didn't hear. I'd just complicated my life a lot more than I'd realized.

I began mixing again and said, "I went to discover what truly happened in high school, you know, to get some closure about the drugs that were found in my car. I had a chance to talk to Harry, and we patched things up a bit. I also was able to talk with Hank for a short while. It was pleasant, but certainly nothing untoward happened," I explained emphatically. "I'm baking the pie because Harry isn't doing well, and I'm hoping to cheer him up if I can. He's been drinking a lot and I think he's lonely. Hank isn't around much, and I think Harry just needs someone to talk to."

"That makes sense, dear," soothed Mamaw. I could tell by her tone that she didn't believe me. Damn, I needed to come up with a better lie, maybe something closer to the truth. I'd never been good with lies; my coloring always gave me away. Besides, Mamaw had a sixth sense about that type of thing. That was part of the reason why I'd only rarely been involved in Emily's hijinks.

I stopped mixing and looked Mamaw's way. "All right, the truth. When I talked to Emily last night, you know, while I was taking my 'timeout' in jail, she almost convinced me that the policeman who arrested me all those years ago didn't plant the marijuana. I went to see Hank today to learn the truth." I returned to stirring, hoping this tidbit of truth would be enough to convince Mamaw of my true intentions in visiting the Waderichs.

"I know you believed it, but I never thought Chief Doeppers planted those drugs either. He seemed honest, and once Emily married him, I was sure. She was a troublemaker, but she had good sense where boys were concerned, at least most of the time." I could almost hear the unspoken "better than you" on her lips. "She wouldn't have dated or married a dirty cop. So, dear, what did you learn at the Waderichs?" asked Mamaw with curiosity.

Damn! I'd given her a story she could believe, but now she wanted details. When would I learn? Now was the time to dissemble. If I divulged everything I'd learned, then I had no excuse to visit the farm again. Furthermore, Mamaw was almost as bad of a gossip as Gladys, and I knew Hank didn't need his name mentioned in any gossip about drugs. "Well, that's the thing," I began. I could feel the sweat on my brow as I started my lie. "I didn't learn all that much. Harry and the house were so disheveled that we never did get to the point of my visit. He actually didn't recognize me at first, so it took a while before we got things settled down. That's why I want to go back tomorrow. I'm hoping to learn more."

"Didn't Harry ban Hank from seeing you, saying you'd drag Hank down into the gutter with you?" I could hear the disapproval in Mamaw's voice. She knew the hurt Harry had caused me.

"That was part of what we needed to work through today," I said.

"And now you want to be kind to that man?" asked Mamaw. I could tell she didn't believe me. She knew me well enough to know I wasn't likely to be forgiving to someone who'd treated me so horribly.

"If I want to learn what happened back then, I guess I need to," I explained. I poured the apple filling into the pie pan, scattered some more flour on the counter and began to roll out the remaining dough for the top crust. "Maybe to be able to move forward, and make a life in Alpine, I need to work through the past," I offered. I'd added the "in Alpine" hoping that she would seize on the idea that I was staying here permanently. I hadn't committed either way yet, but if it got her off my back now, I could deal with her disappointment later if I decided to move. "It may not matter to most people around here anymore, but it still matters to me."

"Sounds like new-age mumbo-jumbo to me," she grumbled. She didn't take my bait about staying in Alpine. A new distraction was in order.

I laughed. "Yes, it does." I finished rolling out the top crust, carefully placed it upon the top of the pie, and used a fork to seal the bottom and top crusts together along the edge and to stab a design in the top. I then moved the pie to the oven to bake. Grabbing a cup of coffee, I joined Mamaw at the kitchen table. "But that doesn't mean it's not true." Time to turn the conversation in a more productive direction. "When did you get a gun, Mamaw?" I asked.

I could tell that Mamaw wasn't ready to let the previous topic rest, but she answered my question anyhow. Maybe we were working our way towards a more fifty-fifty relationship. "Oh, I don't know exactly," she replied. "It was after they started the renovations on that old hotel, but before you moved back to Alpine. I bought it at the Pole & Arms. You know there's a new Chinese restaurant opening next door to the Pole & Arms; they're remodeling the place now. I was talking to Margaret at the diner and she's a little concerned about the competition. I told her not to worry, the food would be different enough that it shouldn't matter. I also told her that if the tourists come like the town council hopes, she may be grateful for another restaurant in Alpine. I'm thinking a Chinese restaurant will be a nice change of pace."

"Did the police determine if your gun was the murder weapon?" I asked. We'd have time to discuss the fine dining options in Alpine, or lack thereof, after the murder was solved.

"You mean for Edward? I'm still cross with you for not telling me about finding the body, you know. I've been on the phone all day, and to think I had to hear from others the details you could have told me directly. If it wasn't for the fact that I had my own part in this story... I'm telling you, Gracie, I'd be much more cross with you."

"What did the police say?" I asked, hoping to avoid more of a speech. Maybe not quite fifty-fifty, perhaps closer to forty-sixty.

"I'm not sure I should say, or if I want to," pouted Mamaw. She took a drink of her coffee, and then started talking again like a kid eating candy on

Halloween. "Everyone is a buzz about the murder, you know, like a bunch of bumblebees in a busted hive. Edward appeared to be such a dear man—'appeared' being the key word. That man had some skeletons in his closet, and the door is opening now. I've heard a few juicy tidbits. I understand that Edward was quarreling with his partners over that beastly old hotel. Some folks believe that they may have come to blows, and the hotel is just across the street from the bridge club, you know. I also heard elsewhere that Edward was having money problems from a few too many trips to those riverboat casinos on the Mississippi. Who knows, maybe he was blackmailing someone. He was a lawyer and seemed to know more than he should about some things. Now, Margaret thought it might be a love triangle, as if anyone could have an affair in a place like Alpine without everyone knowing. You keep that in mind, Gracie. You can't hide an affair in a town this size."

"I have no intention of having an affair with anyone," I replied, rolling my eyes. Great, now we were back to my personal life. This was not the way this conversation was supposed to go.

"You just stay away from married men, ya hear?" She paused and glared at me, and then, to my relief, went on, "I'm thinking blackmail. I think Edward was blackmailing someone to handle his gambling debts. Maybe the payoff was at the club, and whoever Edward was blackmailing got the drop on him and killed him. Either that, or poor Edward was just unlucky. Maybe some Mexican from over at the hotel was trying to rob the bridge club and poor Edward was just in the wrong place at the wrong time."

I knew the speculation could go on for hours, with no facts to back up anything. "What did the police say?" I tried again. "What did you tell them?"

"The only thing that Chief Doeppers told me was that they'd found my gun and wanted to know when I saw it last. I'm not even sure how they knew it was my gun, but I recognized it. I told him where I kept the gun and why, and that I didn't even know it was missing until the officers arrived to take me to the station." Mamaw took a deep breath and then continued, like she was reciting lines. I wondered how many times she'd told this story today, or a variation of it. "He then asked how you knew I'd been brought in, and I told him about my call from the powder room before I left the house. He checked my cell phone, saw the call in the call history, and then looked pretty annoyed. He said he might have more questions for me later and told me to not leave town without consulting with him first. Then he said I was free to go and that an officer would take me home."

"Anything else?" I asked. The story sounded about right, but with Mamaw you never could tell.

"Well," she said. "There was one other tiny item."

"What?"

"Gracie, I'm not sure I should say. I don't think you're going to like it," teased Mamaw.

"Just tell me already,' I said, my voice rising.

"Chief Doeppers asked me to keep an eye on you, and to keep you out of his investigation. He said you were a nuisance and would only make things harder." Mamaw laughed.

"Crap," I muttered as Mamaw cackled. Getting anything out of the station now would be like breaking into Fort Knox. I wondered again if I shouldn't just let the police handle it, but then I was left with whether to tell Doeppers about my encounter with Hank the day of the murder. I was back where I'd started. The only rational solution was to learn enough about the murder to know if I needed to point the finger towards Hank. "Mamaw, who knew about your gun?" I asked.

"Gracie, you sound like an investigator. You aren't sticking your nose into this murder case, are you? Chief Doeppers isn't going to be happy with you."

"I'm just curious," I said. "It's not like I'm doing a full-fledged investigation. I'm just talking to the woman who raised me since I was eight."

"Too bad." Mamaw winked. "An investigation sounds like fun."

"Mamaw." I laughed, then took another sip of coffee. "Okay, say I was interested in learning more. I'd still need to know about your gun."

"Before I tell you anything, you must promise me something."

"What?" I asked, dreading the question.

"That if you learn anything, you tell me first. Well, after the police, that is."

"Deal." I laughed, relieved that she said I could tell the police first. I didn't need to get arrested for withholding evidence because I had to find Mamaw. I got up to check the pie and saw that it was ready. I took the pie from the oven to cool and grabbed the coffee pot to give both Mamaw and me a refill. Seated again, I asked, "Who knew about your gun? Both that you had it and where you kept it."

"I didn't tell many people, just a few. Ada Mae, of course, and I mentioned it to Margaret at the diner. We eat there on Tuesdays, you know, and I wanted her to know about my gun in case she needed it. Gladys knew, since I purchased the revolver in the first place because of the cash in the club and those hooligans working on the hotel across the street. I'm sure a few others knew too. It wasn't exactly a secret, but not something I spoke about often."

I almost groaned in frustration. If she'd told Ada Mae, Margaret, and Gladys, then over half the town probably knew about the blasted gun. Those three, Mamaw, and Ida Bea comprised the heart of the rumor mill. I could guess how the police had found out about Mamaw's gun: they had probably heard about it from several different sources. And yet, I hadn't known.

"And you always kept it in the car?" I asked.

"Locked tight in the glove compartment," she said. "I didn't need it here in the house. I only wanted access to it when I was downtown. I don't know how anyone got my car keys. I always keep them attached to my purse and you know I never let my purse get out of my sight. Do you think someone picked the lock?"

"Maybe," I said, pondering how anyone could have gotten a copy of Mamaw's car keys. Maybe the mechanic made a set when Mamaw had her car serviced? "Didn't you have two sets of keys to the car?"

"Oh, I lost the second set months ago. Not sure where I left them," continued Mamaw. "You see, for a while I was carrying both sets in my purse. I thought I'd misplaced my main set somewhere in the house and grabbed my second set to go out, planning on hunting for the missing set later. Anyhow, while I was out, I found my main set of keys in the bottom of my purse. I'd accidently stuffed them in the purse instead of clipping them to the outside for some reason. Well, from then on I had two sets of keys, one in the purse and one attached to the outside. Eventually I actually did misplace one set of keys, but I didn't realize that the first was missing. By the time I recognized I was only carrying one, I had no idea where I had left the other."

"So," I summarized, "you're telling me that several people knew about the gun that you kept locked in the glove compartment of your car, and that there is a set of your car keys floating around somewhere in Alpine."

"Well." Mamaw frowned. "When you say it like that..."

"Yeah," I said.

"Not too helpful, I guess," replied Mamaw. "I feel just awful. If it wasn't for my foolishness, poor Edward would still be alive." She seemed to wilt before my eyes, and suddenly looked her seventy plus years. Nothing like a little guilt to put a damper on gossip.

"Don't say that," I consoled her. "You did nothing wrong. Whoever killed Edward would have found another gun to use."

"You really think so?" she asked.

"In Alabama, rural Alabama? Over half the houses in this county have guns."

"True, but then why my gun?"

"Good question. Probably because it would be hard to trace back to the killer," I guessed. "The actual killer wouldn't want to use his or her own gun." I stood, stifling a yawn. It'd been a long day and I was ready for bed. "I'm bushed, Mamaw, off to bed for me. Thanks for letting me borrow your kitchen. I'm sure that Harry will appreciate it tomorrow."

"You know, come to think of it, Hank Waderich was at the Pole & Arms the day I bought the gun." She stood and took the coffee cups to the sink to rinse. "He was there picking up some fertilizer for the garden on the farm. Anyhow, Hank even helped me choose which gun to purchase, and offered to show me how to shoot it. I told him I hoped to never actually use the thing, that I was just going to keep it in my car in case I needed it." Mamaw turned back to me and said, "Gracie, are you all right? You look whiter than a sheet."

"I'm fine; just stood too fast, I guess," I lied. Hank knew about the gun and where Mamaw planned on keeping it. He had motive, opportunity and means. Perhaps Hank was the murderer after all.

Chapter 9

Mamaw fussed, but somehow I was able to get away and head home. The pie smelled wonderful in the seat beside me, but my thoughts weren't on pies. I was too busy smelling the stink of the situation I found myself in. I knew I needed to talk to Doeppers about Hank. I'd learned enough to deduce that Hank had motive, opportunity and means. If Edward, no matter how sinful of a man, was to have justice, then Hank needed to be investigated, and not by some amateur sleuth. In my heart I felt that Hank was innocent, but with what Mamaw had said earlier, I couldn't help but wonder if my fond memories from high school were clouding my judgment.

I detoured down Main Street by the bridge club, past the Pole & Arms, and down past Margaret's Diner. There were a few cars about, but not many this late. I got to the corner of Elm and Main, where I could turn left to head to the cottage, or right to the police station. I could feel my heart trying to beat through my chest, and then turned left. I still didn't know for sure that Mamaw's gun was the one used in the murder. It was possible, perhaps unlikely, but still possible that another gun was used. Maybe I was allowing my history with Hank to cloud my judgment, but so be it.

After stowing the pie in the fridge, I changed into more comfortable clothes and caught the end of a horror flick on the television. I didn't know what it was, but I was okay with zombie apocalypses—beefy men in hockey masks, though, freaked me out. I didn't sleep well afterwards, and when I got up with the sun, I wondered if my poor sleep was the result of the movie or the events of the last few days. All I did know was that I had dreamed of Hank wearing a hockey mask, chasing me around the bridge club and smacking me with a marijuana plant. I didn't know what Freud would say, but I figured the stress was getting to me.

I retreated to the bath and got water running in the clawfoot; a long hot shower was in order. Glancing at the mirror, I saw the bags under my eyes. I peered more closely and saw what looked like the shadows of wrinkles at the corners. True wrinkles hadn't appeared yet, but the signs were there.

I suddenly felt the fear and loss returning, and sat quickly on the commode before my legs failed me. I'd wanted to have children; Pierre and I had talked about it often, the life we would build together. And then came the plane crash, the betrayal, the Event-That-Changed-My-Life. Now here I was back where I'd started, thirty-three years old, no children, and with a biological clock that even my reflection told me was ticking. I don't know how long I sat there crying, but when I pulled myself together, the mirror was lost in a haze of steam from the shower. I jumped into the clawfoot, letting the hot water wash away all my anxiety and sorrow. When I finished, I wasn't quite a new woman, but I was the best I could be at the time.

After drying, I pulled my wet red curls into a bun, dropped the towel on the floor to mop up the inevitable water from my lack of skill in using the handheld showerhead, and wrapped a fresh towel around myself. I then headed to the kitchen for the obligatory cup of coffee. I looked through my collection of plastic cups and picked a favorite, one that had a hint of flavor that reminded me of my beloved coffee house in Paris. I could remember sitting outside with a latte on a warm Paris afternoon watching as the tourists walked by with their gaze more on their maps than on the sights along the way to wherever they were going. Occasionally someone would ask me directions to some attraction or another, and I enjoyed the looks of surprise when I answered their question with my southern accent. Pierre had loved the way I talked, and had listened to me for hours, just as I'd enjoyed listening to his sweet French phrases. I felt the tears returning and ruthlessly banished my reminiscing.

I finished my cup of coffee and then brewed a second. While waiting for my next dose of caffeine, I retrieved my notebook and opened it to the Means page. I hadn't been able to write any names on the list before I spoke with Mamaw last night. Now, though, I felt like I had too many names to add. With a sigh, I wrote down Hank and Gladys. I also included Ada Mae, although she had no motive and hadn't even been near the club that day as far as I knew.

I thought about what Mamaw had said: how anyone in the club could have known about the gun. The more I thought about it, the more I realized that getting access to the gun wouldn't really be a problem either, even without using the missing set of keys. Like everyone else playing bridge, Mamaw had placed her purse and umbrella on the center table that day so that she didn't have to keep track of it while she moved from table to table during the play. It wouldn't have been too hard for someone to go to the center table between hands to "grab something" and then palm Mamaw's car keys while there. I had gone to the center table that day to get my purse and retrieve my pack of cigarettes to take a quick smoke; someone else could have done something similar. And with the storm brewing, folks were going in and out of the club between every round. The murderer could have grabbed the gun during one such trip, using Mamaw's keys to gain access, and then could have returned the keys to the table before anyone noticed. That would mean the killer was playing bridge that day, an unsettling thought.

I threw the notebook on the table in disgust and began the second cup of coffee. In the cozy mysteries I'd read, the clues lined up beautifully. There were never more than a handful of suspects, and it was fairly simple for the main character to reduce the list until only one person, the killer, was left. In real life it didn't seem to be working that way. The list of suspects just kept on growing and I hadn't been able to eliminate any of them. The only advantage I had was that I didn't actually need to solve the case. I just had to determine whether I should tell Doeppers about my conversation with Hank that day. I needed to refocus my efforts on Hank, and let the police handle the other suspects.

With new resolve, I tore the three pages from the notebook and tossed them in the trash. Goodbye, *mon ami*, to the little gray cells method. If I was concentrating on Hank's movements that day, I no longer needed to consider motive, means or opportunity. I took a few minutes to tidy-up the kitchen and then headed to my bedroom to get dressed for the day. I was meeting Emily for lunch at Margaret's and then wanted to head out to the Waderich farm to talk more with Harry. I needed to learn as much as I could about Hank.

I reached in my closet and grabbed a new dress that I'd picked up in Atlanta, a flowery print pattern with a scoop neck. It was just above knee length with what at age five I'd called a "twirly skirt." At a glance it looked normal and happy, but if you looked more closely, you could see human skulls behind the floral patterns. I'd liked it on first sight, and it certainly fit my mood today. I complemented the dress with a pair of black sandals and let my hair down to fall at my shoulders. It was still a trifle wet but had curled as I'd hoped. I spent a few minutes on makeup, and when I checked my reflection in the mirror, I felt my self-esteem rise. Damn, I looked good.

It was a little early yet to head to Margaret's, so I grabbed the phone and gave Mamaw a call. I wanted to ask her about playing with me at Edward's Memorial Game on Sunday afternoon. I figured I should make an appearance; plus, I knew that between boards, gossip about Edward would abound. Unfortunately, I was unable to get through. With my cell phone taken as evidence, I knew I wasn't going to be able to ask about the game until I got back to the cottage, unless I took the time to stop by Mamaw's.

I grabbed my purse and keys and headed to the Mustang. The car roared to life, and as I pulled out of the drive, I noticed I needed to fill her up again. That meant a trip to Old Town Auto Supply at the edge of Alpine to get more of the lead-additive canisters the engine needed to run properly. When I bought the car in Atlanta, I hadn't realized how much extra care an older car needed.

The trip to Margaret's was quick, and I was able to secure a corner booth before the lunch rush. I ordered a Diet Coke while waiting for Emily to arrive. I didn't have to wait long, as she appeared before the teenage waitress returned with my drink.

"Girl, you clean up nice," Emily said, strutting towards me like a cock in a henhouse. I laughed and did a quick curtsy pulling on the hem of the skirt so it flared. She snorted as she sat down, and we spent the next ten minutes or so sharing our life stories since high school, although I certainly whitewashed mine in order to stay away from all the painful bits. Emily might have been my best friend in grade school, but I wasn't ready to pour my heart out to her now. The waitress came to take our order, and then we changed the topic to gossip about who went where and with whom. I was surprised that so many of our classmates hadn't moved that far from Alpine. You always hear in the news how small towns are dying with all the young people moving to the city, but apparently Alpine was something of an anomaly. Oh, several people had moved away, but others, like myself, had then moved back. It made me wonder if maybe I could build a life in Alpine. I really hadn't seen myself living here permanently, but I tucked the thought away.

The waitress came to ask about dessert, and Emily and I said pecan pie at the same time. We both called "Jinx!" and laughed like we were back in grade school. The waitress gave us an exasperated smile while clearing a few of our dishes.

"What can you tell me about Hank?" I asked once we had settled down.

"You thinking about starting back up with the Hunk?" Emily teased.

"No," I said, rolling my eyes at her. "We've talked about everyone else so I thought I'd ask about him."

"Well, I don't know much. He went off to Georgia Tech on a football scholarship."

"I know that, Emily," I said. "I was still around then, even though no one talked to me."

"Settle down now, girl," said Emily with a laugh. "He got hurt a couple years in, I seem to remember, but finished his degree. He then got a job down Gadsden way, I think."

"When did he move back to Alpine?" I asked.

"How did you know that?" asked Emily.

Crap, I should have realized a police officer would be able to make inferences from my questions. I should have just let her continue the story on her own. I did some quick thinking. "Well," I blushed. "I did run into him the other day and he mentioned moving back home. It was—interesting—seeing him again."

Emily rolled her eyes, and I knew she didn't quite believe me. "This is the low down," she continued, sitting forward and speaking confidentially. "Hank got married, got divorced, no kids. His mom died about five years ago, and three years ago his dad got drunk and smashed into a pickup truck down off of County Road 43. His dad was in the hospital and rehab facility for almost a year. Hank moved back home maybe six or eight months ago, got rid of the nursing care that had been coming to the house and started taking care of Harry. Not seeing anyone currently in a romantic way, at least no one local."

"How do you know all of that?" I asked, shocked. It was eerie how much she knew just off the top of her head. I wondered if the police had been surveilling Hank after all.

It was Emily's turn to blush. "Well," she said, sitting back and relaxing. "There's this girls' circle that keeps tabs on the eligible bachelors in town. You know, making sure no one is missing out or getting two-timed, that sort of thing. And, well, Hank is on the list."

"Emily!" I objected. "You're married."

"Damn straight," she said. "And happily. But it doesn't hurt a girl to keep informed, and anyhow, the circle uses me as a source. I can hook you up, you know, get you involved in the circle. You may be surprised on what you could learn about the going-ons in this town."

"You are a worse gossip than Mamaw," I said, astonished. I'd have to be careful. The last thing I needed was this circle linking me with Hank. Bad enough the senior circle was possibly already doing it thanks to Mamaw.

"Who do you think I learned it from? Miss Nora's gossiping skills are legendary. I can only dream of obtaining her perfection," intoned Emily, making me laugh.

Dessert came, and we spent a few moments enjoying the succulent taste of Margaret's pecan pie. I knew my time with Emily was about over, and I still had not asked anything about Edward's murder or Mamaw's gun. I didn't want to ruin our reunion, but knew that if I didn't ask now, I wouldn't have the opportunity to ask again. "Emily," I whispered. "Was it really Mamaw's gun that was used to murder Edward Schultz?"

Frowning, Emily finished the last bite of her pie before saying, "I can't talk about an ongoing investigation."

"Look," I backpedaled. "I didn't mean to put you in a difficult spot. Just forget I even mentioned it." I hoped I hadn't offended Emily. I hadn't made a lot of friends since moving back to Alpine. It was hard to meet folks my age; most of the bridge players were older, way older. It seemed like everyone in my generation was busy with family or work or both.

"Oh hell," she said, laughing. "I was just joshing you. You should see the look on your face."

"Emily." I reached across the booth and smacked her on the arm. "Don't do that to me."

"Like a schoolgirl caught sneaking into the boy's locker room to catch a peek," she continued almost choking on her laughter. "I've been saving that line all morning."

"Well," I said, a little annoyed at her amusement. "You going to tell me or not?"

"I really shouldn't, you know. It *is* an ongoing investigation."

"But…" I prompted.

"I was never very good at following rules." She grinned.

"I seem to remember that. I'm pretty sure you broke almost every rule." I laughed.

"Speaking of following rules, what did you do to get Yancey's panties all up in a wad yesterday?"

"What do you mean?" I asked as innocently as I could.

"Yesterday Officer Yancey comes storming into the station cursing and yammering about how she wants to knock you down a peg or two. She's vengeful, that one. You better watch your back."

I smiled. "That's what I have you for."

"And I'm telling you to watch your back or you might find a knife in it, or at least be resting it in a cell. What did you do to piss her off so badly?"

"You really want to know?"

"Hell, yes," she said.

"Trade?" I asked wiggling a pinky finger.

She chuckled. "You are an evil one, you are. Trade." She matched my finger with her own. We did a pinkie shake like we always did back in grade school when promising to share secrets—back when our secrets were much more innocent.

I told Emily about my encounter with Officer Yancey at the Piggly-Wiggly. She laughed at my effrontery and promised to mention something to

Doeppers about possible harassment. I felt a little guilty in getting Doeppers involved, but Emily assured me that it was better to have the Chief warn Yancey now before it escalated. I then told Emily that it was her turn, dreading the answer, yet needing it nonetheless.

"We don't know," she said smugly.

"What?" I asked.

"We don't know yet," she replied. "The caliber is the same, and so it might be the murder weapon, but as of now we don't know. We sent the bullets from the scene and Miss Nora's gun down to Montgomery for ballistics tests. We should hear back in a couple of weeks."

Weeks, I repeated in my head, frustrated.

"Cheater," I accused, looking Emily in the eye.

"Hey, I told you all I know." She laughed. "You just thought I knew more than I did."

"Do you have a suspect yet?" I asked.

"That I won't tell you, even with a pinkie swear," Emily replied. "I could lose my job. Besides, this is police work and anyone else getting involved, even you, just makes it harder to sort out for everyone."

"Can you tell me this? How did you know the gun you found was Mamaw's?"

Emily laughed. "That I will tell you, not that it will do you much good. Did you know that we live in such a backwards country that it is illegal for law enforcement to have a computerized gun registry?"

"What do you mean?" I asked.

"By law, no governmental agency can keep an electronic database of gun ownership—some nonsense about privacy rights pushed by the NRA. Now, I believe in gun rights—hell, I have a couple of guns at home locked up safe and sound, but this is ridiculous. By law, everything has to be done old fashioned, by hand. There is a little town in West Virginia where they keep track of all the gun ownership in paper files. Craziest thing I ever did hear of. You send in a serial number and a description of the gun, and folks there go and try to find the file in the boxes of records. If you are lucky, maybe six weeks later you get a report with the purchaser's name, date and location of purchase, *et cetera*. That's if it happened in a gun store and not at a gun show. Anything purchased at a gun show is like leaves in the wind."

"What does this have to do with knowing that it was Mamaw's gun?"

"Well, that's the thing. There's no systematic and efficient way to keep track of that stuff on a national level. But on the local level, well, that's another story. When Doeppers became Chief, he started making a list of all guns purchased in the county. Handwritten, not electronic, as that would be illegal. He has now passed that job on to me—probably as punishment after I divorced the man. On the first of every month I visit all the establishments in the county that sell guns and copy the purchasers' names, addresses and serial number for each gun sold. The stores are legally required to keep that paperwork. Once I get back to the station, I rewrite the list, merging it with older lists and making sense of all the data. Takes me two work days to complete the thing."

"So when you found Mamaw's gun..."

"We just had to pull the list for that type of gun and look up the serial number. Since she bought it in Corbert County, we had a record of it. Simple as pie." Emily air-washed her hands like she was finished. "Listen hun, I hate to do this but I gotta go. Eliza Anne has a play date this afternoon and I gotta get to the grocery first."

"I understand. Family first," I said.

"Damn straight," Emily rose and took her portion of the bill. "And you are part of mine."

I felt tears in my eyes as I nodded in agreement. We hugged then, promising to get together again soon. I finished what was left of my Diet Coke as Emily paid her bill and left. Once Emily was gone, I went to the counter to pay my own bill.

I drove the Mustang back to the cottage, grabbed the pie from the fridge, and then headed out to Old Town Auto Supply to pick up the canisters of fuel additive. It was not on the same side of town as the Waderich farm, but I didn't think I had enough gas to head to the farm first and make it back to Old Town later.

I arrived at the shop and found the supply of fuel additives where I expected. I picked up half a dozen canisters knowing that it would last me a good couple of weeks. I went to the front counter to pay, seeing Peter Teegarden at the register. The business had been in the Teegarden family for as long as I could remember, and I wasn't surprised to see Peter managing the place. I glanced at the bulletin board near the front counter, where customers could freely post information about cars and parts for sale, and any other thing automobile related. Once again I considered trading in the Mustang for something a little less maintenance ridden. It wouldn't be too hard to write up an advertisement to post.

"What do you think?" I pointed at the advertisements and put my purchases on the counter along with my credit card. "Should I try and sell the Mustang?" Peter and I just missed each other in high school; he was about five years younger than me, with dark blonde hair and a bold nose that would make a proverbial Roman nose look small. His German heritage came through strongly.

"I don't know, Miss Theis." He smiled, checking me out from my head to my toes. "You can't find anything new with that kind of presence on the road anymore."

"True, but it's just such a pain at times," I complained, having a little fun and twirling a bit to let my skirt flow.

"Sometimes we have to deal with a little hassle for the things we love," said Peter, ringing up my goods but keeping his eyes on me.

I nodded, bending a little at the waist to peer more closely at the bulletin board and giving Peter an opportunity to see a bit more of me than before. Out of the corner of my eye, I saw his smile widen and I had to hide a snicker.

"You looking for anything in particular, Miss Theis?"

"Oh, please call me Gracie," I replied with a smile, boldly meeting him in the eye and letting my gaze smolder. I looked away first, pulling my eyes back to the bulletin board. "Not really, just looking at what's for sale at what price." I flicked through a few advertisements, pulling the newer ones up to see those posted below and trying to make a show of it. I hadn't flirted like this in ages and had forgotten how fun it could be.

"Well, this is the place to look, at least in Alpine it is. Nothing's better," Peter claimed.

I flipped up one last advertisement and saw Edward Schultz's name listed on the one beneath. I pulled it off the board and saw that he'd been trying to sell a 1964 Ford Thunderbird for a whopping eighteen grand.

"Yeah, I was surprised when Mr. Schultz came and posted that. He loved that car, rebuilt it from scratch. He did most of the work himself; it must have taken him five years to do it. And he spent a bundle too. I guess his heirs will auction it off or something. Shame, him being murdered and all."

"Did he say why he was selling?" I asked.

"I got the sense that he didn't want to. I figured he needed the cash for some reason. Maybe that old hotel downtown? That could be a money pit if I ever saw one," said Peter. "Just hand that here. I don't expect Mr. Schultz will be needing that post anymore."

"Probably not," I said, handing him the leaflet. I'd lost my desire to flirt, not with a murderer on the loose. I remembered talking to Edward about old cars between hands at the bridge club; he was interested in hearing how I'd gotten the Mustang. At the time I hadn't realized he had his own classic car, although I supposed I should have made the connection.

I grabbed my goods and treated Peter to one last smile before heading out the door. The Mustang started like it was new, and I momentarily felt guilty about thinking of selling. I took the Old Gadsden Road north and stopped at the nearest station to fill up, mixing in one of the canisters I'd just purchased. I paid at the pump, but waved at the teenager who was working inside. With everyone paying via cards at the pump, I figured the poor girl was bored to tears.

With a full tank of gas, a newly baked apple pie, and dressed to kill, I figured it was time to head to the Waderichs. Emily said that Hank had moved back to town after Harry's accident. It might not be a bad idea to look up the details of the accident and the resulting court case. *The Alpine Tribune* should have something on it, and I could find back issues at the public library. At the moment, I was going on Harry's word, and I knew how the old goat could distort reality to fit his own preconceptions.

With the route I took I didn't pass by the old round barn, coming onto the road a little to the east of the structure. It only took a few minutes before I was pulling into the driveway and saw Hank's F150 parked out front. Drat, he wasn't supposed to be here. Didn't he have marijuana plants to be taking care of somewhere far from the house? I saw Hank appear on the front porch as I pulled to a stop beside his truck. I guessed it was too late to just turn around now, and besides, the pie wouldn't keep that well. By the time I'd put the Mustang in park, he was striding down the walk towards me.

"Gracie," he hollered from across the house yard. "I told you to stay away." Yep, he wasn't happy about this, but I wasn't going to let that stop me. I needed to figure out if he was a killer, and fast.

I got out of the car, and before Hank could reach me, grabbed the pie and shoved it his way. "I brought a pie," I said. Hank fumbled but grabbed the pie pan, giving me the distraction I needed to pass him by and enter the gate leading into the yard. "Homemade apple pie," I added over my shoulder.

"Gracie, stop a minute," said Hank as he caught back up. He grabbed me by the arm and twisted me around to face him, all while still holding the pie pan. "What are you doing here?"

"I promised Harry a homemade apple pie, and so I brought one," I calmly replied, hoping Hank couldn't read me as well as he did fifteen years ago. He was angry, and if he were the killer, I might be in a lot of trouble. I willed myself to stay calm and look him in the eye. We stared at each other for a moment, and I saw his anger lessen and his eyes widen as if seeing me for the first time. His eyes went from my face to my toes and back again. My dress was definitely having an effect.

"Gracie, please be reasonable," he said in a calmer voice. "It's too dangerous for you to be here. It's too dangerous for anyone to be here. I don't want to be the cause of you getting into trouble." *Nice of him to be concerned now*, I thought with a small snort. Where was his chivalry fifteen years ago? I gave myself a small shake and reminded myself why I was here. Now was the time to drop the hammer.

"Hank Waderich, what I do or don't do is up to me, not you. I don't think this is all your decision," I said. "As long as Harry wants me to visit, and I intend to see to that," I swished my skirt, "then I will."

I could see Hank's anger rise again. Part of me wondered if I'd gone too far, if Hank had changed to the point of being able to physically hurt me. My heart was threatening to beat through my chest, and I felt a bead of perspiration on my forehead. I wished I'd told Mamaw or Emily about my plans. Then I saw Hank shake and melt, giving me a rueful grin that was reminiscent of a happier time. "Please," I whispered, "let me help. Tell me how I can help."

"You want to help me, Gracie, even after everything that has happened?" he asked. I just nodded and hoped that he would let me. He took a deep breath and said, "Then help me figure out a way to get into that bridge club."

Chapter 10

"What?" I asked, confused. What did the bridge club have to do with John's marijuana operation? This made no sense.

"Let's take this pie on inside," said Hank. "We can cut a slice, grab a beer, and I'll explain everything." Hank kept his hand on my arm and began escorting me up the walk.

I allowed it, knowing this explanation would be a doozy. "You want to drink a beer with my homemade apple pie?" I asked derisively. A smile crept onto my face at the feel of his hand on my arm. I should have known better than to come here. I should have just stayed away from the man. Perhaps my reactions would fade, like paint on the westward side of a house in the Alabama sun. Maybe once I really got to know him again, I wouldn't have these feelings. I just hoped that the happiness I felt at his touch was the shadow of an old learned reaction, and not something real.

"Water then?" he asked sheepishly. "I'm not sure there is much else."

"When I was here yesterday, I saw some lemonade mix in a cupboard. I'll mix some up." I wasn't sure how old it was, but hopefully it wouldn't be too stale. From the look of things, beer, rum, and vodka were the only things that had been drunk in this house since Mildred had died. Hank opened the screen door for me, and I nodded my thanks as I entered the house. Passing through to the kitchen, I saw Harry once again stationed in front of the television in the back room. He was watching a fishing show, of all things.

Harry turned my way and said, "Well, lookie here. You came back, did ya, girl?"

"And brought the pie I promised," I said.

"And all gussied up too. Trying to keep me boy interested?" He cackled. "With that dress, it shouldn't be hard." Hank winked at me and nodded in agreement with his father's statement.

"Not at all, Harry." I twirled around and said, laughing, "This is all for you."

"Well, now, I suppose if that's the case, I might have a slice of that there pie."

I moved past Hank, grabbed some plates from the cabinet, a knife from the drawer, and quickly had three slices prepared. I then pulled a pitcher from above the refrigerator, the lemonade mix from the cupboard, and made us something to drink. In no time, we had Harry settled back in front of the television, and Hank and I retreated to the front porch where we could talk more privately.

Hank sat down on the porch step next to me. He gazed over at me again, his eyes lingering on the scoop neck of my dress. My face flushed despite my willing it not to. I could hardly breathe, but then the shutters came down over his eyes. "I don't know where to start," he confessed and glanced away.

"How about at the beginning?"

"I guess that's better than anywhere else. Okay, the major cause of the money problems, as I said yesterday, is the monthly payments we're making to the bank to cover the loan we got on account of being sued. If we could stop making those payments, then I could stop working for John. We can make enough from the farm to cover our normal costs, just not enough to pay the extra loan amount."

I was puzzled. "You can't just stop making loan payments."

"But we could pay the loan back, and then those payments would go away," Hank said.

"Where are you going to get the money?" I asked. "And what does this have to do with the bridge club?"

"From the plaintiff, because he lied," Hank explained. "And so we can sue him, or reopen the case, or something to reduce the award. Make him pay some of it back."

"Okay, I said start from the beginning, but maybe just skip to the end."

"No, no," continued Hank. "This is easy enough to understand. The plaintiff in the case faked his injuries. He claimed that he could barely walk and had to resort to using a cane. He had doctors back him up and everything. Part of the award was for his pain and suffering, and part of it was for lost earnings, lost future earnings and disability, since he had to stop working due to his injuries. Well, I've heard from a few folks that he barely uses a cane since the trial, only when he's outside in public. It's only been about a year since the trial, so we now have a counterclaim of sorts: Pop and I have been injured by the excessive award and can request the court to make him return some of that money that he didn't deserve. We can then use that money to pay off the bank loan. I talked to Edward Schultz about it and he said it was a possibility. Paid him fifty bucks for a half hour of his time. He said he couldn't take the case, but that there might be a case there. Even gave me a card of a friend of his down in Gadsden who might take it on."

"When did you talk to Edward?" I asked with my heart in my throat. God, I hoped Hank wouldn't say Thursday. If so, the police could be headed here to arrest him.

"A week or so ago, I don't remember exactly when," he replied. I could feel my heart beat again in relief. "Too bad someone shot him. He was one hell of a lawyer. Certainly chewed us up on our case. That's why I asked him about suing; I wanted him on our side this time. I figured he already knew the case and that would help, but he said that was exactly why he couldn't take our case. Something about a conflict of interest."

"So you wanted to talk to Edward again? That was why you were hanging around outside the club on Thursday?" I asked. That was the key question, the cause of all of my anxiety since discovering the body.

"What? No. I was after proof," replied Hank. "I had a video camera in the truck. I was hoping to catch the scoundrel who sued us in the act of walking without a cane so I'd have proof before heading to Gadsden to talk to the lawyer. Unfortunately, with the sudden storm, I had to head home and check on Pop and the crop. I needed to make sure nothing was wrong with the marijuana, or John would have my hide."

"So," I laughed, "you were trying to film someone?" I hadn't realized how heavy of a burden I'd been carrying until it was lifted. I felt like a new day had dawned. Like my life had been black and white and suddenly Technicolor had arrived.

"Yep, what else?" he asked, and I could see the light dawning in his eyes. "You don't think... Edward... you didn't think I had anything to do with that? Oh, Gracie." Hank looked appalled, and I knew I had some backpedaling to do. I guess today was the day for it.

"No, I didn't think that. Not really," I said sheepishly. "All I knew was that I'd caught you acting a little strange, and then Edward showed up dead. I thought you might know something about it. You know, maybe you saw something."

"Well. I guess I can understand that. It was just a coincidence that the jerk who sued us and Edward were in the same place at the same time."

"Who is it? You've never mentioned his name."

"His name is Clovis Jones," Hank said.

"Skeeter?" I asked, shocked.

"What?"

"Skeeter Jones. Clovis Jones. I mean, Clovis goes by Skeeter," I explained.

"Never heard him called that, but if you say so. I guess he was a farm hand around the area for years. Never had a place of his own, and never amounted to much from what I heard. I'd never met him before this case," explained Hank.

"Skeeter does have a cane," I said. "I've seen him. He carries one around but doesn't use it very often." I thought about how on Thursday Clovis had walked me to my car, and then dashed back into the club so quickly. The man was a faker; I had no doubt. He was just putting on a show to not risk his new life. A life paid for by Hank. "But yeah, he *is* faking it."

"Exactly my point," said Hank. "I just need to prove it." He looked at me hopefully.

"And so you want to get into the club…" I began.

"To get a video of Clovis walking without his cane, without pain," said Hank. "I need that proof."

I thought about it for a bit, and then said, "Well, there's only one way I can think of to get you in the club."

"And how is that? I've been racking my brain for a good excuse to just hang out at the bridge club. I've been waiting outside, but that's not working. The man is too careful outdoors, and I can't spend all day trailing him."

"I think you've forgotten the obvious," I said.

"What is that?" asked Hank.

"People go to the bridge club to do just one thing, and that is to play bridge."

Hank looked taken aback at that, and I smiled reassuringly. "Gracie, I haven't played bridge since we dated in high school." I remembered the days we had played around the kitchen table with my grandparents. "I don't remember how to play the game," he said.

"Well, it's a good thing that I'm patient," I said. "Get a deck of cards and let's get started."

Finding a deck of cards in the old farmhouse was harder than what I'd anticipated, but eventually Hank put his hands on an old poker deck. I spread the cards face up and we talked about the different suits and ranks. We discussed the mechanics of play, how the bidding worked and the play of a hand. Hank remembered more than he thought, and we quickly progressed into hand evaluation and the play of the cards.

The afternoon went by in a blur and I had more fun with Hank than I'd had since moving back to Alpine. The bridge play was progressing, but I knew we had a long way to go before we would be competitive. Hank was anxious to try and catch Clovis though, so we agreed to play at the club the next day at the Edward Schultz Memorial Game. I knew it would be brutal, but the first time we played against the more experienced players was going to be that way in any case. Besides, this wasn't about bridge, it was about getting to take a hit at Clovis, and I was up for that. With the setting of the sun, I'd had enough. We'd covered so much that I knew Hank wouldn't be able to remember it all. All he really needed now was time at the table to practice.

With the bats circling above us, Hank walked me to the Mustang. When I got to the car, I somehow found myself in his arms, then his lips were on mine and we kissed like back in high school. I hadn't been that close to a man in a long time and it felt nice. Better than nice—it felt right. When he released me, I knew I had the same smile on my face that I had back on that lazy fall afternoon in the round barn when he first asked me to be his girl.

We said our goodbyes and I retreated with the Mustang down the pecan-lined drive, eventually driving by the round barn on my way back to town. I was so relieved that Hank was not involved in the murder of Edward Schultz; I could just leave it to the police now. There was no reason to try and continue investigating. The police had more resources, more leads, and much more experience in solving crimes than I did.

I turned onto Elm Street to head to the cottage I was renting. I saw a car parked in front of the house, and as I turned into the drive, I recognized Yancey's police cruiser. I sighed, wondering what she wanted now. From what I could tell, everyone important to me was safe from the investigation. I threw the car into park and got out to face Yancey standing there.

"So," she drawled, "where've you been all day?"

"That's none of your business," I said curtly.

"It is my business if I make it so," she replied.

"Look," I said. "I don't want any trouble. I've already said my piece, and have nothing more to add. Why don't you go harass someone else for a change."

"The chief isn't getting anywhere in this investigation. I think he's left a few too many stones unturned."

"What's that supposed to mean?"

"I've seen your type all my life—rich, spoiled girls who think the laws don't apply to them. But I've got your number now. You and yours aren't going to get away with nothing. I'm sticking to you like skunk stank on a hound dog." She headed back to her cruiser. I stood there, shocked to be considered either rich or privileged. "That's the only warning you're going to get. Next time we talk, I'll be arresting you."

I had no reply, no comeback to the threat of arrest. I watched as Yancey slowly pulled away in her cruiser. I just hoped Emily would be able to intervene with Doeppers, and that he could talk some sense into Yancey before I ended up in jail again.

I unlocked the cottage, got a glass of Merlot, and headed to the kitchen to reheat a bit of leftover roast from Wednesday night. As I sipped the wine, I felt the tension leave my body. Yancey could look all she wanted; there was nothing that she would find to link me to the murder. Mamaw had already been interviewed and released, and Hank wasn't even on their radar. Thinking of Mamaw reminded me that I hadn't talked with her today. I needed to tell her about Hank and how I was going to play bridge with him tomorrow. I hoped Mamaw would be able to find another partner, as I was certain she'd want to be in the game for the gossip, if not for the bridge. I missed my cell; I could have called Mamaw while running my errands. I wondered if I was going to get it back or if I should just chalk it up as a loss and get a new one. I wasn't even sure if the thing was salvageable; I'd dropped it into a sink and run water over it, not to mention the pool of blood. Come to think of it, I might just get a new one anyway.

I focused on Hank's problem and how to catch Clovis walking without the cane. I figured that between the two of us we should be able to get a video of Clovis at the club. I decided I'd replace my cell—I needed to be able to make a video clip. I doubted I could find one in Alpine, though, meaning I'd need a trip to Gadsden to replace it. That would have to wait until Monday; I couldn't get there and back before the start of the bridge game. With that decision made, I felt a little better and smiled as I imagined the time I'd be spending with Hank. We'd essentially be on a stakeout until we caught Clovis.

I suddenly sat up straight, almost spilling my wine. If I spent that much time with Hank, Yancey was sure to see us together. I was too central to the investigation, like I had a spotlight trained on me. And now I seemed destined to shine that light on Hank.

Chapter 11

After finishing my dinner, I was able to get Mamaw on the phone. I told her about my day and explained that Hank and I planned to play together the next day at the memorial game. I could tell from her lack of enthusiasm that she was worried about me, but at least she skipped the lecture. We did agree to meet at Margaret's for lunch, as we usually did on Sundays after church.

I spent the rest of my evening reconstructing my three pages of notes, jotting down theories, and thinking about the murder case. If I could finger the killer, then Yancey would have no reason to investigate Hank. I wished Hercule Poirot would appear at my doorstep to exercise his little gray cells for my benefit. I felt there was something here, something that I'd missed, but couldn't put my finger on it.

I went to bed early, hoping to recover a bit from my nightmare-filled sleep of the night before. Alas, that was not the case. This time I dreamed of Hank and me frantically hiding bridge cards from a roving spotlight controlled by Yancey, laughing maniacally—and for some reason, there was the smell of rotten tomatoes. I stayed in bed late the next morning, hoping that a few more hours horizontal would somehow make up for my restless night. I finally conceded defeat midmorning and stumbled into the bath for a quick shower.

I chose slacks and a fashionable hunter-green blouse that was cut just right to emphasize the curves I wanted to accent while hiding the ones I didn't. Normally I didn't wear anything quite so provocative to the bridge club, but I figured if Hank was going to be sitting across from me all afternoon, he should have something pleasant to behold. I chose a pair of suede ballet flats I loved, and after a few minutes adding lip gloss and working with the flat iron, I decided I was ready.

I headed out to Margaret's for my lunch date with Mamaw, the Mustang starting without trouble. I did hear a pinging that concerned me a little. I wondered if I'd have the time to stop by Old Town and see if Peter was willing to take a listen before the bridge game. If there was something wrong with the thing, I didn't want to have car trouble on the way to Gadsden the next day. At least in Alpine I had a mechanic I trusted and knew that he'd treat me fair. Anywhere else and I risked running into some yahoo who would see dollar signs in a female with an old car. I didn't want to have to deal with that hassle.

When I turned onto Main Street, I could see that Margaret's was fuller than usual. I parked on the street under an old elm tree, hoping the shade would keep the car from getting too hot in the sun. We hadn't had a drop of rain since Thursday, but in an Alabama summer that could change in a heartbeat. I entered the front door and glanced around, looking for Mamaw. I didn't see her, but I did see that the place was near capacity. Margaret herself greeted me and led me to one of the last tables. I thanked her and ordered a Diet Coke while I waited for Mamaw to appear. The service over at Grace Lutheran Church must have gone long.

Margaret returned with my soda and set it down. "In case I get too busy and forget, please let Nora know that I looked in the Lost and Found but didn't find her car keys."

"What?" I asked. Mamaw wouldn't have done anything that foolish, would she?

"Nora called yesterday afternoon to see if she'd left a set of car keys here. I told her I'd look and let her know," she explained. "But no keys were left here. At least none that I could find."

I smiled my thanks, hoping my face didn't reveal my concern. Luckily the place was busy, and Margaret hurried off before I had to find something else to say. Mamaw had been a fool. When we'd talked on Friday night, I had asked about her spare set of car keys, and apparently she'd reached the same conclusion that I had. Whoever had that spare set of keys was the most likely person to have taken the gun. It had occurred to me that a discreet search for those keys was a possible avenue of investigation, but I couldn't think of any reasonable way to conduct a search without alerting the murderer. Apparently Mamaw hadn't reached that conclusion though. By calling around town asking about that lost set of keys, she might just have stuck a bull's-eye on her back.

I waved when Mamaw entered, and she came to my table wearing her Sunday best: a sleek gray pantsuit that was just old enough to almost be coming back into style. I suppose it would be labeled vintage now. When she sat opposite me, I asked, "Any luck finding those keys?"

"Oh," she said, having the decency to blush. "You heard about that, did you?"

I fixed her with a firm glare. "What were you thinking, Mamaw?"

"I was thinking that whoever has those keys probably stole my gun," she whispered.

"And did you think that whoever has those keys is probably also a killer? Not to mention that now he or she will toss them in the nearest trash can, easy as pie," I said just as quietly.

"Well, I didn't think about that at the time," she replied. "Anyhow, maybe the killer was seen tossing the keys, or maybe someone else will remember seeing the keys, and we can track the killer that way."

"Or maybe the killer will come after you for asking too many questions." Good grief. The woman didn't seem to realize her life could be in danger. What was she thinking, getting involved in a murder investigation?

"Nonsense." She laughed. "Little ol' me asking about a set of lost keys. Besides, I can take care of myself. I'll be careful." She gave me a look that she thought made her look innocent, but in fact looked much more like a cat with canary feathers on its mouth. Seeing my hesitation, she pounced, "I want to know what your intentions are with that rascal Hank. I see you all dolled up with that low cut shirt and your lip gloss. Are you trying to rekindle that flame? I already told you, Gracie, what's past is past."

"I am not all dolled up," I said. "And my business with Hank Waderich is *my* business. I'm a grown woman. I can handle this, Mamaw."

"I just don't want to see you hurt again," Mamaw said. She looked straight at me. "You've had enough hurt to last a lifetime, child." I could see the sympathy in her eyes, and she didn't even know the worst of it.

"I have to try, Mamaw. At some point I have to start living again." I took a deep breath. "I'll make you a deal. I'll not worry about you calling around looking for a killer by asking about your lost car keys," I lied. "And you stop worrying about my romantic life, or lack thereof."

"You know I can't do that," she said. "I'm not wired that way."

"Well," I chuckled. "Neither can I. But how about we agree to not talk about either of those things for a little while."

Mamaw laughed at that and said, "Deal."

We talked about small things, and I told her how Hank and I had practiced bridge yesterday at the farm. She asked if I thought Hank was ready for duplicate, and I answered that I doubted it, but then again no one is really ready the first time they play competitively. I was happy to hear that Mamaw had found a partner for today's game. She'd called Ada Mae last night after we'd gotten off the phone and made arrangements. I knew that Ada Mae didn't play bridge at the club often, preferring party bridge, so I was glad that she'd made the exception for Mamaw. It occurred to me that Ada Mae and Mamaw would be good opponents for Hank and me to practice against, but I also knew that I was digging my potatoes before they'd been planted. I wasn't even sure Hank would want to continue playing bridge after he got his proof on Clovis, or if he'd still want to see me.

I didn't mention Hank's true motivation for going to the bridge club. I knew Mamaw well enough to know that she would want to share it with just a few close friends, and within the week, if not sooner, half of Alpine would know. I couldn't risk Clovis hearing, not if we were going to be successful in catching him on video. In some ways, I figured Hank's mere presence would have Clovis behaving as if he were up for an Oscar—that is, if he recognized Hank from the trial. He might not, as Harry had been the defendant, not Hank. Besides, Hank had been gone at college and then in

Gadsden most of the time Clovis had been working in the area. My only consolation was knowing that Clovis was in a difficult pinch. If he acted too infirm, everyone at the club would ask him about it, but if he didn't exaggerate his limp, we'd capture him on video. Would his self-esteem or his self-interest win out?

After finishing our meal, I picked up the tab and told Mamaw I'd see her later at the club. She wanted to go home and change into something a little less formal. It didn't look like I'd have the time to drive to Old Town Auto Supply, not if I was going to reach the bridge club at the time Hank and I had agreed to. It was a little early to head to the club, but I figured Margaret could use the table. I knew Gladys would already be there, so I wouldn't be alone.

I parked under an oak tree, just a few spaces from where I had on Thursday, and headed into the club to talk to Gladys. I wanted to see if Hank and I could have stationary seats so that we didn't have to move during the game. If Hank sat against the wall, he should have a good view of the room. I'd warned him already that electronic devices were banned during the game, so he'd have to be somewhat circumspect in trying to take a video of Clovis. Of course, Clovis wasn't going to be the most willing of subjects either.

I felt a little leery entering the building. The last time I was here I'd found a dead body in the kitchen. The lights were on, but the place was empty—or seemed to be. I called out softly, wondering what had happened to my voice, and heard nothing but a faint moaning coming from the kitchen. A picture of Edward floating like an apparition from Ghostbusters flashed through my thoughts and I shivered. I took a deep breath, banishing the vision, and marched back to investigate. The kitchen was empty, thankfully, but I did discover the source of the noise. I found Gladys weeping in the small office tucked behind the kitchen.

"Gladys, what's wrong?" I asked, kneeling next to the chair I found her in.

Gladys took a shuddering breath, wiped her eyes with a handkerchief she was holding, and pulled herself together. She looked up to me and said, "Oh, it's nothing, Gracie. I'm just upset about Edward. I'll be fine in a minute."

She was lying. I knew it in my bones. I'd seen her not forty-eight hours ago and she was chatting to the butcher at the Piggly-Wiggly about the murder. If she were that upset, she wouldn't have been able to act that way then. "Are you sure?" I asked.

"Yes," she cried, but the tears just got heavier, and she put her face back into her hands.

I retreated to the kitchen and got a glass of water, hoping it would help. When I returned, Gladys looked a little better. She accepted the water and drank; I could tell she was on the mend. I tried to make her talk one last time, "Are you sure there isn't anything wrong?"

"Oh, I might as well tell you," she said with a shudder. "The whole club will find out soon enough."

"Find out what?" I asked.

"Someone stole all of the club's money. I don't think there's enough to even pay me this month. I may be out of a job!" she wailed.

"What?" I said, shocked.

"It must have been Edward—he was the club treasurer. Or maybe someone forced Edward to give them the money, and then killed him to cover it up. I don't know. It's all just a mess," Gladys said.

"Tell me exactly what happened," I suggested.

Gladys seemed to be gathering strength as she explained; she almost sounded angry now. "When I went to the bank yesterday to get a cashier's check cut to pay the cleaning service, I discovered that the amount in the account was lower than it should be. I just checked the books—and yes, we're several thousand dollars short."

"How could that happen?" I asked. "Weren't there safeguards in place?"

"Edward put in those safeguards, so I guess he knew ways around them. The cleaners insisted on payment up front before they would take care of... well, you know." A picture of Edward's body lying in the pool of blood flashed through my mind, making me shiver. "I had to get the cleaning done yesterday so we could have the game today," continued Gladys. "Only three of us—Edward, Otis and I—had access to the account. Otis was out of town, and obviously Edward couldn't take care of it, so I had to pay the cleaners. That's when I discovered..." She started sobbing again.

"Maybe we can work something out. Maybe we can find the money to hold things together somehow."

"Maybe," she said doubtfully. Gladys took a deep breath and added, "Nothing I can do about it now, anyway." She stood and straightened her clothes and wiped her face. "It's almost game time and I have a job to do. Thanks, Gracie, somehow it feels better to have told someone."

As we headed to the main room, I told Gladys about Hank, and that it would be his first time playing at the club. Gladys readily agreed to sit us in a stationary position, and then busied herself preparing the game. I took a seat to wait for Hank and the other players and let my mind wander to Edward's murder. Obviously Edward had had a cash flow problem; the fact that he'd tried to sell his precious Thunderbird proved that. Perhaps Edward had stolen the money from the club. Yet he would only have been able to hide the embezzlement of club funds for so long; that money would have had to be replaced before either Gladys or Otis had discovered it was missing. Was the theft related to the murder?

Players were beginning to arrive, and soon I saw Hank. Gladys glanced up from her preparations, and I waved Hank over so that I could introduce him. I swear Gladys looked like she was ready to swoon when Hank uttered his pleasure at meeting her, and the look she gave me conveyed her approval. I felt a moment of dread when I realized Gladys had read more into the situation than what was there. Gladys rivaled Mamaw as a gossip, and I knew that rumors of Hank and me as a couple would soon be in the air.

Gladys told us to sit North-South at table five, and then continued her work. Hank sat against the wall, and I explained to Hank how in duplicate we would only be competing against the other North-South pairs today. I pointed to the collection of plastic containers that Gladys was unloading and explained how each one contained pre-dealt hands—"boards" in bridge parlance—which kept track of each hand as they moved from table to table. Confident Hank had the gist of the logistics, I moved on to more important matters. The room was beginning to fill, and the game would start soon.

"Now duplicate players make some pretty strange bids at times. The good news is that if there is something you don't understand, then you can just ask," I said.

"What do you mean?" asked Hank, flashing me a grin that made my heart flutter.

"If an opponent makes a bid you don't understand, then you can ask that player's partner to explain what the bid means."

"That's stupid. Wouldn't they just lie?"

"They can't, it's against the rules. They have to tell you what their agreement is, but only ask if you need to," I explained. "Any question you ask gives the opponents a chance to exchange information about what they think their partner meant by a bid."

"So first you tell me I can ask the meaning of a bid, and now you say don't ask." Hank laughed. "Which is it, Gracie?"

"Both." I smiled. "Ask if you need to, but don't if you don't need to."

"I'm not sure I'm up for this," Hank said with a grimace.

"I know we aren't up for this, but we're doing it anyhow and we can try and have fun while we're at it."

Hank eyed my shirt and grinned. "I'll definitely have fun." The look he gave me put the butterflies in my stomach into overdrive.

The tables filled quickly, with only a few empty seats remaining. I gave Hank a running commentary of who was who and what to expect. We saw Clovis enter, cane in hand. Hank discreetly used his cell to get some video, but with so many people walking around, I doubted he got what he needed. Clovis was using his cane in any case, as he often did early in a bridge game. It was usually later when he was less diligent in keeping up the show. When Mamaw arrived, we waved, and she joined us at our table, sitting in the East seat. Mamaw was behaving, at least, asking Hank about his garden and if he had any extra tomatoes to give away. I covered my smile, knowing that Hank's garden wasn't exactly the typical vegetable garden. It seemed likely that we would begin against Mamaw and Ada Mae, for which I was thankful. It would give Hank a chance on a decent start and to build his confidence.

With game time approaching, Gladys called for our attention. She thanked Otis for bringing the plate of cheese and crackers, and Wilhelm and Ida Bea for their plate of sweets. All food items would vanish as the game progressed and players sought sustenance. Snacks were an important part of the bridge club community, and there was frequently an informal competition between players to see who could bring the most popular. Gladys explained how this game was in special honor of Edward Schultz, and how he would be missed. Several players murmured agreements at this, and I was impressed by how calmly Gladys handled herself, considering the state in which I had found her only a short while before. Finally she turned towards us, and I suddenly felt like a deer caught in headlights. Gladys smiled at me and said, "And finally I would like us all to welcome a special friend of Gracie's who will be her partner today. It's his first time playing duplicate. Please y'all, welcome Hank Waderich."

Crap, crap and crap. I had forgotten Gladys' habit of trying to make new players feel welcome. She might have just blown our cover. Hank stood briefly and waved as everyone greeted him with soft applause. I happened to be looking Clovis's way, and he didn't seem to recognize Hank's name. The man was happily flirting with his partner for the day, Samantha, and had been ignoring Gladys.

I knew it was going to be a rough afternoon bridge-wise. Gladys had effectively put a bull's-eye on us with her well-meant announcement. Knowing that Hank was new to duplicate and thus inexperienced, our opponents would be much more aggressive. And she described Hank as my "special friend"—she had definitely read more into this situation than what I had intended.

Gladys came by to deliver our boards, handing us hands seven through nine. I gestured to the top board, and Hank pulled his thirteen cards for hand seven out of the slot in the plastic container. I looked at my own cards, and they didn't promise much. It was my beginning bid and I used the green card to pass. Mamaw was up next and she bid One Club, turning to Hank expectantly.

Hank studied his cards, then said, "One Heart." I pointed to the bidding box, and he sheepishly pulled out the One Heart card to place in front of him. He commented on the chances of an afternoon shower and got shushed by Ada Mae. I explained that most folks didn't chat during the bid and play of the hands, only on breaks or between rounds if they finished early.

Ada Mae bid Two Clubs, followed by a Pass from me, and then Mamaw jumped to Three No-Trump. We all passed after that, leaving Hank on lead. He chose the ace of hearts followed by the king, winning both tricks, and then played a low heart, which Mamaw won in her hand with the queen. She then quickly gathered another eight tricks, making her bid. It was a poor defense, which meant a bad score for us.

The next two hands were equally dreadful. On eight, we failed to reach Four Spades, so we didn't earn the bonus that I knew most folks would. On nine we had a competitive auction with Ada Mae winning at Three Diamonds and making it. It looked like we could have made Three Hearts, but I wouldn't know for sure until I could study the hands later that night.

With the play finished, we had time to chat, and Ada Mae started by asking me how long the two of us had been dating. In the silence that followed, there was the sense that she was miffed at Mamaw for not spreading that little tidbit of news. I didn't know who was the most taken aback: Hank or me.

"Hank and I are just friends," I explained. I looked to Hank and wasn't sure if I saw disappointment or relief. Did he want more than to be just friends? Did I? Why couldn't Ada Mae just keep her mouth shut?

"I see." Ada Mae gave a knowing smile. "Just friends then. How did you two reconnect?" she asked Hank.

It was his turn to dance and he lied admirably, explaining how we'd run into each other at the grocery and started chatting. That was followed by a visit to the farm and the agreement to meet again and try bridge. He tried to make it sound like two friends getting to know each other again.

"Humpf," answered Ada Mae. "That certainly sounds like dating to me. Maybe they call it something different these days." Mamaw guffawed and I could feel the heat on my face. Hank caught my glance and winked; the idiot seemed to be enjoying this. Luckily I was saved from further humiliation when Gladys called the round. Mamaw and Ada Mae went on to table six and the East-West pair from table four came to join us. Our new opponents were the Beas, Wilhelm and Ida, and we welcomed them as was customary. We got our new set of boards, numbers ten through twelve, and were ready to start. Sometimes bridge felt like I imagined speed dating would, twenty minutes and then you moved on to the next pair of opponents.

As soon as they sat, Ida began chatting, "You two make such an adorable couple. I just love to see young people playing bridge. I worry sometimes that this game will die out with my generation."

It wasn't a question, so I didn't have to reply. I flicked a small smile at Ida and grabbed my cards. All the cards were with the Beas on the first board, and they easily reached a good contract with Hank and I passing. Hank was on lead and started with his ace of diamonds, a poor choice. Hank was making rookie mistakes, which since he was a rookie, I should have expected.

Wilhelm ended up making the contract with an overtrick. Annoyingly, Ida chatted throughout the play, continuing her thoughts on the state of the game and how we needed to convince more young people to get involved. As we moved on to the second board, I decided to shift the conversation. I still had a murder to solve and I knew Edward had played with Ida the day of the murder. Perhaps he had said something relevant. "I know you and Edward were friends, Ida. I am so sorry," I said.

"He was a good man," she said, with tears forming. Hank gave her a hankie that he had in his pocket, and she wiped her eyes. "He was a good bridge player and a wonderful mentor. I learned so much from him."

"We should play bridge, dear," interrupted Wilhelm, pointing to the next board with a weak smile. I grabbed my cards, a little guilty about making Ida cry, but thought it was nice to see Wilhelm trying to distract her. Hank was the dealer, and so started the bidding in hearts. Ida passed. With a good hand, I didn't want to stop short, so I jumped to game. That was passed all around, putting Ida on lead. I smiled encouragingly at Hank; it was going to be his first time playing as Declarer at the club.

Ida tapped her bright red mouth with a nail that matched the color. She furrowed her perfectly plucked eyebrows in thought and finally led a low diamond. I laid down my hand as Dummy, and Hank called for the queen, leaving the ace on the board. Wilhelm won his king and returned a diamond, which Ida trumped with a small heart. Wilhelm got in later to give Ida a second trump trick, leaving Hank down one.

"That was a killer lead, dear," Wilhelm noted. "Any other suit and I think he makes it."

"Edward was such a good teacher," sniffled Ida as she reached for the final set of cards.

On the last board, I bid a risky Three Spades to win a competitive auction. I was down one, but figured it was a good board, as Wilhelm would have made his bid. Hank seemed disappointed, but I assured him that good bridge did not always mean a positive score.

We had finished early again, so we still had a few minutes to chat with the Beas before the end of the round. I didn't want to upset Ida again, and was saved from hunting for an appropriate topic when Hank jumped in. "How's business at the Pole & Arms?" he asked Wilhelm.

"Spring is the busiest," replied Wilhelm. "When folks are getting their gardens in, but it's been a decent month for a July."

"Edward was such a dear man," said Ida out of the blue. "He was working so hard to make Alpine a destination in these parts. The time and energy he spent trying to get the Carlyle modernized was just one example."

"I heard he was a little short of cash," I said, thinking about the possible embezzlement at the club.

"Oh no. I don't think so at all," she said, looking surprised. Wilhelm snorted softly from his side of the table, but Ida continued on as if she hadn't heard, "He was telling me about the imported Italian marble they were thinking of using in the Carlyle. He called the style 'country luxury' and said it would set a new standard. I just don't know what they're going to do without his vision."

"Hopefully finish it," said Wilhelm gruffly.

"Now, Wilhelm, you be respectful," chided Ida. "You know," she continued in a stage whisper to me that could be heard at the next table. "He was designing a penthouse condominium for the topmost floor."

"I thought it was just going to be a hotel," I said. "Part of the plan to draw tourists to town."

"Oh, it was for the most part," said Ida. "Edward explained it all to me. The majority of space was going to be a hotel, but the top two floors are being divided into condominiums. He said that they'd be the best place to live in all of Alpine, and I believed he was right."

"Were they looking for buyers?" Hank asked. It was a good question; often remodelers got commitments from buyers pre-renovation to reduce risk and help with cash flow, and I knew Edward was in need of cash, even if Ida seemed to think otherwise.

Before Ida could answer, Gladys called the round. The Beas thanked us for a good game and headed to table six, following in the footsteps of Mamaw and Ada Mae. Before our next opponents arrived, Hank snorted and whispered to me, "I bet Edward was trying to sell part of that money pit of a hotel to Ida."

"What?" I said, feeling as confused as a chick without her momma hen.

"Ida wasn't always a Bea," explained Hank. "She comes from the Corbert family and they own half the county. There's money there, I wager." I never realized that Ida came from a background of money; she certainly didn't act wealthy. With Edward desperate for cash, Ida would be a prime target for some scheme or another. It fit, I admitted, feeling somewhat stunned.

Our new opponents arrived, so we had to cut our conversation short. It was the Strange sisters, the octogenarian siblings who'd partnered unsuccessfully for over six decades. I'd played against them before and knew Hank and I were in for an unusual round.

"I'm Mary Sue," introduced the taller of the two, although she was only 5'1 with short gray hair in a tight perm. "And this is my sister, Mary Jane."

"We were named after our mother," explained Mary Jane. "Sue Jane Gilbert Strange was her name." Mary Jane looked like a smaller version of her sister, like she'd gotten shrunk in a clothes dryer. They could almost pass for twins.

"So now we're a pair of Strange sisters." Mary Sue laughed. I smiled at the joke that I'd heard several times in the past, but Hank produced the obligatory chuckle the comment demanded. "You can call me Mary."

"Mary here too," offered Mary Jane.

"A pair of Marys who never got married," offered Mary Sue. Hank gave a pretend groan, which made the sisters laugh harder. "I so love to see young people playing," she continued. "How long have the two of you been together?"

Hank and I exchanged glances, and I let him explain this time. Thankfully our boards arrived before Hank got himself in too deep. The sisters got in each other's way more than we did. We ended the three hands having defended each one and setting two of the three. We finished just as Gladys called the round, and the two Marys headed to their next table. "That was interesting," Hank said, rolling his eyes. "What a pair."

"They are strange." I giggled, making Hank groan again.

I looked to see who was heading to our table next. Our next opponents were Clovis and Samantha. This was going to be interesting.

ChaptER 12

Clovis limped towards us and I gave him and Samantha the expected greeting, welcoming them to our table. Clovis sat and glanced Hank's way but didn't say anything; instead, he turned to me and let his gaze linger on my chest. I could feel my irritation grow; I had worn the green blouse for Hank's benefit, not Clovis's. Eventually he spoke, "Ya know, Gracie, if ya were looking for a break from Nora, I would've been happy to pardner ya. No need to take on some newbie." He stroked his mustache and Samantha frowned. I could tell she was not happy that Clovis was ignoring her for me.

"Now, Skeeter," Samantha said through gritted teeth. "You're supposed to be welcoming to all players. Don't make them call Gladys over here." She forced a laugh, ran a hand through her shoulder length graying hair, and sat up a little straighter, displaying more of her ample chest to draw Clovis's eyes back to her. She was like a cat on the prowl.

"Clovis, we've had this conversation before," I said. I couldn't believe how rude the man could be. Why did I have to play nice when he didn't? "I'm not interested in you as a bridge partner." I wanted to add, "Or as any other kind of partner," but knew I shouldn't.

"Your loss," he said, still staring at my shirt. He turned to Hank and said, "Sorry, fellow. No offense intended, but you're new to duplicate. Just stating a fact."

"True," replied Hank with a blank expression. I'd seen that look before: it was his game face from high school football, before he took to the field and flattened players on the other team.

"Hey, have we met before?" asked Clovis. "I'm Skeeter Jones."

"Can't say that we have," said Hank in a southern drawl I didn't know he had in him. He sounded like Bo Duke from *The Dukes of Hazzard*. A mad Bo Duke. I knew Hank was livid, I just hoped he could keep his anger under control, or we might have a second murder in the club.

"Ya look familiar somehows," replied Clovis.

"I think it's time to play bridge," I said quickly, drawing Clovis's eyes back to me as I leaned over further than necessary to reach the center of the table where our boards had just been placed. I swore I could feel daggers from Samantha's eyes.

I opened One Heart and Clovis jumped in with a Michaels Bid, bidding two of my suit. Hank looked confused, clearly not realizing that Clovis was promising spades. I prayed he would ask the meaning, but after a significant pause, Hank passed. Samantha jumped in spades; I was stuck. To bid anything now would be unethical. From Hank's expression, I knew he held some good cards, but I could only bid based on his Pass. I pulled out the green card.

When the Dummy came down, I almost laughed. We had been skeetered: Clovis had a weak hand. Yet somehow Samantha managed to squeak out the nine needed tricks. I watched helplessly as all of Hank's high cards got trumped and knew that we should have competed after all. Irritated, I itched for a cigarette, not that I could have one in the club.

"Nice playin', Samantha," said Clovis afterwards. She smiled at him and ran her fingers through her hair again.

"Thanks, Skeeter. That was a little on the light side, but I'm glad I could figure out a line of play that worked," she chirped.

The second board was worse. I had a nice opening hand, but Clovis preempted in first seat. When it came around to me, I passed; I didn't have a suit to bid and was afraid Hank would leave a Double in.

On the third hand I opened light to try and get something going. It was a poor choice as we got too high, got doubled, and went down two. Three bad boards, and Clovis was grinning like the Cheshire cat as he stroked that mustache of his.

Gladys called the round and Clovis thanked us both as he almost danced away to the next table. Unfortunately Hank wasn't quick enough to catch him with the cell phone, but I could see Hank's eyes light up when he saw it. The bridge was going poorly, but maybe we could accomplish the main objective today. I didn't know where that would leave Hank and me, but at least it was something.

With four rounds finished and five to go, Gladys called for a break. She said that several members of the club had approached her about wanting to say a word or two in honor of Edward, and that we'd have a short memorial in about five minutes. She asked if anyone else was interested in sharing a remembrance to let her know so that she could organize the speakers. Once she finished speaking, I grabbed Hank and headed outside where we could talk undisturbed.

"Did you see him?" asked Hank once the door to the club had closed, leaving us alone for the moment. "The damn faker. I'll get him on video yet."

"Maybe," I said. "Hopefully. It may be harder than what I'd thought. If he catches you with that cell phone, the game will be up. You'll never see him without a limp again. I almost thought our goose was cooked when he came to play at our table. If he'd recognized you—"

"Well, he didn't. And it's damn hard to have the cell ready, not while playing bridge. I thought you were a good player, Gracie. I feel like we're getting beaten black and blue in there. It seems like every time we bid something, we go down," complained Hank.

I sighed, my mood turning as black as the sky in the west. It looked like we were going to get another one of those sudden summer storms after all. I wondered if we'd finish playing before or after the storm hit. "Look," I said. "In good bridge you take the best score the opponents will allow. Sometimes that means going set."

"I feel that all we do is defend, and when we do win the bid, we go down."

"That's because we aren't used to each other yet as partners," I said. "And our defense is weak. We have to work together on defense to take the tricks we deserve. Once we learn how to do that, then our opponents will know to respect us, and we can win a reasonable auction."

"Well, all I know is that it sucks now," said Hank. "And I thought I'd been taking my tricks." He frowned, and I remembered what a hard competitor he'd been on the football field. The man did not like to lose.

"Look," I said. "We'll work on tactics later. Let's get through the game and see how we actually did. Just be careful with Clovis, and remember, we aren't here to win. We're here to save your farm."

"I know," growled Hank, "but I still don't have to like it." He looked across the street and I followed his gaze to the old Carlyle hotel. The place was abandoned today since it was Sunday, but I wondered if work would continue on Monday. Would Edward's partners move ahead without him? Would his share of the hotel be caught up in probate, delaying the renovation, even if those silent partners wanted to move forward? "It's hard, Gracie," he said, his gaze still locked someplace far away. "My heart says I know you so well, while my head realizes I don't really know you at all anymore."

"I know," I said softly. "Sometimes I feel the same way. When you hugged me the other day, it just all felt right, like in high school. But there's so much we don't know about each other. We aren't the same people we used to be."

"I don't want you to get hurt," he said, still staring into the distance.

"And I don't want you to get hurt either," I interrupted. "We've both had enough pain in our lives." Before Hank could continue, I added, "We may have a problem though. There's this police woman who thinks I may have had something to do with Edward's murder. It's a long story, but the short of it is that she's made it clear that she plans on keeping an eye on me. I wanted you to know—" I stopped as my throat tightened, and then I started again, "I wanted you to know that after this game, if we get the film of Clovis, we need to stay away from each other. We need to stay apart until this murder case is solved." I could feel the tears in my eyes, and found myself in Hank's arms. I let myself remain for a minute, and then stepped back. "It's the only way to keep your secret safe."

"Gracie—" Hank began.

"It's okay," I said. "We can talk more later. Best we return inside now. Maybe you can get the video during the memorial."

We returned to our seats. Hank had his phone ready on his hand. Unfortunately, it looked like Clovis was settled in at the next table with his eyes plastered on Samantha, who preened and cooed at the attention. He didn't look likely to move anytime soon. Several players stood in the center of the room with Gladys, presumably the aforementioned speakers. Otis Greer, the Club President, began by giving a glowing history of Edward's service to the club, ironically enough mentioning his service as treasurer and his role in helping the club gain its not-for-profit status years earlier. He then went on to relate a story about how he and Edward traveled to Birmingham for a regional and won an event that earned Otis his Life Master title. After Otis, Greg Jergensen spoke of Edward and their shared interest in both bridge and classic cars and how Edward had loved his 1964 Thunderbird, but not more than he loved bridge. Several other folks spoke fondly, including a heartrending speech by Evelyn Franklin and another one by Ida Bea about what a wonderful bridge mentor Edward had been. It was a nice memorial, with several members openly weeping. Even Samantha shed a tear or two while holding one of Clovis's hands. Once the last of the speakers had finished, Gladys passed around a box of tissue. After that, the room was ready to continue the game; our honoring of Edward Schultz short but poignant. We played five more rounds of bridge and had a few bright spots in the second half, but mostly it was as rough as I'd expected. Gladys spotted Hank's cell in the middle of the sixth round and forced him to stow it away. We witnessed Clovis walking naturally, but did not get the video Hank needed.

As the game finished, I could tell the room was getting restless. There was thunder, and then rain began punishing the roof. In the center of the room several players were lamenting their lack of foresight, having not brought umbrellas. They looked like hens wandering in the house yard, clucking here and there with no real purpose, the Strange sisters at the center. The lights flickered, and the chatter increased as if a fox was now among the hens. Hank had his cell phone ready, but with the confusion over the rain and the flickering lights, I figured his chances of getting a good video of Clovis were slim. After a few minutes, we gave up, and Hank offered to get an umbrella from his truck. I said that sounded like a good idea and went to find Mamaw and Ada Mae, who were talking to the Beas.

"I think that rain is horizontal," said Mamaw, looking out one of the few windows into the back parking lot. "Oh, hi, Gracie!" She made room for me in the group. "How did you and Hank do? And where is that young man?"

"Not well," I answered. "It's a steep learning curve. Hank went to get an umbrella."

"You and Hank make a cute couple," Ida offered, directing the statement to me.

"They do seem to be spending plenty of time together," said Ada Mae, adding wood to the fire.

"I'm sure Hank will be willing to help you get to your cars safely when he comes back. No use in anyone else getting wet," I said, ignoring the comments.

"Oh, that would be wonderful," Ida cooed.

"Oh, Nora," said Gladys from behind, almost causing me to jump. I moved aside to make room for her. "I'm so glad that I remembered, what with the game and the storm and all."

"Remembered what?" asked Mamaw.

"About your keys. You didn't leave them at the club—at least I never found them. I just thought you'd want to know. You know." Gladys looked around the room and saw that only a few members had left. "We have a big box of those black plastic trash bags."

"Ah, like ponchos," added Ada Mae.

"Exactly," said Gladys before dashing off on her newfound mission.

"So, how long have you and Hank been dating?" asked Ida to me.

"Well, we aren't exactly dating," I said.

"They don't call it dating anymore," Ada Mae explained using air quotes like I used on Mamaw back in the day. "They just spend time together."

Mamaw laughed ruthlessly. "And there's been plenty of that." She grinned at me like a cat playing with a mouse. Really, did the woman have nothing better to do than make me grist for the gossip mill?

"Really?" said Ida dramatically.

I just rolled my eyes and ignored the teasing, hoping Hank would get back soon. Gladys appeared with the box of trash bags and passed one out to each person. The room transformed into a senior citizen Goth party—the lights flickering, everyone dressed in shiny black and still milling around trying to decide whether to brave the rain or wait it out. All that was missing was the loud music and bad makeup. Actually, there was some bad makeup, just not Goth style.

Hank entered, soaked to the skin, with the wind howling behind him. He'd managed to bring in two umbrellas, handed one to Otis, and offered to escort anyone who desired it to their car. The Strange sisters were the first to volunteer, each grabbing an arm and guiding him towards the back lot, where they'd parked. He threw me a rueful smile as they passed, each sister hugging close and chatting nonstop in opposite ears, although on completely different subjects. I was pretty sure Hank was going to have a headache by the time he got back.

Otis looked like he'd been handed a viper, knowing he would be expected to give the same service as Hank. Gladys appeared at his side and said something too low for me to hear. I saw Otis nod and then look towards the front doors. He spotted Samantha laughing at something Clovis had said. She placed her hand on his arm and Clovis grinned. Otis walked over, handed the umbrella to Clovis, nodded to Samantha, and then retreated with Gladys towards the small office. I figured Gladys wanted to show Otis the books, now that Edward's memorial game was over.

Hank reappeared, even wetter than before. He joined our little group and Ada Mae took him up on the umbrella offer. She'd parked in the front, like Hank and me, and they headed in that direction. At Ida's prompting, Wilhelm went to ask Clovis about using the umbrella he was holding. Soon Clovis was taking Ida to her car in the back, and then Wilhelm afterwards. He escorted Samantha next, and then looked for other groupies to lay his hands upon. As the room cleared, an idea started to form. I gestured to Hank and asked him to help Mamaw to her car, and then head around the building and get ready with his phone. Mamaw looked confused, but I told her I'd explain later. Once they were off and I figured Hank had the time to get into position, I approached Clovis.

"Skeeter," I said, forcing a smile. "Would you be willing to escort me next?"

"Where's that newbie of yours?" he asked, eyes drifting towards my chest.

"He seems to be more interested in others than me." I pouted, pinching my arms together just a little to make my cleavage more pronounced. Clovis laughed and took the bait. I told him I'd parked out front, and when he grabbed my arm, his hand brushed the side of my breast. I wanted to smack him but knew that would ruin everything. Hank would owe me big time after this.

The rain didn't look to have slackened at all, and in fact I wondered if it had gotten worse once we stepped out in it. Clovis seemed to almost huddle beneath the umbrella, keeping himself as dry as possible and selfishly leaving me mostly vulnerable to the storm. The umbrella might as well have been left inside for all the good it did me. I wished that I'd taken Gladys up on her offer of a trash bag poncho as the rain made my blouse stick like glue. By the time I had gotten to the Mustang I felt like a wet cat, and my mood wasn't much better than one. Somehow within a week I'd given Clovis Jones two undeserved opportunities to see more of me than I desired. When I got in the car, I didn't even pretend to give a thank you, slamming the door in Clovis's face without giving him a second look.

I waited expectantly and watched Clovis dash back into the club like I'd hoped he would. I prayed Hank had gotten the video, because it would be a good one. There was no sign of a limp at all in Clovis's stride. I looked for Hank but didn't see him. He must have stationed himself out of sight somewhere. The windows were beginning to fog, and I saw no reason to stay sitting there. I desperately wanted to change into dry clothes. I backed up out of the parking spot and headed towards home.

Because of the bad weather, downtown was dead, not that anything much was open on a Sunday. I wasn't surprised to see water at the corner of Maple and Main—that was a perennial problem with quick thunderstorms, but it was higher than I had expected. There were no good detours around the intersection, not without trying roads that were most likely worse. I should have waited, but instead foolishly tried to ease the Mustang through. The damn thing sputtered and died halfway through.

I looked up and down the street but didn't see a soul. Even the parking lot at Margaret's held only a few cars. I instinctively reached for my cell, then cursed when I realized I had no phone to call for help. I'd have to wait until someone happened by, or until the damn car would start again. I didn't have to wait long. I saw a pair of headlights approach from behind, and I felt a sudden chill as I realized I was all alone with a killer on the loose.

Chapter 13

Thankfully, the headlights belonged to Hank's F150. He pulled up and stopped alongside me. I waved at him through the foggy windows and motioned that I'd make a dash to his truck. I opened my door and stepped into flowing water that reached my ankles. It felt more like a stream than a puddle. Hank had his passenger side door open and called to me. I took two cold miserable steps and climbed into the truck, slamming the door closed.

Hank laughed and said, "Gracie, it's a car, not a boat."

"I know that." I grinned.

"What were you thinking?"

"I was thinking of a hot shower and a change of clothes," I replied.

"Hmm..." he continued, staring at my clinging outfit. Somehow, unlike with Clovis, his looks didn't annoy me, but instead I felt a slight thrill.

"Hank Waderich, you get your mind out of the gutter," I teased. "My eyes are up here."

"As if there were gutters here," he replied as he blushed, caught like a coon in a trap. "That's half the problem with the flooding at this corner: outdated storm gutters." He'd had to tear his glance from my soaking wet shirt to the road, which somehow pleased me. "You know we can't leave it here."

"What?" I asked, knowing but dreading what was to come.

"The Mustang. We can't just leave it here in the middle of the street."

"Yes, we can," I tried. "It'll be fine."

"Gracie—"

"Fine," I said, irritated. I knew Hank was right, but that didn't mean I had to like it. "Can't you just push the god-forsaken thing with your truck?"

The look Hank gave me couldn't have been worse if I'd asked him to murder kittens. We'd have to do it by hand. The plan was to push the car thirty feet or so out of the center of the intersection and off into a parking space. We both got out of the truck and quickly got into position at the Mustang. The water had receded a little, but it was still above my ankles. I feared my suede shoes were ruined. I had the driver's side door open with one hand on the steering wheel and the other on the doorframe while Hank was centered in the back. Hank called out to see if I was ready and we began our labors. The car didn't move. Hank cursed and asked if it was in neutral. I jumped in, put the car from drive into neutral and we tried again. This time the car moved, and we rolled it out of danger. By the time we got back into Hank's truck, anything that had been dry was now soaking. The air from the truck made me shiver.

Hank drove me the rest of the way home and I invited him in to dry off. He nodded in agreement, and we made a dash for the covered front porch. I unlocked the door and gave him the grand tour of the two-bedroom cottage as we headed to the bath for towels, the front room opened on the right into an eating area and the kitchen. The two bedrooms were stacked on the left. The bath with the clawfoot was nestled between the kitchen and the smaller of the two bedrooms at the back of the house. I handed Hank a towel from the stack in the bath, took one myself, and told him to make himself comfortable while I changed into something dry. I retreated to the larger of the bedrooms, threw on an old pair of sweatpants and a green sweatshirt, and grabbed a throw blanket from the closet. I had nothing large enough for Hank and figured he could wrap himself at least. I found Hank standing by the mantle, vigorously shaking the towel over his head. When he moved the towel to his sopping shirt, his hair stood on end like a porcupine. I handed him the blanket and asked for his wet clothes. He gave me a sultry smile. I ignored the tingle in my body, and explained that I wanted to toss them in the dryer, nothing more.

While he was changing, I returned to my bedroom and retrieved my own wet clothes. I picked up my waterlogged shoes and set them aside to wait until they dried to see if they were salvageable. I returned to the front room, gathered Hank's wet things, and headed to the kitchen to put the load into the small stackable units hidden in the pantry closet. With the wet clothes in the dryer, I returned to Hank. He looked miserable wrapped in the blanket, like a wet dog after a bath. I sat on the couch and patted the seat next to me in invitation.

Hank gave me a skeptical look, and said, "Gracie, I don't think…"

"Oh, just sit, Hank," I said. "I'm just asking you to sit." I felt that familiar tingle again, but I thought I could handle having him near me. After all, I was a responsible adult.

"I'm half naked under this blanket," he replied.

"So?" I said. "That means you can't sit?" I stood and headed to the kitchen. "What kind of coffee do you drink?" I asked over my shoulder.

"Black," he said. "And strong."

I pulled a Columbian roast for Hank from my stash and a sweeter blend for myself. While the machine was working, I sliced some cheese from the collection I had in the refrigerator and made a plate. I returned to the front room and found Hank sitting hunched on the couch. I set the cheese plate and my cup on the coffee table, handing Hank his cup as I sat next to him.

Hank took a big sip of his coffee. "This is good, Gracie. Really good." He studied the cup like an art history major in the Louvre, and I wondered if he was feeling the same as I was.

"So…" I said, not knowing how to start a more serious conversation. Was I just imagining what was happening between us or was it real?

"So…" Hank said, turning those gray eyes on me.

"Did you get the video of Clovis?" I asked, looking away. I was a coward. A big, fat, faithless pig of a coward.

"You mean when he took you to the car?" Hank growled.

"Yes, silly," I said, amused. "I did that for you. And the way Clovis ogled me in those few minutes… You owe me—big time."

Hank just handed me his phone. It was damp, but seemed to be working. I ran each of the three videos Hank had made of Clovis. In the first, Clovis was too far away to make out very well, and he was using his cane anyhow. The second one was worse, short and jagged. It must have been when Gladys saw him and made Hank put the phone away. I had high hopes for the third, with the trap I'd laid for Clovis. The video itself was decent for a cell, but I knew it wouldn't work. The umbrella covered Clovis's face the entire time. Crap. I'd let Clovis paw me for no reason after all.

I handed the phone back to Hank. "None of those will work, will they?"

"I doubt it," he responded. He looked depressed. He'd spent an entire afternoon being beaten at bridge and had nothing to show for it.

"Well," I said, "we'll just have to try again." I almost felt cheerful that we'd failed, knowing it would mean more time with Hank.

"Gracie, you don't need to do this. You don't need to get involved. This is my problem."

"Hank, I want to," I said, placing my hand on his arm. I felt his heat, and my skin was burning from the electricity building between us.

"You know, if you don't watch it, I might just wrap you up inside this blanket with me," grunted Hank. I looked into his eyes. Decision time.

"Sounds like a plan," I said, pulling my sweatshirt off over my head. By the time I placed it onto the coffee table, Hank had the blanket open, welcoming me into his embrace. His lips found mine and we spent an eternity just kissing. It had been so long, too long, since I'd been in another's arms with romantic intent. I thought I would feel guilt, or confusion, but while I acknowledged that Hank was different than Pierre, my thoughts were on the moment and not the past. Well, perhaps my thoughts were on the far past as if I'd crossed a bridge home again.

I broke our kiss, asking if Hank wanted to go to the bedroom. I felt like a hussy, but why shouldn't I take the lead? It was the twenty-first century after all. Hank nodded yes, and I took his hand to show him the way, our coffees left to cool on the table.

Afterwards, I huddled safe in Hank's embrace, staring at the ceiling. We'd crossed into a new land, Hank and I. I couldn't believe that just three days ago I'd run into Hank by accident outside the bridge club, and now I was naked in his arms. I hoped Emily was right and that her circle of friends had Hank pegged correctly. He hadn't mentioned anyone else, but it wasn't as if he'd had a chance to do so. I needed to consult with Emily and her circle, but then I'd have to admit what had happened. Crap, I'd made a mess of things. What had I been thinking?

"So," Hank said. "A penny for your thoughts?"

"Just thinking how happy I am," I lied. What to do now? Would Hank expect me to do this again? Did I want to? Would he make booty calls and expect me to drop everything to go to him? Would I say no if he did?

"No regrets?" he asked.

"Hank, you aren't… seeing anyone, are you?"

"Well, there was this girl down Gadsden way," he said. "Ow, why did you hit me?"

I sat up, trying to smack him again but missed as he grabbed my arms. "I can't believe…" I couldn't see straight with the tears in my eyes. Mamaw had warned me, but like an idiot I hadn't listened.

"Gracie, Gracie, I was kidding. There's no one. No one but you," he said. "I was just teasing…"

"Are you serious?" I asked. I so wanted to believe him but feared to do so. I'd been fooled before, lied to by those I thought loved me above all others. I was no good at this game of love.

"Gracie, you know me. I wouldn't do that to you," he said.

"How do I know, Hank?" I asked, my chest tightening and the tears blinding me again. "How do I know? I haven't seen you for fifteen years, then you swoop into my life and turn it upside down again. How do I know that I can trust you?"

"Hey now, you've turned my life upside down as well. Trust is a two-way street."

"It's not the same for men as for women. Believe me, it's not the same," I replied venomously.

"Gracie, what happened to you?" he asked with a look of bewilderment on his face. He pulled me to him again and I collapsed into his arms, crying like I hadn't cried since returning to Alpine. All the old hurts were returning, the pain of betrayal and loss. I wasn't ready to talk about it, I didn't know if I'd ever be ready. Yet, if I wanted any chance of a normal relationship ever again, I'd have to find a way to get past what had happened in Paris. I'd have to find a way to trust. What I didn't know was if I should trust Hank after what we'd gone through in high school.

"Could you just talk to me?" I said. "Tell me about your life after... and before... this?"

"Gracie," he said, squeezing me tightly.

"Please," I whispered. "Just be honest with me."

And he did as I asked. He told me about leaving Alpine and heading to Atlanta with what everyone thought was a bright future, but what Hank confided felt like a lost and broken dream. He described how at first he'd fallen into the wrong crowd at school, those from the team who were there to play ball, party, and hopefully land in the NFL for a few years. None of the group had a chance, he said. They weren't willing to work hard enough to be of interest to any scouts; they were chasing fools' gold. He explained how he followed in the footsteps of his friends, enrolled in "easy" classes and didn't take advantage of the opportunities the football scholarship offered him. Playing for the team was like having a job—practice and other team commitments taking up thirty plus hours a week. Hank figured he didn't have the time to attend class regularly, let alone study and try to learn anything. He was there to play football, and that was his life.

It wasn't until he was in the first semester of his sophomore year that all changed, explained Hank. He'd been an idiot, and signed up for the wrong section of the core mathematics requirement, one taught by a professor who actually expected Hank to work and learn something instead of one taught by a faculty member friendly to the athletic program. When it became apparent he was going to fail the class and be ineligible for football the next year, his coach tried to intervene. It was too late to switch to an easier section. Instead he got assigned a tutor and was told that he needed to pass the class. That tutor's name was Sara Newman.

Sara didn't like him at first. She spent more time chiding him for being an idiot and wasting his potential than she did tutoring him. It wasn't as if he couldn't learn the material; the class wasn't that much different than the math classes at Alpine High. But it had been over a year since he'd taken any mathematics, and with football, he felt that he didn't have the time to learn it all over again. In addition to tutoring at minimum wage ten hours a week, Sara bartended twenty hours on weekends and still managed to stay on the Dean's List. That made him understand: he was receiving for free an opportunity that Sara had been working her tail off to get. Out of guilt more than anything else, he began to study for the course, and as he improved, Sara seemed to dislike him less. By the end of the term he had earned a C+ in the course, the hardest grade he'd ever worked for.

That should have been the end of it, Hank explained. He should have gone back to his old habits and his old friends. But at this point he knew he'd never play pro ball. He wasn't fast enough or big enough to make it, and he knew that then. Yet he didn't know how to be a student either—being a student wasn't something he could learn from the team or his friends. He sought out Sara, but all she was able to do was encourage him to take courses in subjects he felt passionate about. The problem was the only thing he felt passionate about was football, and that passion was fading. He asked her to tutor him, but Sara, with her course work and some additional hours bartending which paid much better, had quit the tutoring job.

Not knowing what else to do, Hank took a few courses recommended by the athletics department, and then took another course for which Sara had enrolled, the only one he felt even remotely prepared to take. Sara hadn't been pleased to see him on that first day of class, but he attended class religiously, worked hard, and only asked for her help when he truly didn't understand something. Eventually Sara warmed to him and they began spending time together outside of class. His friends on the football squad accused him of majoring in Sara Newman, but by then they were closer to former friends, as he'd been adopted into Sara's world. When he got hurt at the beginning of his senior year, it was easy to transition fully from football to student.

"Sara and I got married two weeks after graduation," Hank said.

"What happened then?" I asked, getting sleepy.

"We were happy for a time, a couple of years, but we wanted different things in life and eventually that tore us apart," Hank answered, holding me tight. "In some ways my friends had been right; I had majored in Sara Newman. At the time that meant being a good student and sharing her dreams, but when we got out of college, we had different dreams."

"Like what?" I mumbled.

"It sounds silly," he said.

"Please tell me," I whispered. "I want to understand the man that you've become. That Sara helped you become."

Hank took a breath or two and I was afraid that he was done telling his story, and then he began again, "Sara was always more ambitious than me. She came from a small town too, in the backwoods of Georgia, and she had no intention of ever going back." He paused, and I was afraid to speak and ruin the spell. "I wanted to start a family, work for a few years in the city to earn some money, and then move back home to a place near Mom and Pop to raise our kids."

"And..." I said, thinking Hank's dreams didn't sound too bad to me. "What did Sara want?"

"She wanted to continue school and become a lawyer."

"What happened?" I asked.

"We lasted while she was in law school. I was working as a manager at a Dollar General, and she was taking classes during the day and bartending at night. I got a part time gig as a bouncer in the bar where she worked, and on slow days we'd spend hours talking and planning our future. We were living paycheck to paycheck, and the loans we were taking out to cover the tuition for her law degree were frightening, but I think we were happy," he said. "We planned to move to Gadsden when she graduated from law school, where we'd start a family, and where she'd work as a lawyer. We talked about me being a poppa-nanny, taking care of the kids while she worked."

"That sounds nice," I said, giving him a comforting squeeze.

"Well, it didn't work that way," Hank replied, with a bitter edge to his voice.

"What happened?" I asked.

"Sara graduated in the top ten percent of her class. When she started looking for a job, she landed several offers."

"For a job in Gadsden?"

"She had at least two offers there, I think," he muttered.

"And your plans?" I asked.

"She got offered a clerkship with a federal judge in Atlanta," he sighed. "It was something one of her professors had set up, I think, and she said she couldn't refuse. It was an opportunity that was too advantageous not to take: a two-year appointment, and afterwards we could move to Gadsden. She claimed the offers at that point would be even better."

"What happened then?"

"She took the job with the judge. She said we needed to wait for kids. She couldn't be pregnant while serving a federal judge."

"Hank," I said. "What happened between you and Sara?"

"Well, that's the thing," he explained. "It wasn't as if we had some big fight. After the clerkship, the judge arranged for her to work for a Congressman from a district in southern Georgia—just a six-month thing, but that led to a job offer in Washington. Every time, with every opportunity, she claimed she would just finish that one and then head to Gadsden for our dreams. But somehow, our dreams never came."

"And so you left?" I asked.

"I never moved to Washington. I told her that she needed to choose—either me or the job. Her career won."

"I'm so sorry," I said, truly meaning it. I understood how important dreams were and how hard it was when your dreams weren't the same as your spouse's.

"Sara was always driven. I knew that from our college days together. Somehow I always knew that Gadsden would be too small for her, let alone Alpine," Hank said. "She lives in DC now, has a good job up there and took all our debt with the divorce. We talk about once a month or so on the phone. She seems happy."

"And your dreams for a family?" I asked.

"Still dreams," he said, stretching.

I took the cue and shifted away so that he could move more freely. I reached towards the window and shifted the curtain to look outside. The rain had stopped and the sun had set, but it was still light out.

"Look, Gracie, I'd like to stay…"

"But you need to check on Harry," I said.

"Pop can't take care of himself," Hank said. I thought otherwise, but that wasn't something I was going to bring up now. Hank stood and looked around the room, presumably for his clothes.

"I'll get them," I said, quickly putting on panties, jeans and a T-shirt.

"Don't get dressed on my account," Hank said with a leer.

"Letch," I replied as I rolled my eyes at him. "I'm not walking around the house naked." I went to the dryer, got Hank's things, and then left him to get dressed while I put away the cheese and crackers and rinsed out our coffee cups.

"Do you want me to drive you to the Mustang?" he asked, fully dressed when he walked out of the bedroom. "It should start now, I think," he continued with a glance at his watch.

"No." I gave him a kiss while pressing my chest to his. "I'll walk or have Mamaw give me a ride." I could feel his heart beating against me and swore that the pulse was rising.

"Gracie, don't make this harder than it needs to be," he said, placing an arm around me.

"My word, whatever do you mean?" I replied in my best Southern Belle imitation.

"I really do need to check on Pop," he said, but I could tell his will was crumbling.

"I know," I replied, stepping back and letting him go. "But won't you miss me?" I smiled at him and was pleased to see his face flush.

"More than I can say," he replied. He walked to the front door, opened it, and then turned back to me and asked, "Can I see you tomorrow, Gracie? Not for anything... you know." He flushed. "I just want to spend some time with you."

I walked up to him and gave him a lasting kiss. When I broke away I said, "I'd better see you tomorrow, Hank Waderich."

He grinned and left, closing the door behind him.

I stood for a moment thinking about Hank and whether we had a future together. It was possible: we wanted some of the same things, but it was too early to tell if what we'd started here would last. I sighed and turned back to my bedroom.

It took me only ten minutes to get ready, and this time I chose a pair of tennis shoes that were made for walking. I locked up the cottage and left by the back door in the kitchen. When I reached the sidewalk, I saw a police cruiser parked a few houses up from mine. I cursed under my breath as I continued along the sidewalk. What did Yancey want now?

She got out of the cruiser as I walked past and said, "So, who's the stud with the 150? A boyfriend of yours? That was quite a goodbye kiss you gave him at your front door."

Crap, Yancey had seen Hank.

Chapter 14

"What do you want?" I asked without stopping. I wasn't going to talk about Hank. No good could come from that.

"What do I want?" pondered Yancey as she matched pace with me. "World peace, but I might settle for you behind bars."

I laughed weakly and said, "Look, somehow we got off on the wrong foot. I get that, and am sorry for it. But I had nothing to do with the murder. I was just unlucky enough to find the body."

"That seems to be your story, and I admit you're sticking to it. Somehow, though, I think you know more than what you're saying. What are you hiding, Miss Theis?"

"I'm not hiding anything," I said with my heart pounding. "And my story hasn't changed because it's the truth."

"I see." Yancey smiled and turned back to her car. "Don't leave town without reporting to the chief—you're still a person of interest." She got into her cruiser and slowly pulled away.

I watched as she headed up the street past me and then picked up my pace again. We'd been so stupid,

Hank and I. I'd warned him about Yancey, but in the storm and in the moment, that had been forgotten, and now Yancey had seen us.

I needed to warn Hank and wished again for my cell. I considered heading back to the cottage to call from the landline, but hesitated. What could Hank do about the threat? Did he even have time to destroy the marijuana before the police arrived, or would the act of destroying it lead the police to it? Would he even be willing, considering that he'd only started growing the illegal crop as a means to earn cash? And if the police dug into his financials, it would be obvious Hank had more cash flow than he should. There was no way to hide that at this point, and so questions that Hank couldn't answer would arise. If the police investigated Hank, they would inevitably find something. The more I pondered, the more convinced I became that there was just one solution. I had to keep the police from investigating Hank in the first place, and to do that, this murder had to be solved quickly.

I passed beneath tall oak trees that lined the quiet Alpine street and walked by proud Victorian homes. The rain had cleared the humidity from the air, and it had happened late enough in the day that the setting sun had not turned the wet streets into a sauna. The weather was about as pleasant as it got in Alpine in the summer, and soon others appeared to take advantage.

I waved to the few neighbors I knew, but didn't stop to chat. I had plans to make. There was little I could do tonight other than get the Mustang. Tomorrow, though, I'd stop by the police station and see what I could learn. Yancey had reminded me that I needed to check with Chief Doeppers before leaving town, and that gave me the excuse I needed to seek out the man. I'd explain about my cell, and the need to either get it back or drive to Gadsden and replace it. Hopefully I'd learn something about the case while there.

I'd also call Emily and see if she had the time for a coffee at Margaret's. Alpine really needed a coffee shop, and it would fit in nicely with the plans to transform the sleepy town into a tourist destination, but no one seemed to have picked up on that fact yet. Maybe I could open up a little café, modeled after my favorite coffee shop in Paris, that would serve a nice selection of coffees and a few pastries. I couldn't live on the life insurance from Pierre's passing forever. Of course, that was assuming I found a reason to stay in Alpine in the first place.

I arrived at the corner of Elm and Main and waved to Ida Bea, who was sitting on her front porch swing in one of the more impressive homes of Alpine. It had a wrap-around porch on the north and east sides, and a round turret at the northwest corner. The bottom floor of the Victorian was covered in thin wood siding painted a pale yellow, while the upper floor had cedar shingles in a slate gray. The house was topped with dark gray shingles on a steeply pitched roof. Several chimneys reached into the sky. The whole house was trimmed in white, with scrolled brackets at each porch column and a railing patterned like a mathematical fractal that I once saw in a college math class. I knew from the time and money Papaw had spent on his Victorian house that the upkeep on the Bea's would be significant. The house was situated in the middle of a large lot with a circle drive holding their navy sedan. Hank had mentioned that Ida came from money, and that made sense with the house they kept.

I turned onto Main and continued walking towards the Mustang a couple of blocks beyond. The lot at Margaret's was fuller than what I expected with the late rain, but then again with the weather so pleasant, perhaps more folks were willing to venture out this evening. On impulse, I decided that after getting the Mustang, I'd stop in for a bite to eat. I wished I had my cell to invite Mamaw—I never liked eating alone; I always felt self-conscious that others were looking and judging. I'd just have to call from Margaret's and see if she'd join me for dessert.

As I passed by the diner, I heard a voice calling my name. I turned to see who it was and realized with a groan that I should have pretended not to hear. It was Clovis, driving a slick new red pickup with a racing stripe down the side. He pulled up to the curb, crossing traffic to do so, and leaned out the driver's side window to speak to me. "Gracie, a fine thing like yourself shouldn't be alone on a night like this. In fact, a fine gal shouldn't be alone at all." He flashed a practiced smile at me and stroked his mustache. I could hear country music from the radio in the background, as well as the air-conditioning running full blast in the cab.

"I'm fine, Clovis," I replied curtly, continuing to walk and trying not to show my annoyance. "Just out for a stroll."

He put the truck back in gear and followed me down the road like the stalker he was. "Gracie, a woman like yourself needs a man at her side to protect her at night. Why don't I give you a ride?"

"My car is just up there on the next block," I said, trying not to actually growl at the man. "I don't need a ride." I lengthened my stride, hoping he'd take the hint, but of course he didn't. He accelerated the truck slightly to stay apace with me.

"At least let me see 'ya to your car," he begged.

"Fine," I said, stopping. The man was dense, but I could compromise on this. Mamaw would want me to be polite, and Hank still needed a video of the man. I should try and play nice for both of their sakes. Once we got to the Mustang, maybe he would consider his good deed done and go away. I could at least hope.

I walked in front of the truck, opened the passenger-side door, and hauled myself into the leather seat. I explained how the car stalled this afternoon in high water, and I was just getting back to pick it up again. The air conditioning was blasting so hard it felt like winter in New York, but at least Clovis had the decency to turn the music down. Country was not my favorite; I preferred classic rock to the twang currently emanating from the speakers.

We continued down Main in silence until we got to the corner at Maple. Clovis did a U turn in the intersection that threw me against the passenger-side door, then tried a short-stop behind the Mustang, throwing his right arm out to try to "protect me" from hitting the dash. I glared his way and caught a guilty grin. The damn man had hoped to grab a feel with that maneuver. I thought that short-stops were only something that high school boys did to their girlfriends for a cheap thrill. Apparently Clovis had never grown out of that phase.

I got out of the truck, mumbling my thanks, and unlocked the Mustang. I prayed the beast would start and turned the key. I got nothing. I tried, again hoping that something had changed. God, I hated this car sometimes. The water should have been gone by now. What the hell was wrong with it? I tried again. Still nothing.

"Looks like 'ya need more help than 'ya thought," said Clovis right outside my window.

I jumped about a foot. Damn, I thought he'd left when I'd said my goodbyes. Now what? I could walk back to Margaret's Diner to eat, but I was guessing Clovis would follow me, plus that didn't solve my car problem.

"Pop it," said Clovis.

"What?" I asked. The only thing I wanted to pop was his ego.

"The hood," he replied. "Lemme take a look."

"Uh," I said, looking for an excuse. "That's not necessary, Clovis. I'll just call the AAA guy. That's what I pay the premium for." I smiled. Please, God, make him go away.

"Tony's out. I saw 'im headin' down Highway 83 earlier, and in a hurry. 'Probly a wreck off that curve where the road turns to avoid the river."

I was in a pickle. I needed to be somewhat friendly, yet I didn't want to encourage Clovis. That man needed no encouragement from me. Heck, my snubs seemed to be enough. Not to mention that little show I gave him this afternoon at the bridge club. In some way I had Hank to blame for this. Well, maybe myself, but I'd been acting for Hank's benefit. "Fine, take a look," I said, hoping he didn't interpret this as some kind of favor and expect to be repaid in kind. I almost shuddered at the thought of being indebted to the man. I reached between my knees and pulled the lever that unlocked the hood.

Clovis sauntered to the front of the car and opened the hood fully. He spent a few minutes checking it out and then wandered back to my window. "Good news, honey. 'Probly just a few wet connections. I can fix 'em, but 'ya need to get 'er into the shop soon. If ya have water in the oil pan it'll hydrolock 'er and ya don't want that."

"Great," I said relieved. The man was going to be civilized after all. Maybe I'd been too harsh with him. "I'll take it in this week. Thank you, Clovis."

"I said I can fix 'er. Not that I would." He stroked his mustache again and stared at me. "I might need me a wee bit of motivation first. How 'bout we go for a beer and then I'll take care of ya—I mean ya car," he leered suggestively.

I couldn't believe my ears. What a jerk. How could he think I would go on some kind of date in exchange for fixing the Mustang? I glared at him and weighed my options. Unfortunately none of them were good. The man wouldn't leave me alone and I couldn't exactly drive away. I couldn't accuse Clovis of anything, either. He might have suggested a few things that were inappropriate but he hadn't done anything—well, other than that short-stop. I sure as heck wasn't getting back into his truck with him. "Tell you what, Clovis. You go ahead and fix the car. Once it actually starts, I'll follow you for a drink, but I'm driving myself."

"Sounds like we have a deal, ya and I," he said. He spat on his hand and held it out for me to shake. Reluctantly I did so, but I refused to spit first. The man looked like he had just caught a possum in the garden patch. I quickly wiped my hand free of his spittle with a leftover napkin in the car.

He headed to his truck and got a toolbox from the cab. He came back to the front of my car. I watched as he disconnected some wires, dried them with a rag, and connected them again. After a few minutes he asked me to try the engine.

I turned the key and the car roared to life. The idle was on the rough side, and white smoke gasped from the tailpipe. I hoped I hadn't caused worse damage, but the beast settled into a more normal rhythm. Perhaps the Mustang would be fine after all.

Clovis closed the hood and walked back to my window. He leaned down with his elbows on the window and his face inches from mine. His mustache twitched as he said, "Time for drinking, honey. Follow me."

I followed the red pickup through downtown and out past Old Town Auto. Clovis turned onto a side road I hadn't been on since high school and eventually into a gravel drive shaded on either side with pine trees. A rusty sign in front read The Barn, although the N was so thin that I could see someone mistaking it for The Bar instead. The drive widened into a gravel lot with patches of dirt showing through. At the far end of the lot was an actual barn, a tall structure with pitched roof and faded red paint. A scattered collection of vehicles guarded the place, mostly pickups, but a few cars as well. Light and sound leaked out of the structure like it was trying to escape. I hadn't seen a place this seedy in years.

Clovis pulled his truck into the line of vehicles in front, and I parked in the second row behind him. I hoped it wouldn't rain again, or I might find myself trapped in the mud. Clovis got out first and hurried to try and open my car door for me, but I was too fast for him. He didn't bother with the cane, and I knew this must be something like a second home for him. We headed to the entrance together, and Clovis put a hand to the small of my back as he opened the dirty wooden door. I wanted to elbow him but figured now was not the time.

I regretted my deal with Clovis as soon as I walked into the joint. There were only ten or so men and a few women scattered throughout the tables. The men wore dirty jeans and plaid shirts, the women too much makeup and short skirts. Some of those outfits wouldn't be suitable for teenagers, and they certainly weren't appropriate for the ages of a few of those women. The place reeked of stale beer and cigarette smoke, making me itch for a cigarette of my own, and bad country music blared from speakers mounted upon the cross beams.

A tired looking bartender glanced our way, saw Clovis, and glared. Apparently she'd had some experience with the man and wasn't a Clovis fan either. Clovis greeted several of the patrons like family as we headed to an empty booth, and each of the men gave me an appreciative look, which somehow made me feel in need of a bath. Clovis gestured for me to sit in the booth, and then to my surprise slid in next to me instead of across the table. His leg touched mine and I felt an urge to smack the man. I slid as far as I could over to the wall and said, "How about that drink, Clovis?" The sooner I finished that drink, the sooner I could get out of Dodge.

"Sure, honey. I'll be right back." He got up and sauntered over to the bar. Of course he didn't even ask what I wanted. But then again, I suspected there wasn't much choice in a place like this. I certainly wasn't going to find the Merlot I preferred. I watched as he greeted a couple of the men at the bar and winked at one of the women. She simpered and came up to hug him, pointedly glaring at me as she did so. What did they see in that man?

The bartender slammed two plastic cups of beer on the bar, and Clovis gathered them and headed back towards me. Not my first choice of drink, or my second. I quickly scooted to the edge of the booth to accept my cup from his hand, effectively blocking Clovis from sitting next to me. He frowned as he approached, but eventually accepted defeat when I refused to move and sat across from me instead. He handed me the plastic cup with the smaller portion, while taking a long sip from the cup with the larger. I suppose I should have been annoyed, but I was relieved to have less of the swill to drink.

I took a sip—it was worse than I'd anticipated. You'd think in a historically German town you'd get a decent brew, but I was pretty sure this was the same cheap stuff the fraternities had served in my college days. I swallowed with a grimace and looked up at Clovis, who was studying me intently.

"So, Clovis, do you come here often?" I winced as the words came out of my mouth. It sounded like a pick-up line.

He grinned. "Yep, and call me Skeeter now that we're all friendly-like. This here place was where we all used to gather after work, back 'fore I retired. I still come around some to see my buddies."

Retired, right—on Hank's money. I guessed he didn't know I was aware of the history behind his financial success. "I guess that's nice," I ventured lamely. Making small talk with this man was like pulling teeth. I took another sip of my beer and almost gagged. At this rate, I'd be spending the night here before I could finish it. So much for my plan of drinking and running. Maybe I could accidently spill it. It wasn't as if that had never happened in this place. The floor was sticky.

Clovis put his cup to his lips and drank about half of the yellow liquid in one gulp. "Yep. The boys and me go way back. The Barn is about the best place you can be for beer and fun on a Saturday night."

It was Sunday, so maybe that explained it. Then again, maybe not. I was sure Clovis and I had different definitions of "fun." I choked down another swallow as Clovis continued, "All the farm hands used to come here on Fridays after they got their pay. Most still do, I 'spect. Those who don't drink it all away, come back for more on Saturday. Fridays here get pretty wild—a few years ago they had so many fights the county sheriff set up a temporary station in the parkin' lot." He laughed. "Those were the days. Course, after a couple of the worst tempers went to jail, the rest sorta calmed down. Hasn't been a knock-down drag-out in over two years. Miss those days," he said with a grin.

I tried to smile politely as I choked down some more beer. "Really, I've never been much for bar brawling myself."

"Course not, honey. That's for the men. The girls need to look pretty and be the reason for the fight." He looked at me over the table, eyes focused below my face. "If you'd dress more like these other gals, I bet I'd have to get in a fight to keep these other rascals off 'ya. Hell, with the men in here, it would be one to remember." Clovis drained the rest of his beer and set the empty cup down on the table with emphasis.

I resisted the temptation to tell him that it would be a cold day in hell before he ever saw that much of my skin. I looked at my cup and saw it was still half full. Clovis stood up and I thought for a moment he was going to try to sit next to me again. I was relieved when he said he'd be right back and headed to the bar. He ordered another drink from the barkeep and struck up a conversation with the man next to him. I looked around the place, trying not to cringe, and wondered what exactly was on the floor that my shoe appeared to be adhered to. My ears suddenly pricked up when I heard the man Clovis was speaking to say something about Edward.

"The bastard is dead, Jim. I hope he doesn't rest in peace," Clovis responded.

"Yep," grunted the man. "To hell with him. Whoever done him did us a favor. Ya'll were there, weren't ya?"

"I was about," claimed Clovis. "Had nothing to do with it though, hear," he joked with a knowing chuckle that sent a shiver down my spine. Did Clovis just admit to murder? I needed to hear more. "I still don't know what those gals at the bridge club ever saw in the bastard," continued Clovis. "That man was nothin' but a low down, good for nothin', cheat. I never should've let him in our poker game. If he hadn't a been my lawyer at the time, I wouldn't have. Shoulda known. All lawyers are damn crooks."

"After Wednesday's game, I'm surprised you didn't off him then and there," said Jim, grimly. "Caught dealin' from the bottom of the deck. Wonder how much cash he stole from us, the bastard."

"Too damn much if you ask me. He certainly deserved what he got," replied Clovis. "Got it good, he did." Clovis cackled, and Jim nodded like they shared a secret. "I can sure tell ya that."

"Looks like you got some goods for your ownself there, Skeeter," Jim said, glancing my way. I quickly studied my beer, not wanting to give away that I was eavesdropping. "She's quite the looker with that red hair."

"I'm thinking I might get me some tonight. You shoulda seen the way she came after me this afternoon. Hot and cold that one. Just need to get her fire a goin."

"She shore looks like she could get pretty hot. I bet she could burn you right up." Jim laughed. "Bet there be a temper on that one too, ya can tell with the colorin'."

"I like 'em with a temper that matches me own. That there bridge club is like a gold mine, I tell ya," continued Clovis. I shuddered mentally. How crude could they be? I hoped they'd get back to talking about the murder.

"Maybes I'll give it a try then," responded Jim. "I could use a new huntin' ground."

"Ya gotta play bridge, Jimbo. It's been a good week. First I gave it to that bum lawyer of mine, and tonight I be givin' it to that there hottie," he said, gesturing my way.

My heart jumped into my throat. Did I just hear Clovis confess to murder? Time to leave, deal or no deal, while I still could. By God, my last drink wasn't going to be the swill this place called beer. I grabbed my purse and headed for the door. I was just pushing it open when I heard Clovis shout my name. I didn't turn or stop, just headed for the safety of my car.

"Gracie, wait! You still owe me a drink," he called, chasing after me. I made it down the row of cars and got in. Thank goodness the engine turned over, and I began backing out, showering Clovis with gravel from under my wheels as he called to me again. "Gracie, ya owe me. You'll pay for this!" I turned the car around and headed for town without a backward glance.

Chapter 15

As I drove, I began to doubt what I'd heard, or at least what I thought I'd heard. Did Clovis really murder Edward, or was he just taking credit for it to build his reputation? Clovis would be one to tell tall tales. He'd certainly been happy to see the man dead. I suppose that meant he'd been more likely to pull the trigger, but it didn't mean he'd done it. I did know I needed to tell the police about Clovis and fast. I wasn't sure if he'd left the club on Thursday during the game or not, but it was possible he'd palmed Mamaw's keys and stolen her gun, giving him means, as well as motive and opportunity.

I passed by Old Town Auto and slowed as I entered the town streets. The question was how to proceed. I didn't know if Doeppers would be at the station or not, but considering it was Sunday evening, I doubted it. I couldn't risk just showing up at the station—that could be a disaster. What if I got into an interrogation room with Yancey and she was more interested in questions about Hank than about Clovis? I wouldn't risk having to lie to her under bright lights; I didn't think I had it in me.

I almost snorted as the answer came to me, and I

knew who I could tell. I'd call Emily and confide to her what I'd overheard at The Barn. She'd be able to pass the word along to Doeppers and there'd be no risk of having to deal with Yancey. If I had my cell, I'd have called her from the car. As it was, I'd have to return to the cottage.

Elm Street was empty as I turned on it from Main and made my way home. The place looked lonely when I pulled into the carport, or maybe it was just me missing Hank. After everything that had happened today, I felt like a wet rag all wrung out. I couldn't believe I'd fallen into Hank's arms this afternoon, and I was outraged that Clovis thought I'd do the same with him. I entered the kitchen and tossed my purse on the counter to snag the phone and call Emily.

She answered on the third ring, and I tried to tell her what had happened, but I could hear her daughter screaming in the background. Eliza Anne wanted her mommy, and she wanted her now. Emily got the gist of my concern about Clovis, but didn't seem as concerned as I'd hoped. Actually telling her the story made my doubt grow more. Clovis hadn't said explicitly that he'd murdered Edward, but instead alluded to it, and Clovis was not a subtle man. Somehow I blurted out that I'd slept with Hank, and then that dominated the remainder of the short conversation. We agreed to meet at Margaret's for coffee the next morning before her shift at the station. Emily wanted to hear all about my tryst with the Hunk.

And then I called Hank. He was sweet on the phone, explaining he'd been worried about me. I told him about my run in with Yancey, and that I was afraid she'd be watching for him now. I told him about Clovis and The Barn. Hank was not happy about my choices and became more concerned as I told him what I'd overheard. I tried to explain that I'd had no choice and eventually got him to agree, but I could tell he was still displeased. I vowed to make it up to him and shared a few more private thoughts, then we agreed to have dinner together at my place the next day. I told him I missed him before we said our good nights.

I slept fitfully that night, maybe worse than any night since the murder. I couldn't stop the thoughts rolling around in my head. Clovis had hated Edward because Edward had been a cheat. Clovis went back into the club after walking me to my car that day. I had joked to Frank and Gladys, two notorious gossipers, about Clovis being the murderer. What if he had killed Edward and had heard about my theory. Would he come after me with more sinister plans other than the ones I already knew about? He'd promised that I'd "pay." Had it been a coincidence running into him yesterday or had Clovis been stalking me and taken advantage of an opportunity?

I got out of bed, showered, and found a yellow sundress to wear. It had a scoop neck and straight sides with a skirt that hung just below the knee. It was neither the most revealing dress I owned nor the most modest, but it was perhaps the happiest. I wore it because of Hank, although thoughts of Clovis almost made me want to wear a set of knight's armor. I put on a pair of white flats and dropped the suede shoes that I hoped to save into a plastic bag. After some makeup and my second cup of coffee for the day, I stepped outside. The heat was brutal. I wondered if it was going to be a record setting day.

I had plenty of time to stop by Old Town Auto Supply before my date with Emily and headed that way. I wanted Peter to listen to the Mustang and see if he thought I should delay my trip down to Gadsden. With the flooding, and Clovis's warning about the car getting hydrolocked, whatever that meant, I didn't want to take any chances. The beast started right up and I headed down the road with sweat dripping from my nose. I questioned the wisdom of having taken a shower; I'd need one again before seeing Hank at dinner—at least if I wanted the possibility of a little more afterwards. Or maybe I should wait and offer to shower with Hank. That could be fun. The thought made me blush like a schoolgirl, and I grunted at how forward I'd become. Emily would be proud.

I arrived at Old Town and headed in to see Peter working at the front counter as I'd hoped. After a little innocent flirting that somehow made me feel guilty, he agreed to check out the car. Peter even took the Mustang for a spin around the parking lot. Afterwards, he said that I should have a mechanic look at it; if there was water in the oil pan, the engine could lock up at any time and that would mean thousands of dollars. Better to spend a little now than take the chance. I thanked him for his time, all the while cursing under my breath. I'd either have to take Mamaw's car or delay my trip to Gadsden until after the Mustang was fixed.

I headed back into town for my date with Emily, still fuming at having yet another car repair. While waiting to turn into the lot at the diner, I saw Emily's minivan heading towards me, and I was able to pull into the lot right behind her. Emily crushed me in a hug when I got out of the Mustang. She almost seemed happier than I was, and chatted all the way into the diner about destiny and how Hank and I were just meant to be. She explained she'd almost peed her pants when I'd told her about yesterday. We ordered salads and coffee, and claimed a booth at the back of the place to talk.

"So, you, Hank and the rainstorm?" prompted Emily.

I smiled and said, "It was like a Hollywood movie. Dashing to the covered porch together, him taking my hand to keep me from slipping. Rain falling all around us."

"And then…"

"Well, we were soaked, we had to change clothes," I reasoned.

"You are a bad girl, Gracie," she said.

"Funny, that's what Hank said," I returned. I told her the rest of the story, Emily hanging on my every word. When I finished, I couldn't stop myself from asking, "You don't think I was too forward, do you?"

"Honey, you were like a dog in heat," Emily said. "A real hussy."

"Emily!"

"But hey," she continued. "Guys like that. At our age there's no point in being coy."

"I don't think you were ever 'coy'," I replied.

"True." Emily smirked. "I never bought into that game. Let me tell you what I do when I want to get it on with hubby. I wear this little number that pushes here and pulls there. When he sees me, Henry's face lights up like a kid on Christmas morning."

"Emily, that's awful. Where's the romance in that?" I said.

"Romance is for the young. I'd rather have effective."

We both laughed at that. I took a drink of my now lukewarm coffee, and then asked, "Can we talk about the murder case? I want to tell you about Clovis Jones and what I overheard last night."

"Ah, hun, I can't tell you nothing," replied Emily.

"I just want you to listen," I said. "I heard that Mamaw's gun was found in a dumpster at the Carlyle. Well, it's just across the street from the bridge club and I thought—"

"Gracie," interrupted Emily.

"Just listen," I said. I told her about Clovis and The Barn. "So you see," I continued, "he certainly had motive, he had opportunity after he walked me to my car, and he had the means as much as anyone else in this town. He could have easily thrown the gun in the dumpster at the Carlyle when he left the club."

"I'll let the chief know, but girl, just let us handle it. We are the professionals."

"I'm scared," I said before I could stop myself. I could see the look of confusion on Emily's face and knew I needed to continue. I didn't want to drag her into anything, but Emily was the closest thing to a confidant I had in Alpine. Well, other than Mamaw. "I'm scared of Clovis. That man is after me in ways that aren't proper, and if he killed Edward, I think he may come after me next. Not to mention that Yancey is desperate to frame me, and she saw me with Hank. Well, Hank is…"

"Stop," replied Emily, thrusting her hand out to show me her palm. "First of all, Clovis Jones has an airtight alibi. We checked him out first thing. He left the club with Greg Jergensen. Greg followed Jones' car most of the way home. The timing doesn't work; no way he killed Edward. Second, I don't want to know about Hank," she continued. "I can't know if this is something you want to keep from the police." Emily took a drink of coffee and then looked around, as if casing the joint. "Listen," she whispered. "You're wrong about the gun."

"It wasn't Mamaw's?" I asked, surprised.

"Not that, but you got it wrong," replied Emily.

"What?" I said.

"Listen, I could lose my job over what I've just told you. Stay out of it, Gracie." She stared at me, waiting for me to agree.

"I know, I know," I said. "I'm sorry, Emily. I never wanted to get you in trouble. I was just thinking, that's all." So Mamaw's gun was not found at the Carlyle, but then where was it found? I swear Frank had said it was discovered at the construction site.

"All is good," she stated, looking at her watch. "The Chief can't fire me anyway, not with our history and not if he wants to see his boy. And I'll be sure to tell him about Clovis Jones, maybe we can warn him to stay away from you."

"Thanks, Emily." I felt a little better, but my mind was still racing.

"Listen, I hate running out on you again, but my shift starts soon. Jon might not fire me, but he has no problem docking my pay," Emily said, standing.

I stood as well, and we hugged, promising to get together again soon. I gave Margaret a twenty to cover the bill with a little extra, and then left with Emily, telling her of my plans to stop by the station this afternoon because I needed to replace my cell phone. I explained that the Chief had asked me to notify him about any trips out of town. She just shook her head, giving me the same look I remembered from high school when I claimed Hank and I were just studying together. Emily knew I was hoping to dig a little more into the case while at the station.

I got into the Mustang and saw the bag with the suede shoes on the passenger side floor. There was a little shoe repair shop downtown next to the Pole & Arms. I didn't know if they could help or not, but I decided I'd head there first and then go to the station. That way Emily would be able to start her shift, and if I were lucky, Yancey would be ending hers.

The shop was housed in a narrow building with the first floor set back from the others on the street, giving a deep covered entryway that started at about fifteen feet wide and narrowed to ten feet. A pair of wide glass doors gave access to the three-story structure, the top two floors jutting out to match the buildings on either side. I looked up and down the street, seeing a motley collection of other businesses: the Pole & Arms was on the left, and a second hand clothing store on the right. Past the Pole & Arms was the future Chinese restaurant. There was a vacant building across the street, and out of curiosity, I detoured to the empty space and peered in a window. I didn't need to look further; it was too large for the type of coffee house I had in mind. I wanted a tight but comfortable space with good ventilation and good bones that could be transformed into the space I imagined, something that evoked the traditions of the Old Country but was supplemented with the convenience of modern times. Not that I really had plans to open a coffee house, or even stay in Alpine permanently, but it didn't hurt to dream.

I returned to my original errand, crossing the street, and stepping from the sidewalk into the shade of the portico of the shoe repair shop. I found the transition cooling, especially considering the heat of the day. The attached bell above the door gave a pleasant ring, announcing my entry. I saw no one and spent a minute examining the place. The ceiling in the narrow space was surprisingly tall, covered in tin ceiling tiles whose paint was cracked and peeling. The walls were stucco white, patched in places with a mix that didn't quite match and lined with shelves stuffed with dusty odds and ends that clearly hadn't been touched in years. The counter was barely ten feet into the store, completely cutting off the back part of the shop, with an old-fashioned manual cash register that must've weighed 300 pounds. The whole place spoke of a once tidy business gone to seed, almost preserved in amber from fifty years ago.

"I think I heard the bell," said a female voice from the back part of the shop, hidden from sight by a crimson curtain that separated the front from the back.

"What?" clamored another voice. "You thought you heard Mel? He moved away years ago."

"Hello," I called, trying to attract their attention. The voices sounded familiar, but I couldn't quite place them.

"Did you hear that?" asked the first. "Did you unlock the door, Mary? Daddy always said it was your job to open the door."

"I am not a loathsome bore," snapped Mary. "Mel always liked me better than you."

"Anyone here?" I asked a bit louder. The two bickered like a pair of old hens pecking at each other.

"Not true, he was my beau, not yours. And I heard a voice out front," replied the first. "Just go take a look."

"Why would I wanna' bait a hook?" sniped Mary. "Mel did like goin' fishin' though. Although I think that was just to get one of us alone."

"Now that's true, the old rascal. I haven't thought of fishin' with Mel in years."

"I'm out here!" I called again, trying not to laugh at the squabbling pair.

"I guess I'll go look, you lazy bones," replied the first voice with exasperation. The curtain shifted aside and out stepped a Strange sister—I thought it was Mary Jane, but I never could keep the pair straight unless I saw them together. "Mary, come on out here," she hollered to the back room. She gifted me with a wary smile and shuffled towards the counter. "How may I help you?"

I pulled the suede shoes out of the bag and set them on the counter. "I was hoping you could help me with these."

Mary stared at the shoes for a moment, turned to the curtain, and then to the shoes again. She sighed and picked up one of the shoes, putting her hand in where the foot would go. She turned the shoe around to examine both sides, then put it up to her nose and sniffed before setting it back down on the counter. "Mary!" she shouted behind her.

"What?" called the other Mary from the back.

"Come on out here and look at this!" she hollered.

"You want a book on fish?" the other replied. The Mary at the counter sighed, mentioned that her sister's hearing aid was acting up, and grabbed what looked like an ice pick with her free hand to poke at the sole.

"They got wet," I explained, trying to keep Mary from poking a hole through the bottom of my shoe. "I was hoping that you could clean them somehow. Make the suede look like new. Do you have anything here?" I waved vaguely to the shelves on either side of the shop. Mary stopped picking at the sole of my shoe, but before I got a response, the curtain moved and the other Strange sister came through. I'd gotten them straight, I saw with relief.

"Suede shoes. Got wet," snapped Mary Jane, handing the shoe to her sister.

Mary Sue stared at the shoe. Eventually she took the item, glaring at her sister like it was poisonous. She then performed the same little ritual her sister had done, including the sniff. When she reached for the tool to stab the sole, I jumped in, "They got wet; is there anything you can do to clean them?"

Mary Sue pondered the tool, then the shoe, and thankfully put both down. "I don't think you really want to steam them," she said, looking at me with a puzzled frown. "It'll ruin the suede for good; you just need to clean them."

"She said she wanted to clean them," bellowed Mary Jane in her sister's ear.

"Well, I would hope so," retorted Mary Sue. "That's what I said, ain't it? You don't have to shout."

Mary Jane turned back to me and sighed. She watched as her sister picked up one of the shoes, and then continued, "We can't help you. We don't do repairs since Junior passed."

Mary Sue glanced my way. "Junior did all the repairs after Daddy died. He's passed on now. We can't really help you," she continued, echoing her sister's words. Mary Sue adjusted the pair of shoes on the counter, so they lined up perfectly.

"I just said that." Mary Jane sighed, looking to the ceiling like she was beseeching God for intervention. She pulled her watery blue eyes back to me and explained, "Fixing the shoes was Junior's job, God rest his soul. We just ran the register. Best shoe repair shop in all of Alpine. Our Daddy opened it back in '37. We came to work for him, oh, back in '51, it was," she stated proudly.

"We've been open since 1937," chimed in Mary Sue with a smile. "Daddy repaired the shoes, at first at least, and trained Junior up to follow after him."

"But you no longer repair shoes?" I asked, confused.

"We don't drink booze," Mary Sue snapped at me. "Daddy would never approve."

"I wish I had a drink now," muttered Mary Jane to herself. She looked at me and replied, "Not since Junior passed. About six months or so now," she admitted sheepishly. "Daddy left the shop to us when he died. He told us to always keep it open so Junior had a place to be. Daddy worried about that boy something fierce, him being slow and all."

"Junior repaired the shoes, he was a bit off, you know," Mary Sue chimed in. "Re-tard-ed, the school said. Daddy never liked that word. Said we shouldn't use it."

"Then why do you?" muttered Mary Jane irritably. "Hey, don't I know you?" she asked me.

"Hey, don't I know you?" Mary Sue echoed, staring at me intently. I took a step back involuntarily, the two eyeing me like a pair of hound dogs watching a squirrel.

"Gracie," I said loudly. "From the bridge club."

"Why I'll be! It's Gracie from the bridge club. Mary; that's Gracie." Mary Sue pointed at me.

"I heard," said Mary Jane. "I'm standing right here and my hearing aids are workin'."

"I don't think she's here lurking," Mary Sue retorted with a laugh. "What's wrong with you, Mary? She clearly wanted to have her shoes fixed. Too bad Junior's passed on."

"Isn't it a bit strange," I asked loudly, "to have a repair shop when you no longer repair shoes?"

"Well, we are the Strange sisters!" they said in unison. I had stepped right into that one. I laughed along with them, even as I wondered if there was something a little off with the sisters, not just with Junior.

I took my shoes, stowed them back into the bag, and said my goodbyes. As I left, Mary Sue called behind me, saying I should come back soon. Mary Jane looked heavenward again, shaking her head. Once back on the street, I stared at the shop, realizing that it would make the perfect little coffee oasis, and wondered if there was any way I could convince the Strange sisters to let me convert it.

I wondered what the back access was like. I headed around the block and walked down the alley behind the string of buildings. The Cobblers Corner was in the third building, followed by the Pole & Arms and the new Chinese restaurant beyond that. To my right sat an open parking lot maintained by the city that gave adequate parking for the downtown shops. The lot held a scattering of about fifteen or so vehicles, mostly SUVs and trucks, typical around rural Alabama, but there were a few smaller cars and sedans as well. The building with the shoe shop didn't extend all the way to the alley, leaving a small area that held a beat-up old Buick, more rust than green paint on it. An outside staircase led to the second floor of the building, and I wondered what the space was used for and if that was the only access.

I pulled out a cigarette and lit it while I considered the idea of converting the shoe shop into a coffee shop. The size was about right, but the inside would need some major renovation. I almost jumped out of my skin when a delivery truck turned into the alley and honked at me to move out of the way. I retreated to the parking lot and watched as the truck pulled up to the loading dock at the Pole & Arms. The driver hopped out and rang the bell to the loading entrance as I returned to my contemplation. From this angle I could see a back window from the second story of the Cobbler's Corner, and I remembered seeing windows from the front as well. The second story should have decent natural light.

The back door to the Pole & Arms banged open, drawing my attention. I watched as Wilhelm appeared and began helping the driver unload the delivery into the store. I looked further down the alley, but there was little to see. The building housing the future Chinese restaurant mirrored the one with the shoe shop, although the back parking spot was wider and held a dumpster instead of a car. Beyond that were two more stores, each with a loading dock like the Pole & Arms. I wondered if they also got deliveries in the back. If so, the alley might get pretty crowded at times.

I finished my smoke and headed back around the block to where the Mustang was parked. The shoe store was plenty deep to accommodate coffee shop equipment. I could make this work. Then I came to my senses. I wasn't even sure I wanted to stay in Alpine. What was I thinking? I didn't need to take on the responsibility of a business, even if it was only a coffee shop. I shook my head ruefully. I had a murder to solve, and needed to stop daydreaming.

I got back into the Mustang, causing beads of sweat to appear on my forehead. The car must have been twenty degrees hotter than the outside, and that was hot enough to roast a pig. I drove back down Main past Margaret's Diner and turned on Elm towards the police station. I found a parking spot, entered, and saw Emily manning the front counter. Other than the two of us, the place was empty, and I wondered if the chairs that lined both walls in the public area ever saw much use. I smiled as I approached, thinking about sharing the story of my adventures in the Cobbler's Corner. When I got there, she spoke before I did, "The chief can't see you now; he just arrested Gladys Chesholm for murder."

Chapter 16

"What?" I said. I couldn't believe Gladys had shot Edward.

"Listen, I can't tell you anything more," replied Emily in a whisper. "I only mentioned it in the first place because I knew you were worried. Well, it's all over now. Whatever fear you had before can be put to rest. This case is all but wrapped up."

"But—"

"Just stay in Alpine today, Gracie. Don't go nowhere, and tomorrow you can probably see the Chief. He's too busy now to be pestered."

"Can't you just tell me what happened? Why does Doeppers think Gladys murdered Edward Schultz?" I asked. Emily shook her head. I knew she was right. This was police business.

I turned to go, deciding to head to Mamaw's and share the news. As I reached the front doors, I heard someone enter the room behind me and turned to see. It was Chief Doeppers, staring at his notepad as he shuffled through a few pages. He grunted and glanced over to Emily. "Can you radio Lancaster and see if he can—" Whatever task he'd planned to give Emily was forgotten as his eyes scanned the room and landed on me. "What are you doing here?" he barked.

I walked back to the counter and offered the man a smile. If only I could get my hands on that pad, I might know why he thought Gladys was the killer. "Actually, I came to see you, but Officer Stevenson told me you were too busy today to speak with me. I wanted to tell you of my plans to leave town for the day to do some shopping in Gadsden."

"Well, this saves me the trouble of tracking you down. I have a few follow-up questions I need to ask you," said Doeppers as he flipped through his notebook. "If you can give me a half-hour of your time, you can then be off to Gadsden or wherever for the day."

"I'd be happy to help in any way I can," I said. I gave Emily a small grin, which made her roll her eyes. I stifled a snort.

"Follow me," Doeppers commanded, leading me back into the heart of the station. I passed through the double doors and the scattering of desks in the open middle of the structure. Doeppers led me past the holding cells where Yancey had escorted me last time, then past a tiny disheveled space that had "Chief of Police" stenciled on the door, and into a slightly bigger room on the right. Across from the door was a frosted window that let in some natural light, while the wall that was shared with Doepper's office sported a whiteboard filled with childish drawings of cops chasing robbers. The wall opposite the whiteboard held a large mirror, and I wondered if it was one-way glass like in the movies. In the center of the room sat a round table with four swivel chairs, one of which was tilted with a broken wheel. Like most government facilities, this one needed some maintenance.

"Please sit," said Doeppers, taking the chair that faced the door.

I took the chair opposite, although I didn't particularly like the idea of having the door behind me.

"Miss Theis," Doeppers began. "I'd like to begin by thanking you for agreeing to answer a few more of my questions. Police everywhere depend upon the cooperation of everyday citizens to help solve crimes, and I and all of Alpine appreciate your help with this one," he intoned in a practiced way as if he'd repeated these words several times.

"I'm happy to help in any way that I can," I said. Two could play this game.

"Considering our earlier encounters, I'm pleased to hear that," he said, meeting my eyes.

"I would like to apologize—" I began.

"No need," interrupted Doeppers. "Your assistance now is what's important," he said, looking back at his notes. After a few moments he set the pad aside. "I need to ask you about an encounter that happened yesterday at the Alpine Duplicate Bridge Club before the Edward Schultz Memorial bridge game." He looked at me expectantly and I nodded my understanding. "Did you see or speak to anyone before the game?"

I told him I'd gone to the club well before game time, after my lunch date with Mamaw at Margaret's Diner, and had found Gladys crying in the back of the club. I explained how upset she'd been upon discovering that the club bank account was empty and how she thought that Edward had stolen the club's money. I tried to provide as many details as I could remember, like how I'd gotten Gladys a cup of water and how she'd been sitting in the chair. I knew from Thursday's ordeal that Doeppers used these little details to corroborate different stories. If Gladys had relayed this story in an argument for her innocence, I wanted Doeppers to be able to confirm the truth. I also volunteered seeing the flyer at Old Town Auto Repair for Edward's prized Thunderbird, and my conclusion that Edward had cash flow problems. I watched Doeppers' face for clues in how he was receiving my story, but I might as well have been watching paint dry. The man was impassive as ever.

He then asked a few more questions, not only about Sunday but also about the game last Thursday and how the club worked. He was particularly interested in whether I had seen anyone from the time when Clovis escorted me to my car on Thursday to the time when I'd discovered Edward's body. I closed my eyes and tried to recall what I'd seen, but the only person I could remember was Margaret at the diner when I'd turned the Mustang around to head back to the club. The man glanced at his notes a few more times, and then said I was free to go.

I stood, but instead of leaving I asked, "Do you really think Gladys did it? Why? What possible motive could she have for murdering Edward? She didn't even know about the stolen money until after the murder."

He looked at me and asked, "Why do you think that I think Gladys Chisholm murdered Edward?"

"Look, I'm not an idiot. The only reason you'd be asking about what happened yesterday is if you thought Gladys murdered Edward." I sat back down in my chair with a satisfied smirk. I could be as smug as he could.

"Do you think Gladys is capable of murder?" he asked, serious.

"No," I replied, honestly.

"And why is that?" he asked. "When put under enough pressure, even the most unexpected person can commit terrible acts." He sounded like he knew what he was talking about.

"She had no motive," I explained. "She didn't know about the missing money until after Edward was killed.

There was no pressure to make her snap." I felt pretty proud of my deduction.

"So you believe. What if it wasn't Edward Schultz who stole the club money, but instead he was the one who discovered it? What if he accused Gladys of theft and in that confrontation Gladys panicked and shot Edward? Afterwards it would make sense to blame the theft on a dead man."

I thought for a few minutes, but I knew he was wrong. It couldn't have happened that way. "I don't believe it. First that would mean Gladys has the club's money, and if you'd found that money, we wouldn't be having this conversation." I paused and saw a slight tightening in Doeppers' right eye. It was the most I was going to get for confirmation. "Second," I said, "that means there were two people desperate for cash, Gladys and Edward. It's much simpler and more reasonable to assume one person."

"That's a weak argument," interrupted Doeppers. "It's been a tough few years in this town."

I nodded in acknowledgement, and then continued, "Third, and most significantly, I don't think Gladys would have been so cavalier when I saw her in the Piggly-Wiggly on Friday."

"What do you mean?" asked Doeppers, grabbing his notebook. "Tell me about this encounter on Friday."

I closed my eyes to remember the conversation. I told him how I got a hankering to make a pie, although I left out the main reason for it, and had stopped by the Piggly-Wiggly on Friday to pick up some apples. I explained how I'd run into Gladys at the butcher counter and started a conversation with her and Frank about the murder. I mentioned how they'd been gossiping about possible motives, and how Frank had mentioned the case against the Piggly-Wiggly Edward had filed, and how the settlement had gone. I described

Gladys's demeanor and how it had contrasted to when I saw her again on Sunday. I simply didn't believe Gladys was a good enough actress to pull off that deception.

When I opened my eyes, Doeppers was writing down a few more notes in his pad. He asked me a couple more questions about my run in with Gladys and then seemed to be satisfied. Once again he said I could stand, and as I did so I said, "Oh, and when I left the Piggly-Wiggly one of your officers was waiting for me in the parking lot."

"And…" he said, flipping through his notebook to compare several pages of dense script.

"She, Officer Yancey that is, was quite firm in her belief that I was involved in this murder. She was also at my home last night." That got Doepper's attention. He gave me a long look before he spoke.

"I've heard her theories. I'll have another talk with her. You've been quite helpful, Miss Thies. I wish you a good day," he finished, his attention back to his notebook.

I glanced to the whiteboard, itching to ask who could have drawn such adorable artwork, but knew that now was not the time. I headed to the door, but a thought occurred to me. I turned back and said, "One last question." Doeppers looked up, clearly annoyed. "Wouldn't Gladys have had to steal the gun before this imagined confrontation with Edward? She would've had to be prepared, which meant she couldn't have been surprised. She would've had to plan to kill Edward, a premeditated murder. I don't see that in Gladys," I concluded. I watched as Doeppers processed the argument in silence. Eventually he spoke.

"Thank you for your time, Miss Theis," replied Doeppers, his look of irritation growing. "Please see yourself out. And stay out of my investigation."

I walked back the way I'd come, feeling rather pleased that my second visit to the station this week had not resulted in my incarceration. I also felt more certain than ever that Gladys was innocent and that Doeppers believed so too. That meant that there was still a killer on the loose, and while I didn't have access to as much information as the Chief did, it seemed that he was no closer to solving the murder than I was.

I talked briefly with Emily on my way out about my dinner plans with Hank and her plans to take her kids to the park after work. I asked about the whiteboard in the interview room, and Emily laughed, saying it was her kids' doing. The drawings were cute, and her kids were clearly gifted artists. I told her to give me a call if she ever needed a sitter.

I left by the main door and started up the Mustang. It was only midafternoon, and I had plenty of time before my dinner with Hank. Time enough to test a little theory of mine. It wouldn't solve the murder, but it might take care of Hank's problem. I headed out of town past Old Town Auto Supply towards the seedy bar from last night.

As I drove, I pondered what I'd learned.

In bridge, the best players draw inferences on the optimal line of play based not only on what the opponents do, but also on what they don't do. That was always the hardest thing for me to remember: not what the opponents bid but what they did not bid and what that implied. Using these clues effectively meant making fewer guesses and getting higher scores. Could I use the same ideas to solve this murder case?

Now, if there had been a witness to the murder, then Doeppers would have found him or her by now and the murderer would have been caught. He was a competent investigator, and with a witness he would have swiftly solved the case. That meant that there was no witness, and so at the time of the shooting only Edward and the murderer would have been in the building.

By now, Doeppers would have interviewed everyone who remained in the club after I had left on Thursday. He probably would have established the order in which people had departed. Assuming that Edward had never left the club, and with the short time frame, that was a reasonable assumption, then whoever was with Edward at the end would be the obvious suspect. If Gladys had been this person, then she would be under investigation with the only missing piece being motive.

And the missing club money was that motive, at least for Doeppers. Either Gladys or the club president, Otis, must have reported the theft. That would be all Doeppers would need to make the arrest. But Doeppers didn't know Gladys the way I did; he didn't know she wasn't a killer.

And that meant someone must have entered the club after Gladys had left to kill Edward. Someone must have been lying in wait to ambush him.

I turned between the pines onto the gravel drive of The Barn. There were only a couple of beat up old pick-up trucks in the lot—thankfully no sign of Clovis's shiny new one. I pulled up close to the door and threw the Mustang into park. Time to see if there was anything to the look the barkeep gave Clovis last night. Luck was with me because as soon as I entered, I saw she was there, sweeping the floor.

"Sorry, we're closed," the barkeep began. She raised her head and looked at me. "Hey, weren't you here last night? You ran out on Skeeter; best decision you ever made."

"Actually that's why I'm here," I replied. Jackpot, I just needed to figure how to ask. "I'm Gracie, by the way."

"Name is Sally Amanda, but most folk just call me Liz," the barkeep said.

"Liz?" I asked, confused.

"In school Sally Amanda got shortened to Salamander, and then it morphed into Liz. What can I do for ya?"

"Well, Liz, I was wondering if you might be interested in helping out with a little prank of sorts to be pulled on Clovis," I said.

"Ha, Clovis!" She laughed. "I haven't heard Skeeter called that in years. A little prank, huh?" Liz asked, sweeping.

"Well," I began. I couldn't do it. I couldn't lie to her. "It may be a bit bigger than that," I confessed.

"Sounding better and better." Liz put down the broom and took a seat, gesturing for me to take one as well. "Details now."

So I told her about Hank. I told her about the court case, and how Clovis had faked his injuries to get a higher award. I told her about Harry, and how he'd lost his legs in the same accident that Clovis had sued him over.

"Well, I'll be damned," whistled Liz. "So that's how Skeeter's been living so high on the hog. And that's why he keeps carrying that damn cane with him."

"It's not fair, Liz," I argued. "While Clovis is living it up, Hank may lose the farm."

"I agree. Skitter's a menace. He was bragging about punching one of his poker buddies this week, accusing him of cheating. The man needs to be brought down a peg or three. The question is, what are you going to do about it?" she asked.

"Well, Hank thinks that if he can prove Clovis was not as injured as he claimed to be, then he can get the case reconsidered and the award amount reduced. He's been talking to a lawyer, but he needs proof. He needs a video of Clovis walking without the cane, without any pain. I was thinking we could set something up here. Hide Hank somewhere so that he could get a video of Clovis somehow."

"Now, why would you want to go to all of that trouble?" asked Liz. I stared, confused. I thought I'd just explained that. "Just ask, girl," Liz urged.

"Do you happen to have a video of Clovis walking without a cane?" I ventured.

"As a matter of fact, I do. Too many brawls in here not to have a few cameras about. And after you walked out on him last night Skeeter was fit to be tied. Strutted around here like he owned the place. Almost started a fight or two. We got a slick set-up in the back. All hooked up to a computer and such. Give me a minute and I'll make you a copy to take with you," she said, smiling as she stood. I laughed as Liz headed towards the back with a spring in her step. In moments she returned, with a disk in hand. "Now you have any trouble with Skeeter, you let me know. And I'll be happy to talk to anybody you need for that," she said, handing me the disk.

I thanked her and promised to keep her informed as I left with my prize. While the bar itself might be a bit seedy, Liz was a gem. I headed back into town and noticed some clouds gathering in the west. With the chance of an afternoon storm, I decided I'd park on the street so that Hank could park in the drive and have a shorter dash to the house if needed. We had much to celebrate tonight, and I decided on a whim to take a quick shower to freshen up a bit before putting on something special. I wished I'd had time to buy something new, but figured I could find an outfit that would get Hank's motor running regardless. This was a night I wanted to remember.

I pulled in behind a blue sedan, parked the Mustang, and walked down the drive to enter by way of the kitchen as I normally did. I turned on the kitchen lights, looked at the clock, and was shocked to see how late it was. I tossed my keys onto the counter and headed to the shower. The clawfoot called to me, and I got the water running while I got undressed. The warm water soothed tensions I didn't know I was carrying. I reluctantly turned the water off after too short of a time. As always, the floor was soaked, but I wanted to go ahead and get dressed before Hank arrived, although I knew I might not stay so for long. Leaving the mess for now, I wrapped a towel around myself, carefully left the bathroom, and hurried to my bedroom. I let out a scream when I saw a man sitting on my bed with a gun pointed in my direction.

Chapter 17

"I was hoping it wouldn't come to this," said Wilhelm Bea once my scream died. He sat on the bed, gun in hand as if he didn't have a care in the world.

"Wilhelm," I sputtered. "Why?" To me, Wilhelm had always been the type of man you could pass on the street, or play against in the club, without a remark or even really noticing. I was certainly noticing him now.

"There are too many loose ends," he explained. "And before the whole thing unravels around me I must act, I think. I'll provide the police with a nicely wrapped little present that answers all their questions." He was treating this almost like a preempt in bridge, act before the opponents know they have a fit. Unfortunately, that apparently meant an act against me. "You, my dear, will be that present."

"Why me?" I asked, clutching the towel wrapped around me and wondering how I'd found myself essentially naked in front of this man. I should have been worried about the gun, I knew, but somehow the lack of clothes was more disconcerting.

"Because you saw me that day, or at least my car, when I rushed to the store to get a tarp to move the body. Because Nora is searching for her spare keys and eventually either she, or that boyfriend of yours, will remember that she left them at the Pole & Arms the same day she bought the gun. Because the police already suspect you. I heard Ida gossiping about your little display at the grocery, and so they're primed to believe your confession. And lastly, because I saw you snooping around the back of my store earlier today. It was at that point I realized you were too close to discovering what I'd done." He spread his free hand as if displaying his wares at the store. "You see, plenty of reasons why."

"I saw you? And what confession?" I asked. I certainly didn't remember seeing anything, little good that did me now.

"That's why you're still alive, Gracie. It would have been so much easier to shoot you in the shower. But you see, I need a suicide note in your writing, then we can proceed to the more unpleasant, but necessary, task." A small cruel smile appeared on his face, and for the first time I noticed his dead cold eyes. I didn't know how I could have missed it before, but I knew Wilhelm meant what he said. He'd decided to murder me in cold blood in order to try and cover up his murder of Edward. He planned to kill me.

"I'm not writing anything, and there's no way you can make me," I said, putting on a brave front. There had to be a way out of this. I didn't want to die, not now, not when everything was just beginning to get better in my life. I knew running wasn't an option—I couldn't find shelter before Wilhelm would be able to take a shot. I had to keep him talking until I could think of something. I glanced at the clock. It was still too long before Hank would arrive.

"Well," said Wilhelm, standing, "I suppose I could move to Plan B. Of course, I don't think you'll like it any better. You see, Plan B means I shoot you now and then plant the gun on Hank Waderich. Think of it as a lover's spat that went wrong, deadly wrong. He can take the blame for both murders that way. More trouble for me, but there's no rest for the weary, as they say." Wilhelm put his free hand on his chin and began stroking it like Michelangelo's Thinker. "Hmm... a murder-suicide or a double homicide, what will the poor people of Alpine think has happened to their town?"

He dropped his free hand and raised the gun, his mouth twisting into a nasty snarl. I screamed for him to wait as my heart threatened to leap out of my chest, one hand flung out in protest while the other clutched the towel to my body as a shield. Wilhelm tilted his head like a dog hearing a whistle and lowered the gun. I almost swooned in relief.

"Have you perhaps reconsidered?" he asked. "Your suicide at least spares your boyfriend from a murder charge—actually, a double murder charge, I suspect. I doubt the police would think there were two murderers in this sleepy little town. Certainly the people of Alpine would prefer not to think so. So provincial, don't you think?"

"Wilhelm," I said, my pulse racing. I had to find a way out of this. "You haven't thought this through. No one will believe Hank committed murder; he had no motive."

Wilhelm laughed. "Easy enough," he said. "Plenty of folks had reason to see Edward harmed, but I was the only one man enough to act on it. Being sued by Edward should be motivation enough for Hank, considering what that has driven him to. As for you, well, you discovered his little secret and planned to go to the police."

"What secret?" I asked, dread filling me. How would Wilhelm have known about the marijuana? Or was there another secret?

"As if you don't know?" Wilhelm laughed. "Your boyfriend shouldn't buy that much fertilizer for a garden and not plant at least a few vegetables. All that man buys is frozen microwavable meals, nothing to complement homegrown produce. So I figure he must be growing something he shouldn't. It won't be hard to prove once I mention it to Chief Doeppers. I might even get a commendation for assisting them in solving not only a murder but taking down a drug dealer as well." He stood and continued, "Now enough talk. Let's find you something with which to write."

"Can I get dressed?" I asked. I knew it would make no difference, but somehow being clothed felt like the first step in regaining control of the situation.

He looked me up and down, his cruel grin turning a bit more lustful. "I like you better this way," replied Wilhelm. "I think you may be more docile, less prone to trying something foolish."

I almost panicked thinking that Wilhelm planned to take more from me than my life, and then I recognized it as what it was: a potential weakness. I didn't like the idea of using my body to try and distract the man, but considering where this was heading I knew I needed to do something to disrupt his plan, and I needed to do it soon. I was certain that once Wilhelm sat me down at the kitchen table to write my suicide note, I would never stand again.

I walked slowly from the room, Wilhelm following close behind. When I got to the bathroom door, I took a shuffle step and let the towel slip. I pretended to grab at the towel while keeping my eyes on Wilhelm. He took advantage of the opportunity to view my naked body, allowing the gun to wander slightly to the side, as I had hoped. I let the towel drop completely and rose, shoving both hands straight into Wilhelm's chest. He stumbled backwards but kept his balance and did not drop the gun. I jumped into the bathroom, slamming the door shut behind me. I almost slipped on the wet floor, but somehow retained my balance and slid the latch, locking the entry. Only four small screws separated me from a murderer, but that was an infinite improvement from a moment before. I grabbed a new towel from the stack and wrapped it around myself, surveyed the room for anything that could help.

The door handle turned while I was looking, but the latch kept the door closed. "Gracie, don't be unreasonable," called Wilhelm from the hall. "Just come out, there's nothing to be gained by delaying."

"No," I said, stepping into the clawfoot so that I wasn't directly in front of the door. The small window in the bath was too little to squeeze through; I couldn't escape that way. The closest thing to a weapon I could find was my flat iron, not that it would be much good. What was I to do with it, burn Wilhelm's scalp while straightening his hair? My situation was hopeless. If I opened the door, Wilhelm would kill me. If I didn't open the door, he would bust it down and then kill me. I was end-played.

"If you come out and cooperate, I'll still let you write the suicide note. I'll give you the chance to save your boyfriend," Wilhelm said. Thunder erupted outside, and I could hear the rain through the window. Wilhelm could use the gun and no one would think anything of it. It was as if the Lord above was acting in Wilhelm's favor, or maybe he had a contract with the devil. "If I have to break this door down then that option will no longer be viable. The broken door will cause suspicion even with a suicide note. I'll have to implement Plan B."

"Hank will stop you," I cried, praying it would be so. "You won't catch him the same way you caught me." Surely Hank would be safe. Wilhelm was no match for him physically—but Wilhelm had a gun.

"Are you willing to take that chance? Why risk it? You will be dead either way." Wilhelm tested the door again, pushing harder, and I knew the four little screws would not hold for long. Wilhelm might be unassuming, but he was not weak. He would be able to bust his way through the door with a little effort. "I will give you one minute more to decide, and then I'm coming through the door."

"Wait," I said, mind racing. Wilhelm was right. In bridge you never take a finesse that risks the contract in a vain look for an overtrick. You never pick a line of play that contains a potential for loss if a guaranteed line of play is available. Wilhelm was offering me a chance to use my life to buy the safety of my loved ones, and the alternative was to reject that choice and ultimately lose my life and risk Hank's. I should unlock the door and do as commanded, that was the rational choice. I reached for the latch but could not make my legs step out of the tub. I couldn't do it. Life wasn't bridge, and even though it was not rational, I couldn't walk into my own death.

My vision blurred as the reality hit. My legs failed me and I slipped to the bottom of the clawfoot. "I…can't…" I cried as sobs wracked my body. I was going to die, and I wasn't brave enough to do it in a way that gained anything. I was a coward, and as a result I would risk Hank's life as well.

"I understand," whispered Wilhelm. "It's hard to die, I think."

When the door cracked, I let out a scream. I could see the latch barely hanging by two screws. I knew I should brace it or something, but there was no time and

I no longer had control of my body. The horror of impending death had reduced me to a quivering shell of a woman, lying prone in the bottom of the clawfoot, worse even than when I had learned of Pierre's betrayal. Wilhelm hit the door hard a second time and it burst open, his momentum carrying him into the space. When his feet hit the wet tile, they found no purchase. His legs flew out from under him and he landed hard, the jolt causing the gun to go off. I screamed again as the clawfoot rang like a bell, hit by the stray bullet, splinters flying through the air.

My eyes were sealed as I awaited the pain of death. When the moment passed and I heard a gurgling, the horror faded as curiosity bloomed and I became able to act again. I opened my eyes fearing to see Wilhelm's cruel smile hovering over me only to discover empty space. Gathering my wits, I sat up and peered over the side of the clawfoot, and another scream escaped me. Wilhelm lay still on the floor, a bleeding hole in his chest. He held a hand to the wound, but I could see his life's blood seeping from it. His face was turned my way, gray and pale like a fish out of water. I met his frosty eyes with my own, and I knew Wilhelm was dying. I could see his lips moving, but I could not make out his words. I leaned over from inside the tub to hear what he was trying to say, but as I neared, his hand slipped, causing a spray of crimson to flood my vision as moisture soaked me. A final scream escaped me as I realized my face was covered in blood.

My world darkened.

Chapter 18

It took another week with several hours of questioning before Doeppers was satisfied. Thankfully, the man began to grudgingly answer my questions as it became apparent that I'd told the truth, and that Wilhelm had indeed murdered Edward. I learned that Mamaw's gun was found in the alley behind the Pole & Arms, in the dumpster used in the remodeling for the new Chinese restaurant. Doeppers thought that Wilhelm must have thrown it there after the murder, a convenient place to ditch the gun when he'd rushed to the store to get the supplies he needed to move the body. So the gun had been found in a construction dumpster, just not at the Carlyle. Mamaw's spare keys were found as well, in Wilhelm's pocket. No one knew for sure why he hadn't disposed of them long ago, but it did add credence to my tale.

As for why Wilhelm had felt the need to murder in the first place, some papers in Edward's law office indicated that Ida Bea had agreed to purchase the top penthouse in the Carlyle. All that was missing was her signature. Furthermore, Ida had told Doeppers that Wilhelm had no money of his own, that the Pole & Arms rarely turned a profit, and that Wilhelm was against her purchase, preferring to close the store, retire, and move to Arizona. All the evidence pointed to a murder to protect the family fortune, although Ada Mae ventured that Wilhelm may have felt threatened by Edward trying to romance Ida away. Whether Wilhelm felt the need to protect his marriage or to protect Ida's family's money, it amounted to the same thing. Wilhelm had committed murder to protect his unfettered access to Ida's cash.

Brandi Yugler, a reporter for the *Alpine Tribune*, had asked me several times for an interview, but I'd refused. I just wanted to put it all behind me. Regardless of my lack of cooperation, the *Tribune* ran several articles in the following weeks on Edward Schultz's murder and his network of financial dealings, each getting a little more negative as it became clear Edward had built a house of cards. The Carlyle Hotel renovation project was in the red by tens of thousands of dollars, and it was unclear when or even if the project would continue. Apparently to keep the work on the hotel running, Edward had taken advantage of his role as treasurer to embezzle money not only from the bridge club but also the local Methodist church. For a time it was touch and go for both organizations, until the community rallied behind them and donated the funds to keep them afloat. Money came in from as far away as Birmingham and Atlanta, but the anchoring gift was an anonymous commitment to match anything that was given. The rumor was that Ida was attempting to make amends.

While Alpine slowly transitioned back to normal, my life was more unsettled. The cottage on Elm no longer felt safe. Every time I entered the bathroom, my eyes were drawn to the clawfoot and the penny-sized dent in the side where the bullet from Wilhelm's gun had ricocheted and killed him. I was still not sure how long I had laid there surrounded by Wilhelm's blood.

My memories of that day were as hazy as the mist over Cacanaw Creek at dawn on a spring day. All I really knew was that Hank had found me, called the police, and somehow had helped me preserve a modicum of modesty. I hoped that time would help, and that I would find the cottage a home again, but for the moment I was essentially living out of a suitcase. I split my nights between the Waderich farm with Hank and Mamaw's Victorian home.

I hated not having a place I felt was my own. I didn't have much choice though. The Alpine rental market was brutal with few—if any—places available. If I gave up the cottage, I might not find another place to live for several months. Mamaw offered the Victorian, saying I could move in permanently with her. After all that had happened I was sorely tempted, but I valued my independence too much. I didn't know what it would do to me to move back in with her after the trials I'd endured, first with Pierre and now with the murder. Alternatively, my relationship with Hank was too new to consider moving to the farm, and besides, Hank had not offered.

Not that the farm was a particularly good choice. My relationship with Hank was becoming more complicated. We both wanted some of the same things, but the trick seemed to be in agreeing on how to get there. The video of Clovis I'd obtained was a piece of that puzzle, and Hank had shown it to a lawyer down in Gadsden who had agreed to take the case. Much to my relief, Hank was also transitioning out of the marijuana growing business, but that just changed his problems from one with the law to one with finances instead. And there was Harry too, of course. I feared Hank's relationship with his father was an unhealthy one, for both of them. What little I'd seen of them together was of Hank coddling the old curmudgeon, and Harry encouraging it. Hank needed to figure out how to let Harry live his own life, and Harry had to learn how to do it.

And that left me in a pickle, maybe even in a jar of pickles, unsure of where I'd be spending my nights, unsure of Hank and our relationship, unsure of building a life in Alpine. I couldn't live off the life insurance proceeds forever, but there weren't many job opportunities in a town this size. I'd made a few discreet inquiries and learned that Ida Bea, of all people, owned the building that housed the Cobbler's Corner. I also started making lists of what I needed to make my coffee house dream a reality. Unfortunately, I wasn't as circumspect as I thought. Mamaw got wind of my interest, and downright called up Ida Bea and asked if she'd be interested in a new tenant. Nothing was settled, but it was a possibility. While I appreciated Mamaw's help, I also wished I'd been a bit more careful. Mamaw's emotions had been swinging like the pendulum of a grandfather clock between the fear of me opening a business and the joy of me staying in Alpine. And I swore her mood swings were more reliable than the 1870s Gustav Becker clock in the living room of her Victorian.

I heard a knock on the door and knew my time of contemplation was over. Mamaw and I had agreed to watch Eliza Anne and Jon Junior so that Emily and her husband could have a few hours alone together. I opened the door, smiled, and gave Emily a welcome hug. Emily introduced her children, with Jon being very solemn and polite in saying hello and how pleased he was to meet us. Eliza Anne, on the other hand, shyly hid behind her mother's legs. In no time we had the children settled and comfortable. Emily and I had made a trip to Gadsden so that I could purchase a new cell. While there, we'd stopped at a little boutique where

Emily picked up a scandalous outfit that verged on indecent. I knew she planned on getting Henry's attention with it tonight.

Emily hadn't seen the little number I'd purchased. I didn't know if I had a future with Hank or even if I had a future in Alpine. The former would lead to the latter, and I was pretty sure I wanted both. In any case, with what I'd gotten, I knew I'd have some fun while finding out.

About the Authors

Doug and Sheryl Riley have been partners in bridge and in life for 27 years with three wonderful children and two spoiled dogs. Originally Midwesterners, they moved south when they got married, and learned bridge while Doug was an impoverished graduate student. Doug and Sheryl began playing duplicate bridge at the Birmingham Duplicate Bridge Club in 2008 after their third child was born in an effort to get out of the house and save their sanity. This plan allegedly worked, at least until the kids started playing bridge as well. Now the whole family enjoys traveling to tournaments around the country as their work and school schedules allow. Doug and Sheryl have been finalists for the NABC President's Cup four of the past five years. Both are still working towards their Life Master goal. When not playing bridge or writing mysteries, Doug is a mathematics professor and Sheryl is a paralegal.

Overview of Duplicate Bridge

Duplicate Bridge evolved in the 19th and 20th centuries with roots dating back to the English card game Whist. In its simplest incarnation, players are divided into two-person partnerships that are designated as sitting either North-South or East-West. Partnerships are ranked only against players sitting in their direction, but compete against opponents sitting in the opposite direction through a series of 6-12 rounds consisting of 2-4 hands called boards. After a round, the East-West partnership moves to a new table while the boards rotate differently so that all partnerships play the same set of boards (hence "duplicate") but at different times and against different opponents. A sanctioned match of bridge typically consists of somewhere between 21 and 28 boards. Winners have the highest overall score when all of the boards are totaled for their direction, and awards are given which are used to achieve various Master Points Rankings, including the coveted "Life Master."

Each board is built from a standard 52-card deck divided into four 13 card hands, one for each player. Playing a board consists of three phases: bidding, play and scoring. During the bidding phase, or auction, the partnerships compete for the right to name one of the four suits as trump or propose play without a trump suit ("No Trump"). The denominations are ranked in tiers for bidding purposes with Clubs being lowest, followed by Diamonds, Hearts, Spades, and then No Trump. The partnership that bids the highest number of tricks wins the auction, with the tiers used as tie breakers. The player who first proposed the winning denomination for their partnership is named the Declarer with her partner being the Dummy. The opponents are called the Defenders.

Once bidding is finished, the Defender to the left of the Declarer reveals a card, the opening lead. The Dummy then places all of her cards face-up on the table, grouped by suit. The Declarer instructs the Dummy which cards to play throughout the hand. Each player takes turns placing one card on the table, following the suit led if possible, in a clockwise manner. The highest card played in the led suit wins the trick unless the trump suit was played in which case the highest trump wins the trick. The winner of the trick reveals a new card to start the next trick. Play continues in this manner until all 13 tricks have been played.

Once play is complete, one of the partnerships will receive points during the scoring phase. If the Declarer made or exceeded the level promised in the bidding phase, that partnership earns points. The number of points varies depending on the denomination bid with bonuses available at certain milestones based on the bidding. If the Declarer was unable to make the bid, the Defenders earn points for each trick taken over what Declarer could allow while still making her bid. These scores are then compared to the other players sitting in the same direction who also played that board, and normalized to give a score for the board.

Glossary of Bridge Terms

Term	Definition
Bid	A specification of a denomination and the number of tricks over book that a partnership will make if the bid wins the auction. For example, "4 Hearts" promises to make 10 tricks if Hearts is Trump. In addition, Double, Redouble and Pass are legal bids.
Bidding box	A small box on the table which contains a card for each possible bid. Players use the cards to make their bids silently.
Board	One hand of the match typically organized within a plastic container. It consists of one deck of cards divided into 4 sets of 13 cards each. Each Player takes the set assigned to his/her seat, and then returns it to the same slot in the board after play is complete so it can be passed to the next group.
Bonus	Extra points awarded for bidding and making game or slam.
Book	The first 6 tricks earned by Declarer. Only tricks over book earn points.
Bottom	A board where all other partnerships sitting your way have a higher score than you do.
Contract	The final bid which determines the denomination and how many tricks the Declarer must take.
Convention card	A card filled out by both members of the partnership which indicates any and all bidding and playing agreements. The convention card must always be available to the opposing team.
Declarer	The player in the partnership who won the auction who first named the winning denomination. This

person will be the one playing the hand, while the other member of the partnership will lay her cards down on the table for all players to see.

Denomination	One of the four suits or No Trump.
Director	The person in charge of running the game. Specialized training and certification is required to direct games. If there are any irregularities in bidding or playing, the director may be called to the table to make a binding ruling on the occurrence.
Direction	Each seat at the table is given a direction: North, South, East, and West. Players are referred to by the seat in which they sit. North-South are partners, as are East-West.
Double	A bid which changes the scoring if the previous bid is allowed to stand. The double bid has additional conventional meanings depending on partnership agreement. Typically, a double that occurs early in an auction is a request for partner to bid an unbid long suit.
Dummy	The partner of the Declarer. This person lays their cards face up on the table for everyone to see. Dummy can only play the card ordered by Declarer and cannot make any suggestions or comments as the hand progresses.
Face card	Any card with a person on it: Jack, Queen, or King.
Finesse	An attempt to win a trick with a lower card by playing through an opponent who holds a higher card. If the opponent plays the higher card, the lower card can win a later trick in that suit. If the opponent does not play the high card, the lower card will win the current trick.

Fix	A board where the opponents make an unusual bid that ensures a bottom for the partnership.
Game	Bidding and making 100 points or more on one board. Bids which are considered "game" are 3 No Trump, 4 Hearts, 4 Spades, 5 Clubs, and 5 Diamonds. There are scoring bonuses for bidding and making game.
High Card Points	Numerical values given to Honors that are used to evaluate the relative trick-taking strength of a hand. Certain bids promise different High Card Point ranges depending on partnership agreement as outlined on the convention card.
Honors	All face cards plus the Ace and Ten of each suit.
Life Master	A duplicate bridge player who has reached 500 Master Points, at least 50 of which are "gold points" which come from winning in an event at the regional tournament level or higher.
No trump	A bid which does not name a trump suit.
Opener	The member of the partnership who first makes a non-pass bid.
Partial	A bid which wins the auction, but is not at the game bonus level.
Partner	The person sitting across the table, who plays and scores with you.
Pass	A bid accepting the current level and denomination as the winning bid. An auction ends after 3 passes with the stipulation that everyone has had the chance to bid.
Preempt	A bid based on the length of a suit not the Honors in a hand. It is designed to interfere with the

opponents' bidding by raising the auction to a level high enough to prevent the exchange of information.

Round	A set of boards played against one opponent. A round usually consists of 2-5 boards, and players will play 5-12 rounds in a match.
Ruff	To play trump on a trick when a different suit was led. Also known as "to trump." A player can only ruff a trick if they no longer hold any cards in the led suit.
Set	To defeat a contract by keeping Declarer from taking the number of tricks promised by the winning bid.
Singleton	Initially having only one card in a suit.
Slam	A contract to win all tricks in a hand (a grand slam) or all but one trick (small slam). There are significant bonus points associated with bidding and making a slam.
Top	A board where your partnership earned more points than all other partnerships sitting your direction.
Trick	A set of 4 cards, one played by each player in turn. There are exactly 13 tricks in a hand of bridge.
Trump	The named suit of the contract, which is more powerful than any other suit.
Void	To have none of a suit at the beginning of the hand.
Vulnerable	A designation shown on the board which indicates if there will be larger bonuses or penalties for one, both, or neither pair for that hand.